I0721519

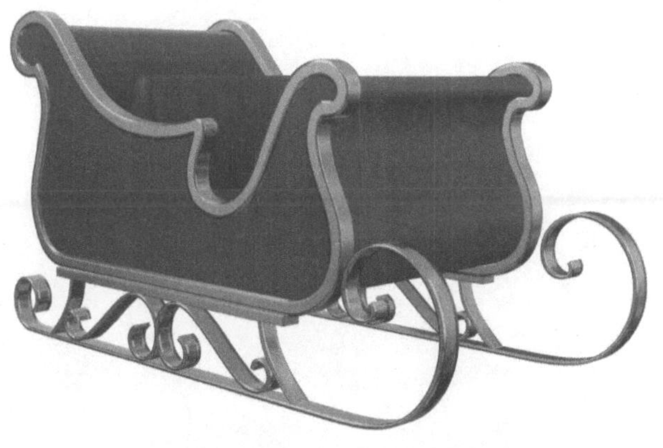

THE MAN WHO WOULD BE SANTA

~ THE NOEL KRINGLE CHRONICLES ~

REBECCA M. SENESE

Also by Rebecca M. Senese

The Noel Kringle Chronicles (in reading order)

Santa Claus: Private Detective

Santa Must Die!

The Claus Connection

The Twelve Deaths of Christmas

Baby, It's Deadly Outside

Do You Fear What I Fear

The Man Who Would Be Santa

Who Killed Santa?

The Elf Who Saved Christmas

Wreck the Halls: 5 Christmas Horror Stories

A Very Zombie Christmas

The Santa Murders

THE MAN WHO WOULD BE SANTA

~ THE NOEL KRINGLE CHRONICLES ~

REBECCA M. SENESE

RFAR Publishing
Toronto, Canada

Trade paperback edition, hardcover edition, and electronic editions designed by Rebecca M. Senese / RFAR Publishing in Vellum Press.

Trade Paperback ISBN: 978-1-927603-74-1

RFAR Publishing Trade Paperback Edition 2024

Printed and bound by IngramSpark.
Australia: Ingram Content Group AU Pty Ltd, Melbourne, Victoria.
US: Lightning Source LLC, La Vergne, Tennessee / Allentown, Pennsylvania / Jackson, Tennessee, United States.
UK: Lightning Source UK Ltd, Milton Keynes, United Kingdom.
Europe: Lightning Source UK Ltd, with facilities in Germany, France, and Spain.

Authorized Representative in the European Economic Area:
Lightning Source France
1 Av. Johannes Gutenberg, 78310
Maurepas, France.
compliance@lightningsource.fr

DEDICATION

For Patricia Highsmith

THE MAN WHO WOULD BE SANTA

~ THE NOEL KRINGLE CHRONICLES ~

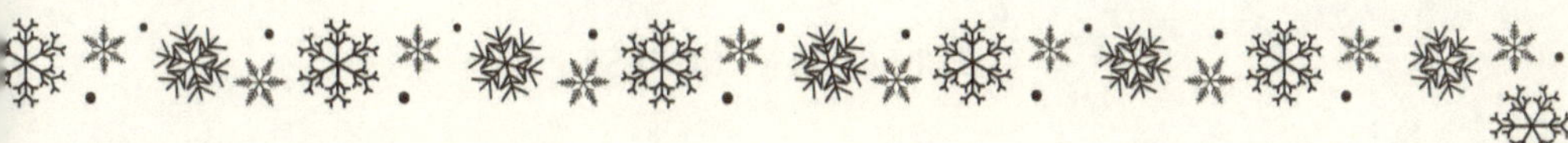

CHAPTER
ONE

Searing sunlight burned against my closed eyelids. I burrowed deeper into my bed, turning my face away from the window. It felt like I'd only been asleep for an hour, how could the sun be so bright?

It was late March and the sun didn't poke its head out until seven or so. Yet I could feel the rays brightening on my eyelids. I refused to open them to check the time. The sides of my head throbbed in time to my heartbeat. My mouth tasted stale and sour. Even closed, my eyes felt scratchy and dry.

Somehow I had made it to my bed.

Exactly how much Gellors scotch had I drank with Mallory last night?

We had been celebrating, I remembered that. With my help, Detective Stan Mallory had broken up a minor robbery ring. The pixies hadn't realized they'd been breaking the law, they just liked shiny objects like sparkling diamonds. A stern warning and a handful of polished marbles had sent the pixies on their way, with a promise that if they wanted more marbles they would come to me.

In return, they relinquished all the gems they'd stolen. Mallory made up a report of finding them with indications that the thieves were gone for good.

It wasn't like he could arrest a group of pixies anyway.

Nor could we send them back to the Magical Realm. They weren't able to describe exactly where they had come through. If it wasn't shiny or full of plants and leaves, pixies didn't pay attention. But I got them settled in a remote corner of High Park where they burrowed under the snow with their marbles to await the spring. Even when winter ended and the trees and grass bloomed again, I knew the pixies wouldn't be any trouble now. I made sure they knew to come to me with any problems and they agreed.

And why wouldn't they? They knew they could trust me. After all, I was Noel Kringle, the second son of Santa Claus.

Mallory hadn't been thrilled to just let the pixies go. But even he had to admit that they didn't seem to really care about the jewels once I handed over a handful of polished marbles. And returning the jewels had garnered him some high praise. So high when he returned to my office a smile had played across his bland face. His dark brown eyes glinted in the rays of the late afternoon sun.

As he settled into the hard back chair across from my desk, he brushed snow off the top of his salt and pepper crew cut that made his head look almost squarish. He'd dumped his beige trench coat on the sagging brown couch in my waiting room. Underneath he wore what I thought of as the Stan Mallory uniform: dark pants, a white shirt, usually rolled up to his elbows unless he was wearing his dark jacket. He'd been wearing the same outfit for the entire time I'd known him, since he had arrested me for a murder I didn't commit. Within the mint green walls of the precinct, I had convinced him otherwise, and of my identity, with the helpful use of discovering his favourite Christmas present, a toy police car that listed to the left.

As far I knew, he still kept it on his desk at work.

Over the years of associating with me, Mallory had come to experience more of the magical side than almost any other person I knew. And he'd managed to maintain his sanity. Now he sat with a satisfied look on his face.

"I think it's time for some Gellors," he said. "You still have my bottle, don't you?"

I raised an eyebrow at his possessive comment. "Your bottle?"

He chuckled. "No one can open it but me, right? You said it was magic that way, so why shouldn't it be my bottle."

I pulled the bottle out from my bottom desk drawer. The metal drawer squeaked a little, not surprising since I'd bought the scuffed metal desk at Goodwill. Along with the squeak, I felt a hint of magic tingling on my fingers. The enchantment I had on the bottom drawer still held strong. I had put a spell on the drawer to prevent anyone but me from opening it. It held anything magical that might be too dangerous to leave lying out in the open.

And the bottle of Gellors scotch I kept for Mallory.

I set the bottle on my desk blotter along with two glasses. Mallory leaned forward and unscrewed the top then he poured. Amber liquid spilled into the glasses.

We each picked up a glass and tilted it toward each other.

"To a successful job," I said.

"In your eye," he said.

We drank.

The Gellors was smooth and delicious. A hint of cinnamon and candy cane lingered on my tongue, the magic in the liquid evoking the flavour, not actually containing it. The Gnomes who made Gellors sure knew their stuff when it came to liquor.

Sooner than I expected my glass was empty. So was Mallory's.

"How 'bout another?" I said.

He poured.

Then he poured again.

I lost track of how many times he poured.

I vague remembered Mallory lolling over the side of the brown couch. Another flash of memory revealed me swirling sparkling lights throughout the office and waiting room while Mallory applauded. Yet another flash of the two of us singing Christmas carols, off key and at the top of our lungs.

And always with a glass of Gellors in our hands.

Then the inevitable despair of the bottle being empty. Mallory fumbling with his cell phone to call a taxi. But I had insisted I could *wink* him home myself. Even at the best of times, transporting another person when I wasn't traveling myself would be a challenge. Why had I thought I could do it while drunk?

Exactly because I was drunk.

Swirling snow, where had I sent Mallory?

I forced my eyes open, still squinting against the too-bright light, as I surged up to a sitting position. I had to figure out what had happened. I had to find him.

Then another flash of memory. Mallory at the main door to my office, waving goodbye as he dragged his trench coat along the floor after him.

He'd left on his own steam after all.

With relief, I sagged back against the pillows. He must have called a taxi after all and I had used my *wink*, my magic to propel me home in the wink of an eye. And then forgotten to turn the bedroom light off.

The bedroom light that revealed white walls with candy apple red trim.

Wait, what?

I opened my eyes wider, blinking the gumminess away as I focused around me.

White walls, red trim, a red door closed. The eight drawer dresser opposite white with red knobs. A matching nightstand of white and red with a lamp sitting on top. The lampshade decorated with Santa on his sleigh and the reindeer.

Damn the halls, I hadn't *winked* my way back to my apartment in Toronto, I'd *winked* my way back to my bedroom at the North Pole!

I started to shake my head but the throbbing in my temples stopped me. Easy, just take it easy. I shoved the covers off me. At least I'd managed to change into my pajamas and not slept in my clothes. One small positive.

I could almost hear the ribbing my older brother KJ was going to give me. KJ, Kris Junior, was the next in line for the Santa Claus job, a role he took very seriously. He would never overindulge because it could possibly affect his efforts to learn every aspect of the job. I could imagine him towering over me with his arms crossed over his barrel chest, wearing one of his favourite red flannel shirts, shaking his head enough that even his slicked-back, white hair would shimmy on his head. He kept his white beard neatly trimmed, enough that I would be able to make out the frown on his face.

I ran my hands through my own wavy brown hair. It didn't feel like it was sticking up too much. Some water splashed on my face, a quick change into my clothes, and maybe I could be out of here before anyone woke up. I knew if I stayed my mother would insist on making breakfast and not just any breakfast, but a huge celebratory brunch for her wayward second son.

My stomach just barely stopped churning at the thought of coffee. Any actual food would cause open rebellion.

As quietly as I could, I stumbled around the room, searching for my clothes. I'd been wearing a light blue shirt over navy pants with black socks. Being as drunk as I'd been I couldn't imagine I'd hung them up or stuffed them into the laundry hamper. They had to be somewhere on the floor.

But the only thing covering the hard wood floor of my North Pole bedroom was the large square area rug that looked like a wrapped present. Even as I groaned my way onto my hands and knees to peek under the bed, I couldn't find my clothes.

Damn the halls, did that mean my mother had found them and took them to wash? Did she already know I was here?

I was going to have to face that celebratory brunch whether I liked it or not.

Maybe she'd let me get away with coffee and a piece of toast.

Maybe two pieces.

Anything more than that and I'd be making a mess all over her table.

Finally I had to admit defeat. I couldn't find the clothes I'd wore here. I'd have to settle for some North Pole clothes.

As long as they didn't have too many tiny reindeer, or presents, or Santa hats. That wouldn't do my image any good when I returned to Toronto. Although I was sure Venir would find it endlessly amusing.

And would never let me forget it.

Of course, being an ex-Christmas Elf, maybe he would

like it. No, that wasn't Venir. He'd definitely take the opportunity to make fun of me, even though he wore countless t-shirts with Santa on them.

My other associate, Palle, would at least have the decency to pretend not to notice. Palle was a nine foot tall troll who used a masking spell to appear as a tall, burly man. I had saved him from an evil entity who had used Palle to cross into the Human Realm and enslaved the troll while it searched for a suitable host. Under its influence, Palle had tried to kill me and when I broke the enchantment, he had vowed to repay me before returning home. As far as I was concerned, he had more than paid me back but Palle didn't see if that way. And I knew better than to argue with a nine foot tall troll with huge tusks jutting out of the sides of his mouth. That along with his green skin, bald head, and pointed ears that curled over his head made for an impressive look when he didn't hide it under the masking spell.

Despite his appearance, Palle was a gentle soul and would not do anything to cause offence.

Venir, on the other hand, had no such restraint.

I sighed. I would have to find the least North Pole-esque clothes here and *wink* home to my Toronto apartment so I could change before I went to the office. It was bad enough that Venir and Palle would be confronted with the wreckage after Mallory and my little celebratory drinking fest, I didn't need to make it worse.

I wasn't exactly sure about all we'd done but I also

seemed to recall something about papering the walls with Christmas wrapping paper...

Trying to remember more just made my head hurt.

I lurched up from the bed and staggered over to the closet. My fumbling gained me a pair of black jeans and a red flannel shirt. Had KJ left one of his shirts in my closet? He'd probably be really annoyed if I wore it.

Which only meant I really had to.

I left the clothing on the bed and stumbled into the onsuite bathroom. The mirror over the sink showed me exactly how rough I looked. My cheeks looked a little hollow. Dark circles hung under my bloodshot brown eyes. My brown beard looked scruffier than ever. My hair stuck up around my head.

Definitely the look of a man who had overdone it with Gellors scotch.

I set the water to hot and ducked under the stream. The shock made me gasp. Then I switched to cold. My body shuddered and jolted upright. I could almost feel the last remnants of the scotch leach out of my system.

I stayed under the shower for fifteen minutes, alternating hot and cold, shocking my system until I felt completely awake. By the time I returned to the bedroom, hair still damp, beard neatened, I felt more myself again.

I dressed quickly and quietly. Maybe if I managed to avoid my mother I could still head straight home. I'd leave her a note with a promise to visit soon and pick up my clothes. I'd even bring her a present from Toronto. There was a place on College Street in Little Italy that sold Montreal-style bagels that she liked. I knew she'd love a dozen of those.

But when I stepped through the door, I caught a whiff of bacon. Mother was already cooking breakfast.

No way to sneak past her now.

I was going to have to face that celebratory breakfast after all.

I headed down the wide, sweeping staircase. Mother had done some redecorating since last I'd visited. The colour scheme still looked the same, white walls, a paler red trim than in my room, offset with deeper green accents. Photos still lined the wall down the stairs. Various shots of mother, dad, myself, the reindeer, the Elves. A few special anniversary Christmas shots before Dad made his run. His two hundredth year. His three hundredth year.

Many of them were the same shots, just moved around on the wall. But something seemed to be missing. I just couldn't put my finger on what though.

Maybe my brain was still a little foggy.

After all that Gellors, I wouldn't be surprised.

As I approached the kitchen, the scent of bacon was joined with the yeasty scent of fresh bread. My mouth watered and my stomach grumbled.

Maybe I'd manage more than two pieces of toast after all.

I stepped into the kitchen. The white motif carried through the room. To the left was the main area. Red cupboards lined the walls. A double-door fridge in sparkling white was directly to my left. The matching white oven sat across, boasting two large frying pans. One held the sizzling bacon.

My mother, dressed in a pale yellow dress with a white apron tied around her waist, stood at the sink, her back to me. Her curling white hair was swept up off her neck and bunched into a messy bun. Loose tendrils hung down along her neck. As she moved her head, I could see more tendrils curling beside her cheeks. She finished rinsing and shut the water off. With a flick of her hands, she cast off the few drips of water and turned to the island that sat in the middle of the room.

Her sparkling blue eyes widened at the sight of me as she set a tomato down on a cutting board.

"Well, look who's up finally," she said. "I thought the bacon would drag you from your bed."

"Good morning, mother," I said. I crossed around the island and kissed her cheek. She smelled of cinnamon and coffee.

"You didn't have to go to all this trouble," I said.

"Nonsense," she said. "You need a hearty breakfast after all your... celebrating." She cocked an eyebrow at me. With neat even movements, she began to slice the tomato.

I felt a flush colour my cheeks. What had I said or done when I'd appeared here? Obviously something that conveyed how drunk I'd been. If I admitted I couldn't remember I might lose all respect in her eyes.

"I'll set the table," I said. "Have you eaten?"

"I ate with your father," she said. "But I'm always up for another coffee."

I carried a white plate with tiny Christmas stockings around the edges to the breakfast nook tucked into the right corner. A window looked out on the expanse of snow that glittered like jewels under the pale March sun. After six months in darkness, even that pale light shone like a beacon but soon the sun would each its zenith and begin its six month stay in the sky. Somehow I'd found those days of constant daylight more disorienting than the months of constant night. At least in the night, the village, workshop and house could be brightened with light, strong enough that it almost felt like day. There was no way to mimic the night.

By the time I finished setting the table, including an extra coffee cup for mother, she was bringing over a platter of food. As usual, she made more than enough for a small horde. Scrambled eggs with flecks of chives, a sprinkling of pepper and grated Parmesan cheese. A small mound of bacon. Roasted potatoes and green onions. Fresh tomato slices. Thick slices of gently toasted bread.

My stomach, instead of churning at the sight of food, actually growled louder.

I took enough to cover my plate but the platter still looked full.

I poured us each a cup of coffee from the pot she'd set in the centre of the table. Mother added a splash of milk to hers and stirred.

I took a sip of mine. The rich, hot liquid warmed down my throat and perked me up even more than the shower. Soon I found myself shoveling egg in my mouth, followed by a bite of potatoes. The bacon and tomato followed, with the bread last. Then I rotated my way through again.

Normally my breakfast in Toronto was a hastily grabbed bagel with cream cheese at the local deli on the way to the office. I hadn't had a real breakfast like this since, well, since I'd left the North Pole.

I ate almost half the food on my plate before I slowed down. My mother was watching with an amused look on her face as she sipped her coffee.

"There's plenty if you want more," she said. "You don't have to eat like someone is going to steal your plate away from you."

"I was hungrier than I thought," I said. I nibbled on a piece of toast, washed it down with a sip of coffee. "You really didn't have to make so much unless KJ hasn't eaten breakfast yet."

A crease formed between her eyebrows. She tilted her head at me as she sipped her coffee. She swallowed and set the cup down on the table top. She rested her hands beside it, then opened her mouth.

"Who?" she asked.

CHAPTER

TWO

I froze, my fork piled with egg and cheese halfway to my mouth.

Then I got it. A joke. Ironic since he was always here and I hardly ever was but I could really see the humour. Maybe he'd done something to annoy her.

I chewed the egg and swallowed, following it with another sip of coffee.

"What's he done?" I asked. "He's not trying to mess around with the workshop schedule again, is he?"

The crease between my mother's eyebrows deepened. "Who are you talking about?"

I set my fork down on my plate. It only rattled a little. I kept my hand away from the coffee cup. I didn't want to risk spilling it.

This had to be a joke. Some strange joke. Maybe a way to

get back at me for just showing up here. But for the life of me I couldn't figure out how.

"KJ," I said. "Kris Junior. My older brother. Your eldest son. C'mon on, mother, you know him."

A slight frown joined the crease between her eyebrows. She leaned toward me slightly and I could see a steady serious look in her eye.

"Noel, you're my only son," she said. "I don't know anyone named KJ."

And just like that, all the food in my stomach turned to lead.

My heart pounded in my chest. I pushed back from the table but stayed seated in the chair. The air in the kitchen, filled with the rich, warm scent of food, now seemed cloying and close. The aroma of eggs and cheese seemed to stick in my throat. The yeasty scent of bread clogged my nose. I felt like gasping for air.

Slow, don't panic. It had to be some kind of joke, had to be. I couldn't imagine the punch line, but there had to be one.

Then I thought of the photos on the wall running down the staircase. Something had been strange about them. Now I knew what it was.

None of them had KJ in them.

I pushed up from the chair. My legs wobbled a little but not from the binge the night before. I steadied myself and headed out, hurrying as fast as I could.

"Noel, where are you going?" my mother called after me.

By the time I reached the staircase, I was running full out. My feet pounded on the steps as I raced up. I stopped halfway. Adrenaline coursed through my system, making my heart race. I clenched my hands into fists at my side as I stared at each photo in turn.

This one, a portrait from almost twenty years ago of my mother, father, and me, standing just outside the reindeer barn. We all wore red parkas with white fur trim. I remembered that one. KJ had left his coat unzipped until mother had seen it and scolded him to zip up. She'd wanted everyone to be dressed the same for the photo. KJ had humoured her by zipping up halfway, then given a thumbs up to the photographer. It had ended up in the photo.

Except he wasn't there anymore.

The spot where he should have been was empty. A blank space. The door behind us filled in the spot, along with the snow piled on our boots.

But KJ was gone.

Gone from another shot of Dad with the Elves inside the workshop. Gone from a photo of Dad with the sleigh, laden with wrapped presents. Gone from a shot with the reindeer.

Gone.

"Noel, are you all right?"

Mother stood at the bottom of the stairs, looking up.

My mouth was dry but I managed to croak, "Be right back."

I stumbled the rest of the way up the stairs.

The white walls seemed too bright. Every door, a rich,

solid oak, was shut except for the room I'd been in. My room. And right beside it on the left.

KJ's room.

Unclenching my hands made my knuckles pop. It sounded like a gun shot in the stillness, making me jump.

Easy, take it easy. Just open the door and KJ's room will be right there. Then we could all laugh at this strange joke. Ha ha, joke's on Noel.

Please let the joke be on me.

My hand barely trembled as I reached for the door knob.

And turned.

The door swung open.

White walls with the same red trim. A sewing table sat in the centre of the room with a sewing machine on top. What looked like Dad's coat was draped over a sewer's dummy off to the left. Tissue paper patterns were pinned to a cork board across from the door.

Nothing of KJ's. No wall calendar mapping out the year's schedule in meticulous print and highlighted in different colours. No bed, no dresser. No clothes, no photos, no cuff links. No sign of this being a bedroom, no sign it had ever *been* a bedroom, let alone KJ's room.

No sign of KJ at all.

"Noel, what's going on?" Mother's voice came from the direction of the staircase. She'd climbed halfway up. "Do you need something in my sewing room?"

If this was a joke it had gone too far. Not even KJ would pull something like this.

I turned back to her. No matter how hard I tried I couldn't stop my hands from clenching into fists. It was the only way to stop them from shaking.

"Where's Dad?" I asked.

THE OUTSIDE AIR WAS CRISP AND CLEAR. THE COLD HAD JUST enough bite that I could feel it on my cheeks as I trudged along the path from the house to the barn. Cold enough that I couldn't pretend that I was dreaming or hallucinating any of it. The crunch of my boots on the packed snow sounded almost muffled as if not wanting to disturb the pristine silence of the flowing whiteness around me.

On my left, the snow was an unbroken field as far as the horizon. It rose and fell in motionless drifts like an ocean frozen in time. The wind, an almost constant here, was a light breeze at the moment, barely tugging at the white fur around the hood of my red parka.

If I looked right, I would see how the hill began to gently slope away, down toward the village that nestled in a small valley below. Even at this distance, the two and three storey buildings broke through the snow, flashing hints of stone even as the snow tried to bury them. It was a constant give and take between the village and the storms, one that always ended in stalemate.

Then ahead of me I caught sight of the stables.

The white structure was two storeys high with a roof that was almost a dome shape, high enough to let the reindeer frolic inside when the weather was too bad for them to fly outside. Red double doors seemed to blaze against the whiteness of the snow. Even in a snow storm they were visible, acting as a beacon for the reindeer.

I pulled the doors open just wide enough to slip inside.

Warmth pressed against my face, bringing with it the thick scent of fresh hay. The floor had been cleared right down to the hard tundra and racked smooth. Ten stalls lined the walls, five on either side running the length of the barn. Only nine were used with the tenth being a spare at the far end on the right. Just beyond them was a large, interior paddock area were the reindeer could mingle together. Even though the walls of their stalls were low enough that they could see each other it was good for them to spend time together.

I stomped my boots to get rid of the extra snow and moved forward into the stable area. Several of the reindeer spotted me over the walls of their stalls. They stomped their hooves and nodded their heads, trying to catch my attention. Probably wanting treats. They always wanted treats, even after they'd just had a treat.

To my left a flash of red light flared up and died.

Rudolph making his bid for attention.

Normally I would wander from stall to stall, dispensing

pets and yes, some treats. But I couldn't linger today. I had to find Dad.

I moved down the centre aisle, heading for the back of the stables where three Elves congregated. They were holding feed-bags and shoveling feed from a canvas bag. I'd come at feeding time. No wonder the reindeer were so demanding for treats.

As I drew close, one of the Elves looked up. I recognized the round face and the brown curls tinged with grey. Bolaris who had just ended his apprenticeship and become a full fledged member of the stable team. He smiled when he saw me and nodded his head.

"Good morning, Master Noel," he said.

The other two Elves glanced up. One was Lectin, a short, round Elf with rosy cheeks and a white beard that grew to the centre of his chest. The other was a taller, thinner Elf who stooped from the shoulders. Bushy grey sideburns high-lighted his narrow cheekbones. For a moment his name escaped me, then I recalled it. Delbar. Normally he was on the night shift with the reindeer.

All three wore the usual stable gear. Brown leather, full body aprons that hung below their knees covering their dark green outfits. Black boots and brown leather gloves topped off the look. They each wore green Christmas hats, the white trim faded and slightly scruffy from being tugged down over their foreheads or snatched away by a mischievous reindeer, like that troublemaker Donner.

"Good morning, Master Noel," Lectin said. Delbar

mumbled something under his breath that could have been good morning.

"Have you seen my father?" I asked. "I'm looking for him."

"He was here, sir," Bolaris said. "He just left a few minutes ago."

Delbar mumbled under his breath, too low for me to hear.

"Pardon?" I asked.

"He said he thought Master Claus had gone to the supplies area," Lectin said. "We were just starting breakfast for the reindeer. Would you assist us?"

All three Elves looked at me expectantly. I remembered that KJ would always assist in every department. It was his way of learning all aspects of the Santa Claus job, a job he had been training for all his life. Dad still had at least another seven hundred years to go but training was ongoing. KJ was insistent on it.

Had been. Would be.

What did you call it when someone disappeared and weren't remembered?

Meanwhile, the three Elves continued to look expectantly at me.

I was desperate to see Dad but I couldn't just walk away without causing a huge stir. Gossip would spread like wildfire, how I thought I was too good to help out in the stables.

"Who gets the first bag?" I asked.

Feeding the reindeer seemed to take forever. The Elves were meticulous about the amount of feed each one received. Only when all nine bags were filled to perfection did the Elves start delivering them. At each meal time, they rotated how they distributed the feed. This time we carried the bags to the stalls near the front door and worked our way back.

"Mixin' up who eats first keeps them on their toes," Bolaris said.

"And stops any of them from feeling resentful for always getting fed last," Lectin said.

Delbar murmured something under his breath that I couldn't hear.

I could feel time slipping away by the time we finished delivering the final bag. It was to Donner, of course, who shoved its head so fast into the feedbag it almost dislodged from the hook on the door. I make a panicked grab for it which caused the Elves to chuckle.

"Don't worry, Master Noel," Lectin said. "Not even that rascal Donner would spill food."

I helped the Elves put away the remaining feed and finally took my leave. It had taken over half an hour to pour and distribute all the food. I only hoped Dad was still in supply or I might end up chasing after him all over the village.

The cold air held a welcome bite after the exertion of lugging the feedbags back and forth. My boots crunched on snow as I took the path away from the house and toward the cluster of buildings that nestled closer to the village. They contained the supply depot, packaging and wrapping, and the prestigious finishing and testing, the final step before presents were wrapped for placement in the sleigh. There was heavy competition to work in the finishing department. It took a meticulous eye and lots of skill to ensure everything was exactly right. Packaging and wrapping was sought after as well. There was nothing Elves enjoyed more than making something looked pretty.

But the supply depot was the lowest and considered drudgery work. There was no glory in keeping everyone supplied with the right amount of wood, metal, screws, or tools. It was the smallest building and the least appreciated by the Elves which was why I knew that Dad always tried to check in on a regular basis to let the Elves working there know that he appreciated them even if the work wasn't flashy.

The door was a single grey metal slab and with handle that pressed down to open. The single word SUPPLY was stenciled in black across the centre of the door. For the Elves, it would have been at eye level. Not that any of them needed reminding of what was in this building.

I grabbed the handle and pressed down. The click sounded strong and the door opened smoothly. I stepped inside to find myself faced with metal shelving that flowed away from the door. It looked like they went down the length of the building and reached almost to the ceiling. Boxes of materials filled each shelf, all meticulously labeled.

Seeing that all the Elves were less then four and a half feet, I had no idea how they would reach the upper shelves. I didn't see any sign of any ladders.

As I stepped in, my steps seemed to echo in the vastness of the building. The floor was white and felt like concrete under my boots. Each step echoed over the last one, fading before the noise got to be too loud.

I knew there was a counter where the Elves did the tracking and logging out of supplies. Usually it was near the door but all I could see were the metal shelves. Someone had gotten tired of that system and moved the desk elsewhere.

The Elves were always doing that sort of thing if they could get away with it. Supply was the only place Dad let them do it. It gave a smidgen of cache to this lowly place.

I headed down the row slightly to the left. Neatly printed labels marked everything available on the shelves. I passed a staggering awry of screws of all sizes and heads. Just after were the boxes containing the screwdrivers for those screws, referencing the box number of the screw for use.

All perfectly in order and perfectly maintained. I didn't understand why the other Elves thoought this was such an awful place. In some ways it was more vital than the workshop. The workshop couldn't run without Supply.

I was glad that Dad appreciated it even if the other Elves didn't.

A few feet away I noticed the edge of the shelving. I had reached one of the four aisles that cut through the rows, allowing the Elves to move quickly and efficiently through the warehouse.

I increased my speed. Maybe the tracking counter was in this aisle and Dad would be there, checking things out.

An Elf stepped into the row from the aisle, head bowed as he checked something on a clipboard in his hand. He wore a faded red outfit, minus the usual red hat. This allowed his white curly hair to float around his head like a cloud. Pointed ears poked up through the edges of his hair.

He lifted his head as he noticed me approaching, allowing me full view of his face.

I froze in shock and recognition.

"Venir!"

CHAPTER

THREE

The slightest frown creased Venir's face as he regarded me. Tension tightened his body. His hands clenched the clipboard.

"Somethin' I can do for you, Master Noel?" he asked.

His tone was flat. His gaze focused on the floor in front of me.

I felt my own body tighten in response. Venir had never reacted to me like this with such veiled animosity. But he'd never been a fan of KJ's, especially after KJ had caused him to be demoted to Supply.

Wait a minute.

With KJ somehow missing, had I been responsible for Venir's fall? Were we not even friends any more?

I swallowed my unease. Something was going on, something that had caused KJ to vanish or be forgotten but had left some of his actions and their effects intact. When I fixed it, everything would return to normal, including my friendship and working relationship with Venir.

Wouldn't it?

Yes, it would. I had to believe that.

"Is my father here?" I asked.

"He was, sir," Venir said. "But he left some time ago."

"Did he say where he was going?" I asked.

Venir's expression tightened. "He doesn't take me into his confidence, Master Noel."

Even in the flat tones, I could hear pain and anger. It made me feel helpless.

But maybe there was something I could try.

"Can I ask you a question?" I asked. "Have you ever heard of KJ?"

I held my breath as I waited for Venir's response. This time he frowned outright, wrinkles deepening on his forehead and around his mouth. I had never seen those lines be so deep before.

Not with the Venir as I knew him.

The Elf shook his head.

"Can't say I have, sir," he said. "Will there be anything else?"

The frown faded, leaving his expression bland and empty. It felt like a chasm had opened between us. There was no sign of the Elf who teased me but was also eager to help.

Who had bullied his way into being my associate in my private detective business. Who had trusted me with his shame of being demoted to Supply.

Instead, I faced that Elf whose spirit had been crushed by that demotion, and in this reality, it seemed it was my fault.

I had to set it right. But first, I had to find Dad.

"That's all for now," I said. "Thank you for your help."

Venir's eyes narrowed suspiciously but he didn't say anything as I turned away. I could feel his gaze, cold and hard, on my back as I walked all the way down the row toward the door.

Only when I stepped outside into the bite of wind did I actually feel warmth again.

AFTER STRIKING OUT AT SUPPLY, I HEADED TO PACKAGING AND wrapping. Again he had been there but I was too late to catch up. Now I had a sense of what he was doing. He was making the rounds, checking in with every aspect of Christmas production.

Knowing that, I could maybe jump ahead far enough to intercept him.

After packaging and wrapping, I knew he would check in with sorting. Last in line would be the workshop itself. The beating heart of Christmas production.

The workshop was a large, single storey building on the edge of the village. It consisted of a large, open room with two long tables running the entire length. At the far end, tucked into one corner was a small office for Dad but he hardly ever used it. Usually he was on the workshop floor with the Elves or dealing with other areas of production.

Benches sat on both sides of the two long tables in the workshop, allowing multiple Elves to work on the same toy from two sides. A narrow conveyor belt stretched along the centre of each table. It allowed for a flexibility in building. Some Elves preferred to build a toy from start to finish, others specialized on specific tasks.

As of late March, no Elves should have been working in the workshop but Elves were never very good at taking time off, even when my mother mandated it. She had various projects to keep the Elves away from toy building, ranging from repainting all the exterior walls of each building, to organizing a massive party for the entire village. Still a few Elves managed to slip back into the workshop to tinker and when I opened the door and stepped inside, I found a couple doing just that.

The three Elves that gathered together at one end of the table on the right started at my appearance. They all wore the usual green outfit with the leather work apron tied around their waists. One of the Elves, shorter and squatter than the other two, twisted to hide the table top from my view.

"It's still too early to be making toys," I said. "My mother would be disappointed that you aren't taking time to relax."

"We aren't making toys, Master Noel," said one of the skinny Elves. I recognized the voice. His name was Fentor. His voice had a funny squeak at the end of each sentence as if he was part mouse.

"What are you building then?" I asked.

Nervous looks passed between the three Elves. Finally Fentor gave a quick nod. The squat Elf turned to look at me and I recognized his round face and bulbous nose. Renalor who was a master of delicate machinery. He bowed his head at me.

"We're makin' a present for the mister and missus," he said. His voice was a low rumble. "Present for their anniversary."

Of course the Elves were keenly aware of all important dates regarding my parents and went out of their way to express appreciation. I couldn't help but be touched by their thoughtfulness.

"Dad will be heading over shortly," I said. "Finish up as fast as you can."

Fentor blinked. "You aren't wanting to be checkin' it out?"

I smiled. "I would hate to ruin your surprise any more than I already have."

Renalor bowed his head again. A smile made his face even round.

"Thank you, Master Noel. We'll be but a few minutes. Any chance you could delay Santa a few minutes?"

"Sure," I said. "I'll keep him at the door."

I could hear their collective sighs of relief as I stepped back outside and closed the door behind me.

As the door clicked shut, I heard the crunch of snow under boot. I turned.

My father, Kris Kringle aka Santa Claus, moved smoothly down the path. He was a large man, both in stature and girth. He wore a red parka zipped to just below his chin. A red scarf with white snow flakes decorating it was tied around his neck. His white hair was trimmed and styled around his bare head with not a strand out of place, even in the constant breeze. His beard was trimmed along his jaw line.

At the beginning of December both his hair and beard would grow and become bushy, taking on the usual Santa Claus look, but for now he was able to keep it trim and neat.

A smile blossomed on his face, making his round cheeks even rounder and jolly. His eyes sparkled. Even in late March, the Christmas magic flowed off him with ease.

"Noel, my boy." His voice boomed across the space between us. "If I'd known you were going to join me on my rounds today, I would have waited for you. Glad to see you're so eager to learn, son."

He reached me and put a hand on my shoulder. I could feel his warmth flow through me.

"I'm glad I caught up to you, dad," I said. "I wanted to talk to you."

"Of course, of course," he said. "Let's step inside out of the cold."

I thought of my promise to keep Dad at the door.

"Let's stay out here," I said. "It's not that cold and it's nice to see the sun again."

Dad chuckled. "You say that now but I know you'll be gripping in a few months."

"I don't gripe any more than you do," I said.

That earned a full laugh from Dad. His entire body shook with laughter, especially his belly which wasn't nearly as large as people thought. It was mostly the bulkiness of the coat he wore during his one night a year trip, designed to keep him well insulated in the upper atmosphere.

Finally his laughter trickled away.

"So what's this topic of conversation, son?" he asked. "Could it have something to do with the present the Elves are making in there?"

I kept my expression carefully neutral. It didn't surprise me at all that Dad knew something was up inside the work-shop. Knowing who was naughty and who was nice wasn't an instinct he could turn off. There were aspects to the Santa Claus magic that even I didn't understand.

And I was counting on it to help me figure out what had happened to KJ.

"That's not what I want to talk about," I said. "I want to ask you about... KJ. Kris Junior."

I let my brother's initials and name drop into the silence between us and waited, watching my father's face carefully. No flicker of recognition. No frown of confusion. One eyebrow twitched, a slight hint of curiosity. But no other reaction.

"Who?" he asked.

The single word hit me like a punch to the gut. I almost doubled over. My breath whooshed out of me as if I had been actually hit.

Concern flickered over Dad's face. He reached out a hand toward me.

"Noel, are you all right?"

"You've never heard of KJ?" I asked.

He shook his head. "Should I?"

I pressed my lips together. Decision time. Dad's Santa Claus magic might be able to help me figure out what was going on but asking him to invoke it outside of Christmas was a dangerous thing. The magic held at the North Pole was a delicate balance between the Human Realm and the Magical Realms. Only at Christmas was the full power of the Santa Claus unleashed to assist Dad in his single night's journey around the world. The only time it could be used outside of that event was during an emergency.

If there was any time that was an emergency it was KJ vanishing, not only without a trace but without anyone remembering him.

Except me.

I had to take the chance.

"Listen to me carefully, dad," I said. "This will probably sound a little strange but I have an older brother named Kris Junior. We all call him KJ."

Dad's brow crinkled but a hint of amusement played across his face.

"Does your mother have something she forgot to tell me?"

"I get that you think I'm an only child," I said, "but I remember KJ. I grew up with him. He's the one who's supposed to train and eventually replace you as Santa Claus. I left the North Pole and moved down to Toronto for work."

"Really?" I could tell from his tone that he was humouring me. "What kind of work do you do down there?"

"I'm a private detective," I said. "At least I was until I woke up this morning. I went to bed at my home in Toronto and woke up here."

Dad gave a slight chuckle. "You've always had such an imagination. I told your mother we shouldn't have let you read too many of those books."

"It's not books, dad," I said. "It's not a story, it's not made up in my head. It's real. I woke up here and suddenly no one remembers KJ but me. And there's no trace of him. Not his room, not in any of the family photos. But he's real, dad, and something has happened to him."

The twinkle of amusement faded from my father's face. He regarded me seriously.

"This isn't some kind of trick," he said. "You really believe this."

I nodded. "I do."

His expression became even more sober.

"I didn't realize how tired you were," he said. "I know being Santa Claus is an incredible burden and you've always worked so hard to learn everything. I shouldn't have let you take on so much at this point. It isn't necessary."

"Dad…" I started but he held up a hand to silence me.

"It's obvious you're feeling a great strain, creating an older brother who would take the burden from you," he said. "I never should have let you push yourself like this." He put a hand on my shoulder. "This is what we will do. You will step back from any Christmas duties for a time. You will rest and recover. If you wish, you can even take a trip. And when you return, we'll take it slower, my son."

His hand squeezed my shoulder affectionately. Compassion and concern radiated from his eyes.

He didn't believe a word I'd said. Instead, he thought I was overtired, stressed, possibly delusional.

And for the first time since I'd woken up that morning I was wondering if he wasn't correct.

I RETREATED TO MY ROOM, EVEN REFUSING MY MOTHER'S OFFER OF fresh hot chocolate. I needed to think, to figure things out.

I sat on the side of my messy bed, staring out the window

at the expanse of snow glittering in the sun. Everything looked solid and real. The white walls with candy apple trim. The firm mattress under my rump. The snow outside my windows with the occasional eddy of loose flakes swirling up as the breeze caught them and made them dance.

Was I losing my mind? Had I somehow convinced myself that I had an older brother who would inherit the Santa Claus mantle other than me? Having two children was unprecedented for a Kringle so me being an only child made sense. Only one child to learn the Santa Claus job and take over when Dad retired.

But if that were true, if I'd made KJ up in my head, why did I remember him so clearly?

Building snow forts when we were kids, his constant teasing about being Santa Claus, his disdain when I left to work in Toronto. His occasional trips to my office where he put his boots up on my desk and grumbled when I insisted he take them down. Him helping me, him getting in trouble. Him complaining about me wasting my life.

All so clear.

How could I have made that up? Sure I had imagination but not that good.

Something must have happened to him, something that upset the balance, the time flow, that left me as an only child to take over the Santa Claus mantle.

But if that was right, had I never gone to Toronto? Had I never become a private detective?

What had happened to my cases?

I felt a chill run through me even though my room was toasty warm.

Had anyone helped those people, solved those mysteries? What had become of my clients?

I had to find out.

Dad had said I should get away.

I decided to take his advice.

CHAPTER

FOUR

"What do you mean you're leaving?"

Mother stood at the sink, her hands paused in the act of wiping themselves on a tea towel. Beneath her white apron, her yellow dress looked as soft as butter. Several strands of her white hair had escaped the bun at the back of her head and curled beneath her ears. Other loose wisps curled by her cheeks, heightened them. Even with her slight frown, she looked lovely.

I stood opposite her beside the breakfast nook where only a few short hours ago I realized I wasn't just visiting but had somehow woken up in some kind of alternative life.

"Dad says I should take a break," I said. "I think he's right. I've been working too hard. So I'm going to take a trip."

She squared her shoulders and lifted her chin. "Kris Kringle, you come here right this minute."

Her sharp command echoed through my mind. I remembered that summoning. Usually it was for KJ and I when we were late for dinner.

Or maybe it was just for me. I couldn't be sure and I had to find out.

A moment later a popping sounded as the air was displaced by my father. He appeared just inside the back door, standing on the mat. Immediately, the snow crusted on the tops of his boots began to melt.

He'd thought of that in the instant he'd heard my mother's call and landed on the mat so he wouldn't ruin the floor she'd worked so hard to keep clean.

KJ and I had never thought of that.

Dad wiped the edges of his moustache down. "Yes, dear?"

Mother crossed her arms over her chest.

"Did you tell Noel to leave?" she asked.

"That's not exactly what he said..." I started.

A sharp glare from my mother shut me up.

"I merely said maybe he should take a break. Go away for a bit. He's been working awfully hard lately. We're not even into the season yet, Mary. There's lots of time. He could go away for a bit."

"And I am not consulted about this?" she asked. "You don't wonder if maybe I have things he could do to help me?"

"Now Mary, you know if there's anything you need I will help you."

She pressed her lips tight together until they formed a thin line. Then she puffed out a breath of air.

"And what about this older brother he talks about?"

Worry crinkled her brow, making it easier for me to hear the fear in her voice.

Dad stomped on the mat, knocking the rest of the snow loose from his boots. Then he crossed the kitchen to wrap an arm around my mother's shoulders.

"That's why he just needs a break," he said. "Noel will go sort himself out and come home good as news. Right, my boy?"

Beneath my father's bravado, I could hear a faint whisper of worry.

Was he wondering what he would do if I couldn't be convinced I was an only child? If I held fast to this belief of an older son who somehow didn't exist anymore? If I was somehow losing my mind?

I pushed that away. I had to go to figure out if my memories were real or something I had imagined. I couldn't do that here.

"That's right," I said.

"See Mary?" Dad tightened his grip around her shoulders. "It's going to be just fine."

Mother blinked several times and I realized she was blinking back tears. A hint of a smile touched her lips.

"We'll be waiting," she said. "You'll always have a place with us."

My chest tightened around my heart. Part of me wanted

to assure her I wasn't going to go but I had to stand fast against that instinct. Instead, I nodded.

"There's just one thing," I said. "I want someone to come with me. And I know exactly who."

VENIR FROWNED AT THE BLUE JEANS AND GREEN CABLE KNIT sweater in his arms.

"I'm not sure I'm the one for this duty, Master Noel." His voice was stiff and gruff, with a hint of impatience.

More like the Venir I knew but to see if I could trigger any memories, I had to get him out of the North Pole environment.

And it would test my own as well.

"You're exactly the Elf I need," I said. "I need someone who will watch my back but not just be a Yes Elf."

The faintest flicker of a smile crossed the Elf's face. "So a little informality is all right?"

"Yes," I said.

He hefted the clothes in his arms again. "Okay, kiddo, I'll do it."

Now that sounded like the Venir I knew.

A moment later, a shimmer appeared around him and the clothes vanished from his arms, magically appearing on his body. He shifted his shoulders and kicked out his legs, as if testing the feel of the clothing. A perplexed expression settled on his face.

"They feel odd," he said.

"You'll get used to them," I said. "Make sure to put on the parka and boots as well. It's still winter down where we're going."

He gave a snort. "Winter," he grumbled under his breath but a moment later another shimmer flashed over him. Brown leather hiking boots covered his feet and a green parka covered his body, hanging almost to his knees. He tugged on the sleeves.

"A little too big," he said.

"Never mind that," I said. "Now remember while we're down there you'll need to mask your ears and not engage in any overt forms of magic."

He nodded. For a moment, his pointy ears wiggled and then vanished beneath the white curls of his hair.

"How's that?" he asked.

"Perfect. Make sure it holds."

"Yes, boss."

His voice held an edge of sarcasm but the words sent a forlorn pang through me. In my memories as a private detective with Venir as my associate, he always called me boss and with no irony or sarcasm. We'd become true associates and friends through the cases we'd worked on.

Would I be able to get that back?

I took a breath. First things first. We had to leave the North Pole and I had to figure out what happened to KJ, where he was and why no one but me could remember him. Then I had to set everything to rights again.

Because if there was one thing this experience was showing me, it was that I did *not* want to become Santa Claus.

"Okay Venir, let's go," I said. "Next stop, Toronto."

I grabbed hold of the sleeve of his puffy parka and focused. My magic surged through me, strong and alive at the North Pole. I had to remember I wouldn't have this power while I was in Toronto. I would have to rely on my wits, such as they were. But for now, I relished the feeling of energy sparking through my body.

And pulling Venir along, I *winked.*

IN THAT WINK OF AN EYE, I TRANSPORTED US FROM THE NORTH POLE to a street in Toronto. Because of how quickly that instantaneous transportation was, I always called it a *wink.*

We landed in a snow drift, piled on the side of a shoveled sidewalk. The air was filled the stench of exhaust. Other odours fought for dominance: garbage, perfume, sweat, wet fabric, mold. All the smells of a city.

The smells of home.

Beside me, Venir wrinkled his nose.

"Boy, it's smelly. And ugly."

The day was overcast. The sky was the colour of slate grey with clouds hanging heavy as if they were about to drop onto the city. We had landed at the edge of the parking lot of my office building. Situated in a run-down area of the east end, the snow covering the ground actually hid the cracked sidewalk and asphalt of the parking lot.

Along the sidewalk at irregular intervals, thin, spindly trunks of tree stuck up through the snow, branches empty of any leaves. They looked more like stick drawings of trees than actual trees.

I turned my back to the road and faced the building at the edge of the parking lot. So familiar. Faded red brick. Windows covered in grime.

I trudged over the snow-covered path to the stairwell door and opened it. The same, familiar disused look. Bland beige walls. Concrete steps leading upward.

By the time we stood outside the frost door of what should be my office, my hands were trembling. But instead of my name on the door, it was blank and the office beyond was dark.

"So are we goin' in?" Venir asked from behind me. I realized I'd been standing there for several minutes.

I grabbed the door knob and twisted, pushing the door open. The air smelled stale and damp, reminding me of the first time I'd visited the office. I fumbled for the light switch and hit it.

Pale light filled the space. The empty space. No brown sofa sitting against the left wall in front of the door. No plastic yellow chairs lined up to the right of the door. No small table tucked into the far right corner beside the door that led to the small half bathroom. No coffee table in the middle of room filled with old magazines.

Nothing but dust.

What should have been my waiting room was nothing now.

The door directly across was closed. My breath caught. I didn't want to see behind that door. It should have been my office, with my old, scuffed metal desk that I'd found at Goodwill. My creaking leather chair tucked behind it. Two hard back, wood chairs for guests in front. A metal filing cabinet tucked into the corner. Everything was so clear in my mind's eye, I didn't want to not see it in reality.

But I had to be sure.

My steps seemed to echo as I crossed the empty not-my-waiting room. As I reached the door, I heard Venir step in behind me and give a snort.

I opened the door to what should have been my office.

As empty as the waiting room.

A film of dust covered the window that would have been directly behind me when I sat at my desk. The parquette flooring was empty without my desk sitting on it. A thin layer of dust was undisturbed, showing how long this place had stood unused.

"Yesh, what a dump," Venir said.

I turned to regard him as he stood in the centre of the empty waiting room. He gestured around him.

"This should be my office," I said.

Venir cocked his head at me. "What office?"

"I was...am a private detective," I said. "Or I should be." I shook my head. "It's complicated."

Venir crossed his arms over his chest. "Uh huh."

I stared across at him. The urge to tell him everything was strong and I should have been able to, after all we were friends, colleagues. But that was a different Venir. One who knew me as the youngest son, the one who left the North Pole, who took a chance to confide in me about a plot against Dad.

This Venir was someone completely different. Who knew me as the only son of Kris Kringle, the heir apparent to Santa Claus.

Would he trust me?

Then again, how could I expect him to if I didn't take the chance and trust him.

"Remember earlier in the Supply Depot, I asked you if you'd ever heard of KJ?" I asked.

The Elf tilted his head. His arms were still crossed over his chest.

"Yeah," he said.

A flat tone. He wasn't even curious.

I blundered on.

"KJ is my older brother. Kris Junior. You don't remember him, do you?"

Now Venir's head shifted back on his neck. His expression was carefully neutral, like he didn't want to cause me any upset.

"Can't say that I do, sir."

I sighed. I was going to have to tell him everything.

"Before I woke up this morning, everything was different," I started.

And I told him. All of it. Growing up with KJ. Moving down to Toronto to be a private detective. The cases I worked on and how Venir had joined me. At that, the Elf began to shake his head but he didn't interrupt. I continued through to celebrating with Mallory and then waking up at the North Pole this morning.

By the time I finished, I felt winded. Dust scratched at the back of my throat. I wished I had some water.

The half bathroom just off the waiting room. There was a sink in there.

I crossed the room. Puffs of dust followed in my wake. The door to the bathroom creaked as I opened it. I fumbled for the light switch and flicked it on.

The plain, white porcelain sink to my left and the toilet to the right. Just ahead was the towel bar where I usually hung two bath towels, white with Christmas Santas on them, a gift from mother.

The towels hung there.

"Venir!" I shouted.

The Elf appeared on my right side. "Yeah, what?"

I pointed at the towels. "Those were mine," I said. "If everything I said was wrong, they shouldn't be here."

Venir frowned.

"It's just a coupla towels."

"But they're *my* towels," I said. He crinkled his nose, not getting my point.

Mind you, I wasn't sure what my point was either but I knew those towels. I knew they were mine.

I hadn't imagined it all.

I turned to speak to Venir, then caught a glimpse of shimmering over his shoulder.

For a moment, the atmosphere in the room shifted. The thick scent of dust vanished. Across the room, my brown couch appeared. The yellow plastic chairs. The coffee table. The little table with the coffee machine. Everything appeared.

But none of it was solid. It looked faded like an old photograph. Even as I watched, it began to shimmer and fade again.

I grabbed Venir by the shoulder and spun him around.

"Hey..." he started. Then stopped as he caught sight of the fading furniture. After a moment it was all gone.

I felt a tingling in the air, like static electricity.

Residual magic.

"Do you feel that?" I asked.

Venir nodded. "Powerful spell. Somebody got ridda that stuff right quick."

"My furniture," I said.

The Elf looked up at me. "You weren't kiddin'? You really were a private detective?"

"I wasn't kidding," I said. "I was and you were my associate. And my friend."

Venir still didn't look entirely convinced but he seemed less hostile to the thought than before.

"So if that was the case, then what's going on?" he asked.

"That's exactly what I'm trying to figure out," I said. "And you're here to help me."

"Okay," he said. "So how do we do that?"

I took a deep breath and let it out. "I'm thinking about that."

My mouth still felt dry. I turned back to the sink and took a quick glance at the towel rack.

The two Christmas towels that had been hanging there were gone.

CHAPTER

FIVE

Without an office and a computer of my own, I was going to have to find one that I could use. Staying in my non-office wasn't a good idea, not with something magical affecting it. I had to find somewhere in the city I hadn't been before, something untouched by whatever was happening.

Then I thought of the perfect spot.

The library was in a red brick building up a long curving walkway. I stepped out of the shadows of the apartment building across the street. After a moment, I felt a tingle as Venir *winked* into place behind me.

I waved to him and we crossed the street.

The air was still chilly but the sun seemed to be making a weak attempt to penetrate the cloud cover. As I followed the curve of the path, a faint hint of a shadow led the way. Then as I passed under the overhang of the building, I felt the temperature drop as I moved out of the range of the sun.

When I pulled open the door, warm air rushed to greet me. I felt it envelope me as I stepped inside.

The library spread out before me. To my right, a pale grey counter curved like a snake away from the door. Several monitors sat spaced along the counter in regular intervals. A wide space stretched from the counter to several display tables on the left. Books were arranged in themes on the tables. Beyond them, three long, rectangular tables about ten feet long filled the space, sitting in front of heavy wood book shelves.

Just ahead past the counter was a set up of six computers on a table, three per side. Four of the computers were being used.

"Let's get one," I said to Venir. We crossed the grey carpeting. Just before I reached the desk with the computers, I spotted a sign sitting on the end of the table, instructing anyone who wished to use the computers to sign up with their library card.

Uh oh.

I didn't have a library card.

Venir stopped beside me as I paused. "What's up?"

"I don't have a library card to sign up with," I said.

The Elf waved away my concern. "Watch this."

He turned and marched over to the counter. Because of his height, the counter came up to his collarbone.

The librarian, a young Asian girl with square black

glasses and straight black hair, peered down at him.

"May I help you?" she asked.

"Yeah," Venir said. "I wanna use one of those boxes with the screen."

"Do you have a library card?" she asked.

Venir tilted his head. "Yes."

The word was spoken with force and a heavy dose of magic behind it. I could even feel it tingling along my skin from several feet away.

The librarian behind the desk didn't stand a chance.

She stood, revealing a long black skirt under her pale blue blouse. With quick steps, she hurried around the edge of the counter and crossed to the closest computer. A few clicks on the keyboard and the monitor lit up.

"You enter your card number here," she said. Her voice sounded distant.

"You do it," Venir said.

For a moment, she hesitated and I thought her natural inclinations would override Venir's suggestion but then she started typing. When she hit enter, the screen cleared.

"Thanks," Venir said. "No sense in remembering this."

He waved her away. She turned and walked away, not heading directly for the counter. It took her a moment to reorient herself and return to her spot. For a brief moment, a look of puzzlement creased her forehead then smoothed away.

Venir gestured to the screen. "Does that work?"

"It does," I said. "That wasn't entirely necessary."

"Really? You got time to futz around?"

He had a point, and one he made sounding more and more like the Venir I knew.

I sat down at the computer before I could say something embarrassing.

Without my files, I couldn't remember every one of my cases, but I could remember some of them. If I was now the Santa Claus heir that meant I had never come down to Toronto and those cases would never have been solved. Not by me anyway and probably not by anyone else. They weren't exactly regular cases.

I began searching.

First, I discovered that Regina Marcus who worked for the Way Station Mission had disappeared a number of years ago and never reappeared. Disappearances around the city rose, causing a clamour for answers from the police. But they had their hands full.

Charred, stone-like bodies appeared every other month and had been for years. The count was up to twenty and growing. At the same time, there were reports of a large creature smashing things. People claimed to have glimpsed something huge and green. They had nicknamed the monster the "Hulk."

My heart dropped. Palle Grubrand. He was a troll who had been hijacked by an evil entity and crossed over from the Magical Realm. I had rescued him while stopping the evil entity. But in this reality it had never happened. The charred, stone-like bodies were the devastating remains of the entity's quest to find a body that would hold it. But there wasn't any here. It would burn through the entire city before it found anyone.

And it looked like it was trying to. Meanwhile, Palle remained its prisoner.

The string of deaths went on, including a rash of murders of prominent Torontonians just before Christmas. With dismay I reviewed the names. Eleven in total, just missing the magical number of twelve that Grinela had aimed for to crush Christmas.

I flipped to another report. And another.

More and more strange happenings all year long. A popular neighbourhood haunted house attraction shut down due to unexplained deaths. The city seemed darker than ever before. Phrases like 'unexplained' or 'unknown' littered the stories but I knew what they really meant.

Unchecked magical phenomena rampaging through the city. How long before the effects started to ripple outward, extending across the province, across the country, and then across the world?

That gave me an idea.

I widened my scope and focused northward. A rash of disappearances from Camp Cristain last summer, five miles north of Toronto. I reviewed the list of names and stopped at the last one.

Robbie Trombley.

Shirl's nephew. The nephew I had helped rescue along with his friend.

I could find no mention of Shirl herself. What had happened to her?

Shirl Trombley was my resident computer expert and friend. She was excellent with research, had a not so secret love of Christmas, and made a tart and tasty lemonade based on her grandmother's recipe.

She'd made the switch from hacking to using her computer skills for good. I liked to think I helped along the way.

But what had happened to her in this revised world?

I had to find out. Just like I had to find Mallory.

I pushed away from the computer and stood up. Venir who had been peering over my shoulder stumbled back.

"What's all that stuff?" he asked. "Are places down here always like this?"

"No, it's all wrong," I said. "All of the cases I worked on, they're rampaging across the city. Magic is breaking loose and we weren't here to stop it."

"We?" the Elf said. His voice squeaked a little.

"We," I said. "You helped me with this, Venir."

But already the Elf was shaking his head. I could almost see the tips of his pointed ears shaking in the movement.

His fear was palatable. This wasn't the Venir who risked everything to bring me the information about the threat to my father and who had then joined me, whether I liked it or not. This was a different Elf, spirit weighed down under his demotion, still despairing. Would he be able to rise to help me?

He had to, he was the only Venir I had right now.

I grabbed his shoulder and turned him toward the door.

"Let's go. I've got someone I need to find."

THE INTERIOR OF THE POLICE STATION LOOKED THE SAME. SAME scuffed counter in front of a bored-looking officer in uniform. The same stale air with a hint of dust and exhaust from outside. Just beyond the desk, I even spotted the mint green walls leading deeper into the precinct.

The bored-looking officer sighed as he regarded me. He could have been anywhere from forty-five to seventy-five with deepening wrinkles lining his mouth and forehead. Light brown hair was brushed back from his face, only high-lighting his receding hair line. He had his folded hands resting in front of him.

"What was the name?" he asked for what felt like the fifth time in a row.

"Mallory," I said. "Detective Stan Mallory."

He tilted his head at me. "Malloy?"

"Mallory." I mimed spelling it out on the faded counter, emphasizing the letter R.

"Mallory," he finally said. "Let me check."

He turned away and his head dipped down as he looked at a monitor set below the counter. I heard keys tapping as he typed.

"Mallory," he repeated. "Sam."

"No, Stan," I said.

"Gotcha." He tapped a few more times before sitting back. He scratched his chin.

I waited.

Venir stood beside me. His eye level was just below the counter and he kept standing on tiptoes trying to see over.

"What's happening?" he asked.

I shook my head.

"Here we go," the officer said. "Stan Mallory."

"That's right," I said. "Is he here? Can I see him?"

The officer shook his head. "Who did you say you were again?"

I caught an undercurrent in his voice, a hint of suspicion. He hadn't turned his head toward me but I could feel his gaze.

Something was wrong here. If I pressed I could get into trouble. But I had to know.

I leaned on the counter and focused on the officer. Taking a deep breath, I drew on my magic.

I felt the power surge up inside me stronger than it had ever been while down here before. Of course, in this reality I was still strongly tethered to the North Pole. I had more access to my magical power but the longer I was down here the weaker that link would become.

For now, I would take advantage of it.

"Do you like Christmas, officer?" I asked.

His body stiffened and then relaxed. He got a soft, dreamy look on his face. From his mind I could easily pluck out the image of his favourite Christmas present, a cowboy play set, complete with hat, badge and spurs. It was what had directed him toward law enforcement, even if he couldn't be a sheriff.

"Tell me where Stan Mallory is." I pitched my voice low and let my magic do the trick.

His fingers twitched. I could feel him trying to resist telling, trying to do the right thing. I wanted to force him, could feel the magical energy within me eager to leap out but I held back. It was always better to give any spell time to work.

He shook his head but his mouth dropped open.

"Suspended," he said.

The word shocked me. Mallory was suspended? How could that be? He was an honest, hardworking police detective. What could he have done to be suspended?

I wanted to ask but there wasn't enough time before the magic wore off and I had another question to ask.

"Give me his home address," I said.

I had just enough left in the spell to get that and then I could find Mallory and ask him myself.

THE HOUSE WAS A TINY BUNGALOW IN THE NORTHWEST END OF THE city. Snow softened the edge of the dirty, yellow brick and hid most of the faded, grey tiles on the angled roof. A blue sedan sat in the driveway, the trunk and back window covered in snow. No one had driven that car for some time.

Venir followed me up the driveway. I could feel his boots crunching on the snow I kicked out of the way. As I neared the front door, I noticed that the curtains were drawn across the front window.

Was anyone even here?

I reached the front door, a pale brown that looked more steel than wood. I pressed the door bell and heard the off-key notes echo. I waited a beat.

Venir sniffled and rubbed his nose. When I glanced back at him he was looking back at the road, a bored expression on his face.

I rang the bell again.

"Nobody's here," the Elf said.

"We'll give it a minute," I said. My voice sounded confident and determined but what would I do if Mallory wasn't here? What was my next step?

How was I going to figure out what happened to KJ that caused my world to turn upside down?

Then the lock clicked and the door was yanked open.

"Who'er you and whadaya want?"

Stan Mallory stood in the doorway, swaying from side to side as if we were on a cruise ship. His normally neatly cropped salt and pepper hair had grown long enough to stick out in various directions around his head. The beginnings of a scrappy beard dotted his chin and cheeks. Instead of his regular crisp, white shirt and black pants, he wore a grey t-shirt so faded I couldn't read the logo on it over khaki sweat pants. His feet were bare.

The scowl on his face was the most animated I'd ever seen him and the glare was enough to convince me to take a half step back to avoid being punched.

If he could see straight enough to punch.

"Detective Stan Mallory," I said.

The glare which had wavered to just left of my face snapped back into place.

"Who're you?"

"I'm Noel Kringle. We should be friends. It kind of a strange story. May I come in?"

He grumbled but stepped back, turning away as if something else inside had caught his attention. He just left the door open which I took as an invitation to come in. Venir followed close behind.

"He's snookered," the Elf said in a low whisper. "It's not even noon."

"Hang on to my coat." I shrugged off my parka and dumped it in the Elf's arms. That would give him something to focus on.

I stepped into the living room. Pale light filtered around the curtains of the window on my right, giving suggestions to mounds in the room that were probably furniture. A large lump was against the wall to my left. Another, smaller lump was set to my right, closer to the window. In the far left corner, I caught a suggestion of movement. Mallory.

Shifting slightly to my right, I felt my knee bump into a table. I touched it to steady it and felt the base of a lamp. I switched it on.

The lumps coalesced into furniture. The fabric was a woven, darker taupe colour on the couch against the left wall. A matching armchair sat just to my right. Mallory slumped in another armchair in the far corner. On the coffee table, a collection of used glasses were piled near the armchair. A relatively cleaner glass sat on the end table beside him. It was half full of a liquid that reminded me of Gellors scotch.

Mallory blinked and frowned. "Who're you 'gin?"

"Noel Kringle," I said. "Youngest...son of Kris Kringle. Santa Claus."

Behind me, I heard Venir gasp. Telling a normal human was severely frowned upon.

Mallory shook his head. "I'm not drunk 'nuff for this."

He reached for his glass.

I flicked my hand, causing the glass to skitter away. It floated off the end table, following the line of my finger as I directed it toward the coffee table. It landed on the end closest to me, away from the pile of used ones on his end.

Mallory's gaze flicked from the empty spot on the end table to where the glass rested now and back.

"How...," he started.

"I told you. Son of Santa. I'm magic." I glanced back at Venir. "Is there a way to sober him up fast?"

The Elf shrugged from under the pile of my parka.

Great. I was going to have to do this the hard way.

"Where's your kitchen?" I asked. "I'll make coffee."

Mallory was leaning forward, his hands resting on the arms of the armchair as if ready to push him up. I felt his gaze more focused on me that it had been since I walked in.

"You said something about we're friends," he said. His voice came through strong and clear, as if he was willing himself to be sober.

"I said we're supposed to be friends," I said. "Something has gone wrong. My life isn't the way it's supposed to be."

The tension in his arms faded. "Who's is?"

"I'm supposed to have an older brother who is taking over the Santa Claus position," I said. "I'm supposed to be a private detective here. You're my friend and we've worked together on several cases." I jerked my thumb back at Venir. "He's supposed to be my associate."

"I am?" Venir squeaked.

"Another of my associates, Palle Grubrand, is still stuck out there under the influence of an evil entity, the one who's been leaving burn, stone husks all over. Shirl Trombley is supposed to be my go-to for computers."

"Shirl Trombley." Mallory spat out a laugh. "She's in prison for multiple counts of computer crimes."

My stomach clenched. Shirl in prison. Mallory had referred me to her as part of his plan to help rehabilitate her. Somehow it hadn't worked.

Was it because I wasn't here to ask her to work for me?

It felt like I was trying to grab an armful of sand that was slipping away through my fingers. Every piece I found just showed me how broken everything was.

How was I going to fix this? How was I even going to figure out what was happening?

Focus. I had to keep Mallory's attention.

He had sagged back into the chair again. His gaze fixed on the glass on the coffee. I flicked my hand again, causing the glass to move farther away from him. He glanced back over at me.

"I need your help," I said. "My brother is missing and no one remembers him but me. It's causing all of these problems. If we can find him I know everything will be set right."

Mallory snorted.

"How can you be sure you even have a brother?" he asked. "Maybe you're the one who's misremembering."

Beside me, Venir sniffed. I glanced over at him and he shrugged at me. But his expression was carefully neutral.

He didn't believe me either. He was only here because I'd commanded it. As I was the heir to Santa Claus, he couldn't refuse me.

But that didn't mean he had to believe me.

But I knew KJ. I knew it had to be real. My life here in Toronto was real. I would find a way to prove it. To fix it.

I crossed over to Mallory. Grabbing his arm, I pulled him out of his seat. He didn't resist.

"Get dressed," I said. "We'll get you some coffee and then you're coming with us."

"Where we goin'?" he asked.

"To see Shirl Trombley," I said. "We're going to need her help."

CHAPTER
SIX

By the time Mallory was dressed in a rumbled white shirt and creased black pants, he was starting to sober up. His eyes looked blurry as he squinted at me from across the kitchen. The bitter odour of coffee hung in the air between us. While he'd dragged on his rumbled clothes, I had made coffee and forced a mug into his hands. Now he leaned against the counter, both hands bracing the mug as he sipped.

Venir stood off to the side and shook his head.

"Visiting hours aren't until two more days," Mallory said.

"We aren't visiting," I said. "We're getting her out of there."

Mallory's fingers tightened on the mug.

"You're talking about a crime," he said. "One I can arrest you for."

"You aren't going to arrest me," I said. "You want to know what's going on as much as I do."

His eyes narrowed over the edge of the cup as he took another sip. He swallowed.

"All I know is you're some kind of nut. One who might be delusional and dangerous."

"Dangerous enough for this?"

I held out my hand. Inside was a small Mattel police car. It had been Mallory's favourite Christmas present. He'd written his name on the bottom. The little car had been so loved and played with that it listed slightly to the left when it moved.

I had given this car to Mallory the first time we had met. He still kept it on his desk at work.

Now his hands tightened on the mug. The tips of his fingers bleached white. He gripped the mug so hard I thought it was going to break in his hands.

"Where'd you get that?" His voice sounded hoarse.

"I conjured it from your memory," I said. "It's your favourite Christmas present. I showed you this the first time we met."

I refrained from saying he'd been questioning me as a murder suspect at the time. Why confuse the issue?

"This whole story, this nonsense about Santa Claus and magic." He waved in the direction of the coffee table behind me. "This all is true?"

I nodded.

He took another sip of coffee and I could see him turning

the idea over in his mind. He wasn't quite ready to fully believe me yet but he was getting close. Or at least he was getting sober.

"So how do we get to see Shirl Trombley?"

I smiled. "I thought you'd never ask."

THE EARLY AFTERNOON SKY HAD DARKENED AS CLOUDS MOVED IN. From the road where we had landed, the prison looked like an elementary school made of concrete and glass. If the school had been behind a fence and had windows with bars across them.

A driveway led from the road toward the building, interrupted by the fenced gate. A guard's booth sat to the left of the road. The brick structure looked large enough to be a small cottage.

Mallory stared across the road and shivered. He was wearing a beige winter coat but I knew it wasn't the cold temperature that made him shiver. He hadn't really believed it when I told him that Venir and I would take care of traveling to the Greater Basin Institution for Women. With concentration, Venir and I were able to coordinate enough to carry Mallory along with us while we *winked.*

I only hoped we'd be able to do that with Shirl as well. If we could get in to see her.

"Okay," Mallory said. There was only a slight shake in his voice. "So we're here. But I tell you they won't let us in to see her. It's not visiting day."

"We're aren't visitors," I said. "You're a detective and she's got information. You're here to interrogate her."

"And we're your assistants," Venir said.

"You think they're really going to buy that?" Mallory asked.

"We'll help convince them," I said. "We just need a few minutes."

Mallory frowned. "Look, I believe you're....special but I don't like this plan of yours. Breaking a criminal out of prison."

"She shouldn't be in there," I said. "You know that. You tried to help her."

His face paled even in the dull, afternoon light.

"How do you know that?"

"I know because you gave me her name when I needed computer help and I hired her as my computer expert. She lives in an apartment on Bathurst in an apartment filled with computer boxes."

"That's where we picked her up for computer fraud," he said. "Maybe you know that because you were one of her clients."

"I was one of her clients but not the way you mean," I said. "You helped her, Stan. You wanted her to get into a more legitimate line of work and it worked. She shouldn't be in prison."

"And this is all because your brother is missing," he said.

"That's right."

He glanced over at Venir and I could almost hear his unspoken message of 'do you believe this?' Venir lifted one eyebrow and gave a noncommittal shrug.

Mallory sighed. "Okay, what do I do?"

I jerked my thumb toward the guard's booth. "Get us through the gate."

"They're going to wonder why we don't have a car," he said.

"I'll take care of it."

Mallory pursed his lips in his typical gesture of annoyance. It was eminently familiar to me. I had annoyed him more times than most.

But he didn't argue. He turned and headed up the drive, the snow crunching under his boots. I followed, gesturing to Venir to keep up.

The Elf lagged behind, forcing me to slow to let him catch up.

"Are you sure he ain't gonna turn us in?" he asked. He pitched his voice low, staring at Mallory ahead of us to be sure the detective hadn't heard him.

I wasn't sure, not completely. This Mallory wasn't exactly the same as the Mallory I knew, just like Venir wasn't exactly the same. The experiences they had had without me had changed them slightly, just enough that I couldn't completely predict how they would react.

But I had to hope. It was the only way forward.

"It'll be all right," I told the Elf, avoiding his question.

Ahead of us, Mallory had reached the guard's booth and was already talking to someone inside. I saw him gesture at Venir and I.

My stomach tightened. Now or never. If Mallory was betraying us Venir and I would have to beat a hasty retreat. I focused my magic, felt the tingle along my spine and the tips of my fingers. Beside me, Venir jerked. He'd felt the build up. After a moment, I felt an answering tingle of magic from him.

We were both primed, just in case.

As we approached the guard's booth, I caught a whiff of cheap cologne mingled with sweat. The snow crunched and crackled under my boots. My heart beat heavy in my chest.

Beyond Mallory, a guard stuck his head out of the booth. He wore a beige parka over a beige uniform shirt. Short brown hair was smoothed back from his narrow forehead. His skin was a darker shade of beige than his uniform. He gave me a quick appraisal and then nodded to Mallory.

"I'll have to call up and get permission for the interview, lieutenant," the guard said.

Mallory nodded. "Of course." His voice was strong and confident, the tones carrying on the air.

He stood with his hands shoved into the coat pockets, feet braced apart, body ready but relaxed. No one looking at him would have realized he'd been drunk just a short time before.

The guard ducked back inside the booth. Mallory spun toward me.

"Are you sure I won't be implicated in this?" His voice was a low growl. "My job is on the line."

"I'll make sure," I said.

He glared at me. "You damn well better."

At that moment, the door of the guard's booth opened again. "You can head in. They're bringing her to private visiting room A. You can question her there."

Mallory nodded his thanks and turned away, heading for the fence. Just before he reached it, it began to slide back. Wheels grated along tracks filled with ice making it crunch and pop. The gate opened wide enough for us to slip through and no farther.

Another guard met us as we passed through security on the way into the building. We left our coats, a pen from Mallory's pocket, and the hat Venir had used to hide his pointed ears. As he tossed it onto the pile, I caught a hint of a pointed ear before his hair thickened to obscure it. The Elf gave me a quick nod. A subtle illusion to hide his pointed ears.

The guard waited patiently for us to finish then led us to visiting room A. He closed the door after us and I heard a click of the lock.

The room was small and bland. The walls were painted a nondescript beige, with brush strokes still visible in the paint near the ceiling. A scuffed, round wood table with a metal bar bolted in the centre sat in the middle of the room, surrounded by four wood chairs with cushioned seats. As I sat I discovered the cushion was about as dense as a snow flurry. It flattened against wood beams that dug into my rump.

From the look on Venir's face I knew his chair wasn't much better. Mallory had no reaction, instead staring at the closed door opposite the one we'd entered.

A moment later the door opened. A short, slender black woman walked in. She wore an orange jumpsuit. Her black hair was cropped short against her skull. Gone were the long braids she used to wear piled on her head to give height to her shortness.

Her movements were slow and cautious as she regarded us. The guard behind her nudged her forward. She shuffled to the remaining chair. The guard pulled it out and pressed a hand on her shoulder, pushing her down. Shirl sat and lifted her hands. They were cuffed.

She cocked her head at the guard. The guard looked at Mallory.

"Uncuff her," he said.

"To the bar, sir?" the guard asked.

"No, leave her."

"Sir, our regulations…"

"I don't give a fuck about your regulations," Mallory said. "This woman could be a material witness to a major felony. I'll take responsibility."

The guard hesitated again. I leaned forward, resting my folded hands on the table. If I needed to I would be able to influence him to unlock the cuffs but I didn't want to use up the magic. It was going to be enough trying to *wink* away with two additional people.

The guard unlocked the cuffs and left the room. As soon as the door was closed, Shirl whirled on Mallory.

"You gotta lot of nerve showin' yer face here, Mallory," she said. Her voice was a low growl. Her hands balled into fists, resting on the edge of the table.

"Settle down," Mallory said. He nodded to me. "You know him?"

She barely gave me a glance. "Why would I know some pasty-faced white boy?" She gave a snort.

Venir stifled a laugh.

"Do you ever see your nephew, Robbie?" I asked. "I bet you don't want him to see you here."

Her head jerked up. She pressed against the back of the chair as if recoiling from a blow.

"How you know about Robbie?" she asked. "Who the fuck are you?"

"I'm Noel Kringle," I said. "I'm supposed to be one of your clients, one of your legitimate clients after you went straight."

She shook her head, glanced over at Mallory. "I don't know what he's talkin' about."

"I'm the son of Santa Claus, the youngest son and I'm supposed to be a private detective down here but my brother KJ is missing and no one remembers him but me. According to this time, I never came to Toronto and the cases I worked on never got solved. It's created ripple effects that threatened the stability of this realm. There's too much unrestrained magic. We have to find my brother and restore everything to normal."

She stared at me.

"You crazy." She turned to Mallory. "He's crazy."

"Yeah," he said. "He's also kind of convincing."

Shirl crossed her arms over her chest. "So Santa boy, what you want me to do about it?"

"I need your computer skills," I said.

She barked out a laugh. "You see any laptop in this room? I ain't even seen a computer in the last eighteen months."

"If we get you one, will you help me?" I asked.

Her eyes narrowed as she studied me. The look was so familiar. I had to remind myself this wasn't the Shirl I knew. The Shirl I knew was sarcastic and caustic but ready and willing to do whatever she could to help. But she'd never gone to prison, not endured what this Shirl had endured.

"Whada I get in return, pretty boy?" she asked.

I resisted the urge to glance at Mallory. He wasn't going to like what I was going to say but it was the only offer I knew she'd consider.

"Freedom," I said.

Mallory made a noise of disapproval. Shirl leaned forward.

"You got the papers?" she asked.

"Are you going to help?" I asked.

She made a show of mulling it over but I could already sense her agreement in the eager way she leaned forward.

"I help you," she said. "You show me the papers first though."

"There are no papers," I said. "We don't need papers." I stood up, kicking the chair back. Venir hopped off his chair.

Shirl looked from me to Venir.

"You bring some dwarf in here and not my papers?"

I gestured to Mallory. He rose and moved to stand between me and Venir.

"Like I said, we don't need them," I said. "We just need this."

I grabbed her left wrist. Venir grabbed her right one. She tried to pull away with a yell.

Venir and I *winked.*

CHAPTER
SEVEN

We ended up in the only place I could think of.

My not-office.

Dust puffed up in the air as we landed. Venir caught the worst of it, coughing enough that he lost control of the glamour that hid his ears. As he bent at the waist, coughing into his hands, his pointed ears quivered above the curls on his head.

"What the...his ears," Shirl said. "And where the hell are we?"

"This should be my office," I said.

"Sorry for your loss," Mallory said dryly.

I hit the light switch on the wall. The bare bulb flickered on, illuminating the empty would-be waiting room.

Shirl slowly circled the room. She touched each wall as if

she couldn't believe she was actually here. She stopped in front of me.

"You weren't kidding," she said.

"No, I wasn't," I said. "I even know your favourite Christmas present."

I touched her hand, projecting into her mind the image of the doll she had tied a piece of fabric onto, simulating a cape. She jerked her hand away.

"And he's an Elf," she said.

"That's right."

She swallowed. "Santa always go around jail-breaking felons?"

"You shouldn't be a felon," I said. "Just like Mallory shouldn't be suspended."

"Suspended?" she glanced over at him. Mallory looked away.

"Like I said, it's because my brother KJ is missing," I said. "You have to help me figure out what happened to him and how to restore him."

"You said you wanted computer help." She gestured to the empty room. "Don't see no computer here."

"Stan..." I started.

Mallory held up a hand. "No."

"But..."

"I said no. I helped you find her. That's it. I'm done. I don't care if you're the Easter Bunny." Tension deepened the lines on his face. "They've got my name at that prison. As soon as they find her gone, where do you think they'll start looking?"

I glanced at Venir who had finally recovered from his coughing fit. The Elf wiped his nose on the back of his hand.

"Venir, can you take care of that?"

"Sure thing, boss."

The Elf *winked*.

My mouth felt suddenly dry. The way he'd called me 'boss' was so much like the old Venir.

I felt a wave of homesickness that ached in my heart. I'd worked so long to distinguish myself here, to build these friendships, this office, this work, and these people who should be my friends were looking at me like I was a stranger.

"Just so I got it," Shirl said. "You wanna find this older brother so he can be Santa and you can be some private detective with a crap office?"

"That's right," I said.

She gave a snort. "Wouldn't see me givin' up a one night a year job."

"It's not just the one night," I said. "That's the night the deliveries are made, but there's work all year round."

She shook her head and mumbled under her breath. I thought I heard 'nerd.'

A mound of coats appeared in the middle of the room. I spotted two arms wrapped around them and a wisp of white curl poking over top.

I hurried forward before Venir dumped them into the dust on the floor.

"Thought I'd get our coats while I was at it," he said.

"To hell with the coats," Mallory said. "What about the records?"

Venir waved a hand in directions. "Ain't no records and nobody remembers nothing."

"Are you sure?" Mallory asked.

The Elf turned on him. Hands on his hips, he lifted his face up to the detective, chin jutting forward.

"You think I'm a hack like you? I don't get suspended for nothing."

"Venir," I said. "How is the Supply Depot?"

The Elf whirled toward me. His face went from pale to red. His lips pulled back in a snarl.

"Weren't my doin'," he said. "Someone listened to bad advice, someone who didn't know *nothing*."

He finished with a shout, glaring at me, hands in fists at his sides.

"You're right," I said. I kept my voice calm and even. "You shouldn't be there. You should be here, working with me as my associate." I gestured around the room. "None of this is how it should be, none of us are where we're supposed to be. Are you going to help me set it right?"

He blinked and jerked back as if I've taken a swing at him. Then he bowed his head.

"Yeah, all right."

I turned toward Mallory, ignoring the Elf, giving him a chance to gather his dignity.

"You're in the clear," I said. "There's no trace of you at the prison now. You can back away from this if you want but I could really use your help too."

Mallory pressed his lips tight together into a thin line.

Shirl moved over to stand on his right side. She nudged him with her elbow.

"C'mon detective, you can't tell me you ain't curious," she said. "I wanna know where this ride ends up. Don't you?"

He grunted, his expression turning more into a frown but I sensed that he was acquiescing.

"So, Santa boy, what you want me to be doin' with this computer?" Shirl asked.

"I want you to find a troll," I said.

SHIRL LAUGHED BUT SOON STOPPED AS SHE REALIZED I WAS SERIOUS.

"A troll? How am I supposed to find one 'a those?" she asked.

I noticed she didn't even bother to question my request. After *winking* her out of prison, revealing myself as the son of Santa Claus, and learning Venir was a Christmas Elf, she seemed to take hearing about a troll in stride.

"People have been spotting something they call the Hulk," I said. "I want you to trace the most recent sightings in the city. I can narrow in from there."

"You said you wanted to see where the ride went," Mallory said dryly.

Shirl gave him a sidelong glare then turned her attention back to me.

"So I'm supposed to do this search from his place, I assume," she said, jerking a thumb in Mallory's direction. She plucked at her orange jumpsuit. "Pretty obvious, ain't I?"

I handed her my parka. "This should cover you until we get you some regular clothes. Keep the hood up over your face."

Mallory looked ready to protest again but then shook his head. He snatched his own coat and started putting it on.

"Are you going to whisk us back to my place?" he asked.

"I can't, sorry," I said. "I've got my own work to do. I'll be in touch later today."

"You'd better be right about this," Mallory said. He took the coat from Shirl's hand held it out for her. She shoved her arms into the arm holes and he draped it over her shoulders. The parka swamped her small frame, making her look like a child. With it zipped up, it hid her orange jumpsuit easily. Mallory took Shirl's arm and began to steer her toward the door.

"You try anything funny and I'll shoot you," he said.

"Yeah right," she said.

The door clicked shut behind them.

"What now?" Venir asked.

"Now I have some others I need to talk to," I said. "Some who might have an idea of how this could have happened."

"Who?" he asked.

I shook my head as I focused inward. I really wished I had my cane. It was a perfect magical focal point being magical in its own right. I had brought it from the Magical Realms when I'd helped stop a rogue faerie bent on disrupting the peace between the Summer and Winter Courts, a peace my father just happened to have brokered.

Of course in this reality, that had never happened. I had never stopped the rogue faerie because Venir had never come to me with a tip about a plot against my father. Was the faerie still working toward disrupting the peace? Had he been successful and was even now bent on stalking Dad?

Even though the empty room was chilly, I felt sweat bead on my back.

I couldn't think of that now. I had to focus and reach out. Without the cane to assist me, I had to use all the magic I could muster.

The air grew colder against my skin. Without my coat I was only wearing a red flannel shirt over black jeans but that should still have been enough to keep me warm in the empty office. Even with the heat cut off, residual heat from other offices had kept the room warm enough.

But now I felt the temperature plummet. A moment later, I felt tingling on my skin. My hair prickled on my head. I breathed in deeper, pulling more and more of the North Pole magic to me.

I could feel it swirling around me, plugging the room into frigid cold. If I opened my eyes, I knew I would see my breath.

Instead I focused inward and pictured where I wanted to be. The cavern, deep in the mountain. Shadows and darkness hiding creatures I couldn't see but who reached directly into my mind with vibrations I couldn't understand until they finally spoke aloud in words. Creatures of unfathomable power who made it their mission to guard the realms and protect all life and magic.

The Council.

When I had met them, trying to save Venir from a black void where he had been trapped, they had given me the ability to contact them. Call them and they would answer.

I remembered it and I knew how to do it.

I just hoped it would work here.

I focused.

The cavern, the mountain. Shadows and darkness. I breathed in, tasting dust and sulphor on my lips. The floor under my feet felt uneven, like I was no longer standing on tile but was perched on stone.

"Master Noel!" I heard Venir call but it sounded distant, like he was calling me from another room, miles away. His voice faded, leaving a brief echo that faded to nothing.

"Who called us?"

I opened my eyes.

I stood in the centre of a pool of white light. In four corners around me, torches burned at head height but they didn't give off any warmth or light. They were there to give credence to the white light that surrounded me.

Beyond it, I could see suggestions of ground falling away. Hints of walls curving around me.

The cavern. And in its depths I sensed beings around me.

"It's me, Noel Kringle," I said. "We met some time ago. You put me on retainer."

Silence answered me. I could feel their presence beyond the reach of the white circle of light. I knew they were still there.

But no response.

I wanted to fidget and had to force my hands to stay still at my sides. Being in the centre of the white light made me feel exposed, especially with no coat around me. I didn't even have the comfort of the cane with me this time nor did I have the presence of Stromgrankhaur, the gatekeeper of the Underwell who had escorted me into the Council's presence the last time.

Finally I couldn't wait any longer.

"Um, anyone there?" I called.

"We are here," a voice said. "We wonder why are you?"

So that was it. They were waiting for the reason for my visit. That made sense.

I cleared my throat. "My older brother KJ is missing and no one remembers him but me. I need help to figure out what happened and restore everything to right."

More silence but this time I had the sense of communication flowing around me at a level I couldn't access. They had done this the first time I had visited but had then started talking when I couldn't understand them. Had they already forgotten they needed to talk aloud to me?

"I can't hear what you're saying," I said. "Can you talk me in words?"

"Of course," a new voice said. It was low and deep, resonating in the air until I couldn't tell what direction it came from.

"We were discussing what you have said," it continued. "We have only one question."

"What's that?" I asked.

"Who is this KJ?"

Tension tightened in my gut. My mouth felt dry. Settle down, I wasn't going to assume anything.

I cleared my throat again. "KJ is Kris Junior, my older brother."

"You do not have an older brother," the first voice said. "There is only one child born in the Kringle family per generation, one child to carry on the Santa Claus position."

My stomach clenched. My heart pounded in my chest. It felt like I couldn't get enough air into my lungs. The white light around me seemed to dim.

It couldn't be possible. It couldn't be.

The Council didn't remember my brother either.

Whatever had happened didn't just affect me and the world around me.

It stretched out through the realms. Through the Human and the Magical Realms.

No one remembered KJ.

No one but me.

The light dimmed. My heart pounded so hard I thought it would burst. I could feel it throbbing in my temples. I tried to put my hands on my knees, bend over to breathe deeply, but I felt myself falling as the light faded into total darkness.

CHAPTER

EIGHT

Sharp pain yanked me awake. I felt my left cheek mashed against my teeth. Dust tickled my nose. I tried to sneeze but felt my nose squished against something hard.

I managed to blink. My eyes focused on parquette flooring. A moment later, I felt the rest of my body, crumpled on the floor. I managed a groan as I rolled over onto my back.

Hands closed on my right arm and shook me.

"Master Noel, Master Noel, are you all right?"

I turned my head. Focused.

Venir's bulbous nose was less than two inches from my own. I could smell candy canes on his breath.

I lifted my left hand and pushed him away.

Sitting up took some effort. My body felt shaky and exhausted. When I finally pulled myself up, I felt lightheaded and had to rest my head on my knees. Meanwhile Venir hovered around me, reaching out toward me then yanking his hands back as if afraid to touch me.

That was when I remembered the sharp pain in my cheek. I lifted my head from my knees.

"Did you slap me?" I asked.

"I had to," he said. He clasped his hands in front of him. "You were just standin' there shaking and twitching. I had to do something."

Shaking and twitching?

"Did I vanish?" I asked.

The Elf shook his head. "You just seemed to go into a trance. It was all right until the shaking and twitching started, then it wouldn't stop. I tried calling to ya but you wouldn't respond. So I had to..."

"Right," I said. "I got it."

With a groan, I managed to pull myself into a standing position. I still felt weak and I wished there was somewhere other than the floor to sit. I had to settle for leaning against the wall.

So I hadn't vanished, I hadn't travelled to the cavern where the Council resided. I had travelled only in my mind but it was certainly enough to cause physical sensations.

"Did you talk to them others?" Venir asked. "The ones who could tell us what's going on? How it happened?"

I glanced across the room at him. The Elf stood in the centre of the floor, his hands in his pockets after he confessed to slapping me. With the green sweater and the jeans, he looked so much like the Venir I remembered and although he was starting to sound more like that Venir, he wasn't quite the same person. He was here because I had ordered him to accompany me, not because he really believed me or felt like he wanted to help.

What would he say when I confessed that the creatures I thought were all-knowing, all-powerful didn't recognize the name of my missing brother either?

Would he believe me? Could I believe myself?

I pushed that thought away. Of course there was a KJ. I remembered everything about him. His impatient looks when he found me annoying, his focus on all things Christmas, his fondness for boots. How even though he took the job seriously he occasionally slacked off, like when he insisted I find new sleigh runners when he'd forgotten to order them on time.

He had been real. He was real. And I was going to find a way to get him back.

I straightened, pulling myself away from the wall. My legs still felt a bit shaky.

"They couldn't help," I said. "They didn't remember him."

The Elf's eyes widened. Then his gaze dropped away. His feet shuffled on the parquette floor, causing tiny puffs of dust to rise into the air. The particles danced like snowflakes.

"So are we headin' home now?" he asked. His voice was a low mumble.

"No," I said. "I'm not done here. There are still places I can search."

Venir tilted his head at me. "Like where?"

Good question. Most of the time KJ had visited me here at my office which wasn't my office any longer. Not only was there no lingering trace of him here, there was nothing of me here either.

Although there had been. For the briefest moment, my Christmas towels had been in the bathroom. I'd caught a glimpse of how my office had been.

A crack in this version of reality, showing how it really should be. And if there was one crack there would be another.

And I'd find a way to pry it all the way open to break it apart.

Where to find the next crack?

It had to be some place where KJ and I had been together.

I could think of at least one place.

I pushed away from the wall and this time my legs felt steady and sturdy.

"Good View Mall," I said, plucking at the front of my flannel shirt. "Since I've given away my coat I'll pick a new one while we're there."

Venir frowned. "Is this really the time to go shopping?"

"It's not for shopping," I said. "KJ was there. Maybe there'll be a trace of his presence."

Venir didn't look convinced but he didn't protest either. Instead he gave a loud sigh.

"So where is this place?" he asked.

THE GOOD VIEW MALL LOOKED QUITE DIFFERENT SINCE THE TIME I had worked their Christmas in July promotion. Snow drifts piled along the edges of the parking lot that surrounded the mall. The sky was overcast, the colour of slate grey rather than the bright sunny heat of a July day.

I shivered as I hurried toward the main door. My flannel shirt did little to cut the icy wind that whipped across the parking lot. We had landed on the edge in a cusp of trees, out of view of anyone who might notice a man and a short Elf appear out of nowhere.

Ahead, the mall stretched out, two wings angled inward as if they were arms embracing the cars parked in the lot. The concrete which had seemed white and gleaming in the sun now seemed dull, reflecting the greyness of the sky.

I avoided the worst of the puddles of slush as I hurried forward. My breath left a trail of vapor every time I breathed out. I could feel the damp cold sinking into my torso. This was exactly the kind of weather my mother warned would give me a cold.

I picked up the pace and then glanced back.

Venir followed leisurely behind, his hands stuffed in his pockets. He had his jacket half unzipped. The wind made his curls dance and bop around his head. The tips of his ears quivered. Although his cheeks looked pink, he didn't seem to be bothered by the cold. Christmas Elves always seemed more impervious but it had never annoyed me more than watching Venir saunter along while I was freezing.

"Hurry up," I said.

He waved a hand at me. "You go ahead. I'll catch up."

Fine. I ran for the door and yanked it open.

Warm air enveloped me, carrying a hint of toasted buns and the tang of cologne. White tile spread out before me in a wide swath. I recognized a few of the stores that lined the path. A nail salon, eye glass hut, gaming store, and there at the corner, a men's clothing store.

The door creaked open behind me and Venir stepped inside. I pointed at the clothing store.

"I'm going to get a coat and then we'll check out the spot I came to see."

The Elf shrugged. "Sure."

I hurried forward, catching a few curious glimpses from several of the scattered shoppers. Most wore coats, a few carried them in their arms, but none were missing a coat like I was.

Avoiding their gaze, I ducked inside the clothing store. The air held a hint of musk that seemed to follow me as I moved past the first few racks. Neat rows of men's pants on one side and crisp white shirts along the other. Against the far wall, jackets of various shades and styles were arranged in a diamond pattern.

As I reached the end of one row, I spotted the cashier counter in the centre of the shop. A tall man with dark brown hair swept back from his face was bent over the counter. He wore a grey suit, similar to the ones on the rack, with a dark purple kerchief in the breast pocket. As if feeling my gaze he glanced up and gave me a professional smile, bland and unthreatening but not insincere.

"Outdoor coats?" I asked.

He lifted his hand, thin fingers grasping a pen, and pointed behind him.

"Back of the store, sir. Is there a particular style you were looking for?"

"No, I'll just take a look around," I said. Before he could offer further help, I slipped by the counter and headed for the back wall.

Wool, cashmere, and puffy parkas hung on different racks. I headed toward the parkas, when a fabric coat caught my eye.

A navy pea coat.

A wave of homesickness washed over me. I'd worn a pea coat exactly like that during my first case. I remembered crouching in the underground cave, watching the goblin, while I wore that coat. Seeing it felt like a message, like I was on the right track.

As I turned toward it, I felt a presence beside me.

"That's a good choice, sir," the clerk said. "A classic style and although it's not terribly warm for winter, it's easy to layer underneath to keep warm. Good for spring and fall wear as well."

His hand reached past me and plucked up one of the coats.

"I believe this size will fit you," he said.

"Thanks." I took the coat from him and slipped it off the hanger. He held onto it while I slipped the coat over my shoulders. He nodded at the fit.

"Fits you perfectly, sir. You can see how the edges of the cuffs reach here." He pointed to a spot just past my wrist.

I felt a strange sense of deja vu. A Yule Lad had sold me a stingy brim hat a while ago in the middle of December when I was trying to hide my then white hair and beard. As a son of Kris Kringle, it didn't matter that I wouldn't become Santa Claus, every December my hair and beard turned white and became bushy.

I went through a lot of hair dye and scissor trims during that month.

Wearing a stingy brim hat, a close cousin to a fedora but with a narrower brim, had hid my hair and made me look less like Santa.

And the clerk who had sold me that hat, a man named Brendon had turned out to be a Yule Lad, who had been manipulated by an imposter and forced to kill.

Was this one of his brothers, still enslaved and waiting for the proper time to carry out a murderous mission?

Or maybe I was just letting the strain get to me.

I moved away, heading for the mirror at the end of the

aisle. The coat looked perfect, exactly like the one I had always had.

"I'll take it," I said.

"Shall I wrap it or would you like to wear it out?"

Only one cocked eyebrow let me know that he had noticed that I had come in with no coat and was looking to buy a coat.

"I'll wear it out," I said.

"Follow me to the cash and I'll cut off the tags."

A few snips of the scissors and the tags came off. He then rang the coat up. The register showed four hundred and seventy-five dollars. A lot more than the nothing I had in my pockets.

Fortunately I had North Pole magic on my side.

I touched a finger to the credit card machine. The register flashed paid and let out a soft ding.

Behind the machine, the man let a slight frown play across his face before it settled back into a bland expression.

"Thank you, sir. Come again."

He made a slight motion with his hand for me to move along.

I knew I should go before the spell I'd cast wore off but something made me hesitate.

"Do you have a brother name Brendon?" I asked. "He works in a closing store on the PATH."

The man's expression didn't change but I sensed a hardening around his eyes.

"No sir, I do not."

"Sorry to waste your time," I said. I hurried out before he could respond.

It wouldn't do to call him a liar to his face.

I almost collided with Venir in the doorway.

"Got a coat, huh," he said. "So where do we go now?"

For a moment I felt disoriented. My cases were getting mixed up in my head. Where was I? Good View Mall. Right. KJ had covered for a missing "Santa" during the Christmas in July promotion while I was trying to uncover a plot to kill Dad.

And the room where KJ had entertained the visiting kids was down that hall to the left.

"This way," I told Venir and headed off.

Now that I had a coat on I didn't feel like everyone was staring any more. People shuffled along, looking bored or blank-faced. March doldrums seemed to have taken hold. I detected no enthusiasm, no interest, even as people strolled by.

A sensation of wrongness filled me. I hurried down the corridor on the left to get away from it.

The door to the room where we'd held the Santa visit part of the promotion was just ahead on the left. As I expected, the door was locked but with my stronger North Pole magic that didn't cause much problem for me.

"Keep an eye out," I said to Venir. I shielded the door knob with my body. I turned it while I whispered a short spell.

Magic tingled in my fingers, causing the door knob to

warm under my palm. After a moment I heard a click and the knob turned freely. I pushed the door open and stepped inside.

The room was shrouded in darkness. I fumbled along the wall beside the door until I felt a switch. I hit it and flourescent lights lit up the room.

It was full of an assortment of stuff. Metal folding chairs were stacked against the far wall. Sheets of plywood leaned against the wall to the right of the door. The walls were painted off white. No sign of the fake clouds. No cotton snow. No golden throne. No cardboard candy canes holding a golden rope. Nothing to indicate that once this room had been used for a Santa display.

I stepped farther into the room. There had to be something here, some indication that KJ had been here. He'd spent hours in this room, days. He'd been so popular the line to visit him had stretched all the way down the corridor.

There should be some sense that he'd been here, some indication. Even some residual sense of his magic.

I could feel nothing.

Venir came up beside me. "Well, that's a pile a junk." He glanced up at me. "What's wrong?"

"He was here," I said. "For several days, acting out the part of Santa, listening to kids talk about the toys they wanted as they sat on his lap. There should be some trace of that."

Venir opened his mouth to say something and the door behind him slammed shut.

CHAPTER

NINE

I pushed past Venir and grabbed the door knob. It wouldn't turn.

We'd been locked in.

I pressed my ear to the door. Through the wood I could hear a voice mumbling. The tone sounded familiar. The clerk in the clothing store. He must have watched us head down this corridor and followed us. Why?

I didn't have time to find out. Through the mumbling I could make out a few distinct words like 'security' and 'police.'

Time to get out of here.

I turned back to Venir.

"We have to go, security is coming," I said.

Venir gave a curt nod. "Where?"

"Mallory's house."

We joined hands to ensure we travelled together. I took a deep breath and we *winked*.

MALLORY'S LIVING ROOM WAS MORE BRIGHTLY LIT THAN THE FIRST time we had visited. The place looked a little neater and I realized the pile of dirty glasses had been removed from the coffee table, leaving only a newspaper folded neatly in the centre.

The aroma of coffee and grilled cheese floated in from a doorway on the left. I followed the scent and entered a dining room.

Shirl sat with her back to me as she hunched over a keyboard on her lap. She had one leg tucked under her, the other swinging free. A laptop sat on the table in front of her. An empty plate sat on the right, holding crumbles of what must have been a grilled cheese sandwich.

For one disorienting moment I pictured her in her apartment, sitting at her large, L-shaped desk, surrounded by three monitors. Instead of an orange jumpsuit, she should be wearing a bright yellow sleeveless top that would shine against her dark skin and khaki capri pants. Her long braids would be piled high on her head or tied to hang down her back. Instead she looked almost child-like with the short afro on her head and the sleeves of the ill-fitting jumpsuit rolled up to her elbows.

She glanced back as I entered.

"Better be good, Santa's back," she called out.

On the right side of the dining table, a cut-out window through the wall showed the kitchen on the other side. I caught movement as Mallory poked his head through the window. His hair was brushed and he'd shaved.

"Sit. I'll bring coffee and you can tell me what you've got."

Shirl tossed an amused look in my direction. "He's been bossy ever since we got here."

I took the seat on the end with Venir on my left. Shirl sat on the right, still tapping on the keyboard.

"Any luck?" I asked.

"Got lots of sightings," she said. "Most of them unverified. I wouldn't trust 'em. The ones who do seem a little more credible are here."

She tapped the notepad beside the computer. The list was pitifully short with only two items listed.

Mallory entered carrying a tray with a coffee pot and four cups. He set it down in the middle of the table then retreated back into the kitchen. A moment later, he returned with sugar and a small carton of milk.

"No cream?" Shirl asked.

"No, you have to suffer," he said.

After the coffee was poured and cups distributed,

Mallory sat at the other end of the table across from me. Both hands cradled the cup in front of him.

"As you see I got her back here," he said, nodding toward Shirl. "She's been looking for that troll you mentioned without much luck."

"I told 'em that," Shirl said, wagging the notepad.

"I tried a couple of things myself," I said. "But I didn't have much luck either."

Mallory frowned.

Shirl tapped the notepad. "Will this troll have any answers?"

I sighed. "No, he's in thrall to an entity that's leaving burned, stone corpses behind."

Mallory flinched.

"So why am I searching for 'im?" Shirl asked.

Why indeed? I had thought that getting everyone I knew together again would help me find KJ. That somehow even if I hadn't come down to Toronto and become a private detective, these people, my friends, would recognize me in some way. As if we had some kind of bond that transcended this reality.

But from the looks on Shirl's and Mallory's faces that bond didn't seem to be there and wasn't necessarily growing, no matter how hard I pushed.

A wave of helplessness washed over me. I took a sip of coffee to hide my confusion and was grateful that my hand didn't shake.

What was I doing? I'd done everything I could think of,

even going to the Council, but no one knew KJ, no one had even heard of him, and I couldn't find any trace, not even in the one place it should have been.

I was out of ideas and afraid to admit it to these people. They weren't the people I knew as much as I wished they were. The Stan Mallory, Shirl Trombley, Venir, and Palle from my memories would have stood by me even if I admitted I didn't have any idea at the moment. They would have known I'd think of something or they would help come up with an idea.

But these people, even with their familiar faces, weren't the same and I had a feeling they wouldn't be so forgiving.

Shirl tapped a couple of keys on the keyboard and sat back. "So do I keep lookin' or what?"

"I think 'or what' is the answer," Mallory said. His voice was flat. "We're no closer to finding this brother of yours, are we? No closer to fixing what you say we should be fixing."

"No," I admitted. "We aren't."

Mallory slapped his hands down on the table, using the momentum to push himself up from his chair. He picked up his cup and carried it back into the kitchen. I heard the splash of liquid and then the water running as he rinsed out his cup.

Shirl threw a wary look toward the kitchen and then turned to me.

"You pulled me outta prison, you can't send me back," she said. Her voice was a low whisper, pitched so Mallory couldn't hear her. "You can't let him send me back."

I opened my mouth but no words came out. I didn't know what to say. I didn't know what to do. I'd come looking for answers and only managed to make a mess of everything.

She cast a quick glance back at the kitchen.

"Can you give me an hour head start? Hold him off me for an hour?"

She was going to try to make a run for it.

The mess just kept getting deeper and deeper.

Mallory appeared in the doorway. He had his arms crossed, tugging his t-shirt against the waistband of his pants, revealing the holster clipped onto it.

"Thinking of going somewhere?" he asked.

Shirl pressed her lips tight together. She looked at me and raised her eyebrows.

Now what?

I had to think of something else we could try, some other avenue to explore. I'd brought us together to find KJ but those fragile bonds were unravelling and I was no closer to my brother.

"Kringle, what's the next move?" Mallory asked. He used the same closed tone as he did with Shirl.

He'd already made up his mind. There would be no other moves as far as he was concerned.

I swallowed. The coffee had left a sour taste in my mouth. I pushed the cup away and stood up. I opened my mouth.

And inhaled a faint hint of candy cane and cinnamon.

Venir inhaled sharply. He'd smelled it as well. It wasn't my imagination.

The air in the room went completely silent. Even the background hum of the refrigerator went still. In the doorway, Mallory paused in a half-turn toward me. The furl between his brows only beginning. Shirl sat hunched in her chair, both hands on her thighs. She'd pulled her leg out from beneath her and placed both feet on the floor. She looked like she was just about to stand up, to make a run for it.

But she was frozen, both of them were frozen.

The candy cane and cinnamon smell intensified. Air popped as it was displaced. On the other side of the table, opposite Shirl, Dad appeared.

He wore the red Santa coat with white fluffy cuffs, undone over a dark green shirt. His hair was brushed back but several strands had come free and curled at the sides of his face.

"Noel, it's time to come home now," he said.

"You said I needed a break, time away," I said.

"Yes, I did and I thought it would be helpful for you," he said. He crossed his arms over his barrel chest. "That was before you visited the Council with this nonsense."

Burning coals, the Council had squealed to my dad.

"How do you even know about them?" Dad asked. "You weren't to be told until you took up the Santa Claus mantle."

"It's a little hard to explain," I said. I couldn't very well tell him about contacting them through the gatekeeper of the Underwell, the prison for magical beings who had broken the covenant of the Human or Magical Realms. It had been in service of one of my cases. A case I hadn't worked on here, in this time, in this reality.

Trying to reconcile my thoughts around what I remembered and where I was was giving me a headache.

"You've tampered with these people's lives, Noel," he said. "Kringles can't do that. I know you're having a challenging time and I confess I can't completely understand it but I do know the pressure of being Santa Claus. It can feel overwhelming, having that responsibility."

He moved around the table until he stood by my chair. He placed a hand on my shoulder. I felt soothing warmth flood through me.

"It's time to come home now, son," he said.

I wanted to protest, to say I couldn't because I hadn't found KJ but I hadn't found any trace of him out here in the world. If I couldn't find any in the back room at the Good View Mall where he had spent days entertaining children as Santa, I certainly wasn't going to find any trace of him anywhere else. The only other place he'd spent any kind of time in was my office and that was empty now.

I sighed. My father removed his hand from my shoulder and stepped back. I stood up from the table. I felt as if I was inside a photograph. The tableau of Mallory and Shirl had not moved. Nor did they register any notice of us, but they wouldn't. My father had a knack of being able to slip in between the beats of time.

It was the only way he could deliver presents all around the world in one night.

"What about Stan and Shirl?" I asked.

"I'll set things to right," Dad said. "Time to go."

I noticed Venir had already stood from his chair and moved to my father's side. Just like an obedient Christmas Elf. Especially one who was probably angling for a way out of the Supply Depot.

There was nothing else I could do. No one else who could help me. I gave one last glance to Shirl and Mallory, standing frozen in position. Once Dad had set things to right they probably wouldn't even remember this visit, never mind their relationship to me in my other life.

Goodbye, my friends.

I turned back to Dad.

"Okay, let's go."

CHAPTER

TEN

Life settled into a routine at the North Pole and I found myself slipping deeper and deeper into it. All the minutia that I had never learned because I was the second son now filled my day to overflowing.

It was my job to oversee the workshop schedule. Every shift I moved to a different section of the production line to learn the ins and outs of that area. I assisted with the care, feeding, and training of the reindeer. I helped Dad deal with the ever-changing present orders. I took point on ensuring the workshop was fully equipped and every time I found myself in the Supply Depot, I could feel Venir's cold, accusing stare on my back.

He probably thought I'd lied to him, that it was some weird, elaborate prank to make him think we were friends and colleagues, but I didn't know for sure. He never spoke to me after we returned to the North Pole.

Not that I had time for socializing. I felt like I was running from the moment I got up to the time I went to bed, and no matter how hard I tried, I could feel myself slipping farther and farther behind.

None of this came naturally to me, not the way it had come to KJ. He'd seemed born to the role. He'd worked hard on it, yes, but he'd excelled at it with an ease I could never match. Even in this reality, where I was supposed to the only son of Kris Kringle, I was nowhere near suited for the Santa Claus role.

With every passing day, it became more and more obvious to me.

It had to be obvious to mother and father too, although they never said anything. Still I noticed the slight furl between my mother's eyebrows as she made me breakfast or the half sigh my father gave as he repeated an instruction he'd already given me twice the day before.

Had KJ ever struggled like this? I didn't think so but then I'd never really paid attention.

I wished I had now.

As the spring months flowed into summer, the workshop began to gear up. At Dad's direction, I took over scheduling the Elves in the workshop. I spent hours pouring over time sheets matching them to the scheduling report, trying to make sure every shift was covered while giving each Elf a suitable break. That was the real challenge, forcing the Elves to take their breaks. They wanted to keep working and would do so until they dropped. Creating the schedule was as much about policing the Elves to make sure they left at the end of their shift as it was about figuring out their hours and posting the schedule up.

I took over a small office in the main workshop building. It was a half flight of stairs up, overlooking the workshop floor. Wooden slat blinds covered the window that looked down onto the floor but I kept them shut. I didn't want the Elves to think I was watching them. They always seem to smile wider and burst into song whenever I was around, eager to please me and share their joy at building toys.

It depressed me.

So I kept the blinds shut and sat hunched over the exquisite oak desk that took up much of the space in the office. The walls were painted a warm burgundy. The chair was rich, dark brown leather with wheels that seemed to float over the wood floor. Filing cabinets made from a matching oak lined the back of the office, with any required items easily available in which ever drawer I opened. In the corner by the door was a beautifully wood coat tree, with every hook carved into the curling shape of a candy cane. The air was a mix of warm cinnamon, fresh wood, the tang of metal, with a touch of crisp coolness from the snow outside.

The entire office was warm, inviting, prosperous, and efficient.

And I hated it.

I missed my slightly lopsided, squeaky leather chair. I missed my second hand metal desk from Goodwill with the burgundy desk blotter that covered the scuffed surface. I missed hanging my navy pea coat on the nail behind the door, because I kept forgetting to buy a hook and didn't have space in my squished office for a coat tree. I missed the rattle of the air conditioner in the window behind me as I sat at the desk. I missed the faint hint of dust and exhaust that drifted in from outside. I missed my laptop computer that Shirl had set up for me. I missed the two hard backed chairs that sat in front of my desk for visitors. I missed my cases.

I missed my life.

Nothing showed me that, although I was Kris Kringle's son, I was not destined to be Santa Claus more than sitting in that office, reviewing workshop schedules and listening to the Elves sing Christmas carols.

A Kringle I was but Santa Claus I would never be.

Except that in this life, I was going to be.

Eventually.

I missed KJ more than ever.

But I still had no idea how to find him, and as I stared at the scheduling sheets or took a turn feeding the reindeer, I began to wonder if I hadn't just imagined him all along.

From beyond the door, I heard the Elves finish their most recent rendition of "Here Comes Santa Claus." Their voices, in perfect tune, faded, the melody drowned out by the clink of tools being placed on the tables, the scrape of benches as they were pushed in. Footsteps followed as the current shift of Elves left. There would be a brief few minutes break before the next shift came in and got to work.

I pushed away from the desk. The leather chair glided smoothly away until I stopped it. Getting up, I moved to fetch my red parka from the coat tree. I slipped it on over my red flannel shirt. It carried the faintest hint of cinnamon and nutmeg. I'd left the coat hanging over the back of a chair in the kitchen and it had absorbed the scent of mother's cookies overnight.

The door opened silently and I peeked out. Below, the workshop floor was empty. Partially finished toys were lined up in a row along each table. The conveyor belts were full of finished toys and moved smoothly along, carrying them to the back of the workshop where they would be retrieved by Packaging.

I hurried down the stairs and headed for the door near the back of the workshop. As much as I liked the Elves, I didn't want to spend another ten minutes greeting each one individually as they arrived for their shift. They insisted upon paying their respects to me as the next Santa Claus. It didn't matter that they'd done it the day before and the day before that.

You enjoyed working here, you were delighted that I would be the next Santa Claus, you looked forward to working with me then, blah blah blah.

There was only so much unrelenting cheer I could take.

I reached the back door and yanked it open just as the front door creaked and the sound of chattering Elves filled my ears. As fast as I could I darted out and closed the door behind me, making sure it shut as silently as possible. With those great big, pointed ears, the Elves could hear almost anything.

Cold air enveloped me as I turned and hurried away from the workshop building. The path from the back door wasn't as used as often so the snow came halfway up my calves. I gave a wave of my hand and the snow fell away from my pants. Ahead of me, the path began to smooth out, the snow shifting to the sides, clearing the way.

The freshly cleared snow sparkled in the unrelenting sunshine. Summer at the North Pole meant constant sunlight, whether it was nine in the morning, nine at night, or three in the morning. I'd been used to the schedule as a child growing up here, six months of endless night and six months of endless day, but only a few years in Toronto had acclimatized me to a regular twelve hour sunlight, twelve hour nighttime day.

Except in this life, I'd never moved to Toronto.

But I still remembered it. At least I think I did.

Just like I thought I remembered KJ. Even as part of me was starting to wonder about that too.

Was it possible I had made it all up in my head? Maybe I didn't feel the calling to be Santa Claus, not the way mother and father wanted me to. Not the way the Elves expected. Dad was right about one thing, the pressure of being Santa Claus was intense, more intense than I had imagined. I'd always preferred reading the mystery novels mother left lying around when I was younger, maybe I'd only fantasized about leaving to be a private detective.

Maybe I had created the image of KJ in my mind, the perfect son to be Santa Claus. One who took it seriously and had a natural gift for it. I'd imagined him as the first born so *he* would take up that mantle and leave me out of it, free to pursue my own dream.

Being a private detective, away from here.

It made sense. Ever since the Kringles had been tasked with the Santa Claus duty, they had agree to have only one child per generation to carry on the duty. Why would my parents have had two sons? Why would they break with tradition like that?

They wouldn't of course, so there couldn't be a Kris Junior born ahead of me. There was only me, Noel Kringle, tasked with inheriting the Santa Claus mantle when Dad was done.

It was a great honour. A great duty. A great pleasure. A great joy.

A great nightmare.

I shook my head as I trudged along the path. Loose snow crunched under my boots. A breeze tickled the hair on my head but I refused to pull the hood up on my parka. Noise from the workshop faded as I moved farther away.

This path swung up around the back of the stables before turning toward the house. I knew my mother would be finishing with dinner now, waiting for both Dad and I to join her. It was just past the six pm shift change. Dad always made it home for dinner.

I on the other hand, often skipped dinner, citing the need to keep working, keep learning. If either of them knew it was an excuse they never let on. They were understanding that way.

Too bad I didn't understand anything anymore.

I reached the back of the stables. A fence made of snow and ice circled a large clear space at the back, a paddock for the reindeer, as if they couldn't fly over top of the fence. They didn't because Santa asked them not to and they listened to him. Well, most of them did. Donner did when he was in the mood.

Snow drifted almost a third of the way up the white sides of the barn. The top was a soaring dome which enabled the reindeer to frolic inside when the weather outside was too blustery for them. The front door was painted a deep, rich red so it was easy to spot, even in a snow storm, but the back door was white like the rest of the structure.

I yanked on the great, round brass handle. The door gave a slight creak and then began to slide open. I pulled it open just enough to let me enter. It could slide open almost all the way, letting the reindeer out into the paddock area as a group rather than one at a time. It also helped with the harnessing and staging of the reindeer in preparation for the Big Night.

But with the Big Night still more than six months away, I didn't need to pull the door open too far. As I stepped inside, warmth pressed against my face. I inhaled the musky odour of the reindeer along with the sweet scent of fresh hay.

Just ahead on the right, Donner stuck his head over the edge of his stall. He wiggled his ear with excitement. Being at the end of the row of stalls, he usually had to wait to be greeted by whomever came in from the front but when someone came in from the back, he got first pets.

Donner gave a loud snort and shoved his nose toward me. Apparently I was taking far too long in the petting department. How dare I not spring toward him immediately?

I scratched his nose and rubbed along his jaw line.

"Hello, Donner, you little devil."

The reindeer half closed his eyes in pleasure. He gave another soft snort of approval. I was allowed to pet him for another few seconds before I heard the stomp of a hoof beside him.

Comet wanted attention.

I wandered my way through the barn, saying hello and petting noses and necks of each of the reindeer. I wasn't allowed to miss anyone or spend too much time on one rather than move on to the next. The reindeer were very particular and very demanding of attention.

I ended up at the other side of the barn beside the tenth, empty stall. With only nine reindeer, the tenth stall was used as storage. Beside it, Blitzen hung his head over the stall door and nuzzled my hand.

Leaning back against the wood, I scratched the side of his neck. He gave almost a gurgling sound of pleasure. The other reindeer poked their heads over their stall doors, patiently waiting for another round of pets. Now that I had greeted each one, they were more willing to wait for more attention.

I let out a sigh. The barn felt like the only place I could relax. The reindeer didn't care whether I was the heir to Santa Claus or not, they just wanted to be petted and fed. Not always in that order. They were indiscriminate in their demand for attention. They didn't care if I was able to juggle the scheduling properly or if I learned the best route to take around the world. As long as I pet them, they were happy.

It was the least demanding location in the North Pole so I stole as many moments here as I could.

I was about to cross back over to the back door when I heard the creak of the front door opening.

Damn the halls, someone was coming in. If it were Elves I would have to spend a sufficient amount of time greeting them and conversing before I could sneak away.

I did not feel like talking.

I ducked into the empty stall beside Blitzen and eased the door closed behind me.

"...so I told Delbar and you know what he said?" said a voice I recognized. Felric, one of the regular stable Elves.

"What, sir?" A high pitched voice almost squeaked in response.

"Let 'em try shovellin' to hammerin' and see which is easier." He broke off into loud guffaws. The Elf with the high voice chuckled along, the way you would with a boss you were trying to impress.

The laughter trailed off and I heard the rustle of feed-bags. In their stalls, the reindeer snorted and stomped their hooves. It was time for the evening meal.

Which meant the Elves would be coming into the empty stall to get the feed.

I scrambled back into a dark corner of the stall. A large roll of hay was pressed up against the wall. With a few shoves, I managed to roll it just enough to hide me.

Footsteps sounded closer. The stall latch clicked open.

I heard the crinkle of a bag.

"This one's almost empty. Kelstio, grab the full one in the back," Felric said.

The bag of feed was right beside me. I pressed myself against the back of the stall, feeling the grooves of the wood dig into my back. Maybe before they reached the stall I could have announced myself but doing it now would be embarrassing, ridiculous, and insulting.

"Will Santa come by tonight?" Kelstio asked. I caught a glimpse of the sleeve of his green outfit as he grabbed a bag of feed.

"He usually doesn't come out at night," Felric said. "Sometimes the heir comes out, pets the reindeer. Good he pays attention to 'em. I don't know why the workshop Elves back talk about 'im."

Kelstio had been dragging the bag forward. He stopped.

"The workshop Elves back talk about Santa?"

"No, no, about the heir, you know," Felric said. "Master Noel."

"What do they say?" Kelstio's voice was soft, almost hushed.

I heard the scrape of a boot on the floor, then Felric's voice sounded almost as hushed as Kelstio's, but closer.

"They say he's clumsy, doesn't remember the easiest things. Santa's always reminding 'im. They think he's the worst candidate for Santa they've ever seen." Felric gave a snort. "Like they seen any others. Most of them are too young to remember when Kris Kringle was just learnin' the ropes. Besides, ain't like he's gotta take over any time soon. Ol' Kris has still got seven hundred years on his contract. Could even squeeze in a few hundred more I bet if Master Noel still needs more seasoning."

"The workshop Elves really say that?" Kelstio asked.

"Eh, just a few disgruntled ones. There's always one or two of 'em. Always flapping their gums. Now hurry up with that bag."

The bag hissed against the floor as they dragged it along. Then I heard the click of the stall door. Their voices continued on a conversation as they fed the reindeer. I recognized the sound of the feed pouring to the feed bags and the eager munching of the reindeer.

But I didn't move. Instead I huddled behind the roll of hay, feeling my face burn with embarrassment. My fumbling and pathetic efforts hadn't gone unnoticed. Maybe only one or two of the Elves had the nerve to talk about it but that only meant many more thought the same thing.

I was nowhere near Santa material, and they knew it.

I hunched against the back of the stall until I heard the Elves finish feeding the reindeer and leave. Only when the door shut and I listened to several minutes of uninterrupted munching did I dare move.

I dragged myself out from behind the roll of hay, brushing stray strands from my parka. Beside the stall, Blitzen snorted then settled back in with his bag.

The stall unlocked with a click and I stepped out. Ears flickered in my direction but none of the reindeer looked up. They were too busy eating. Even petting wasn't as great a draw at the moment.

Somehow this place that had always felt like an escape and a refuge didn't feel quite so much like that anymore. Now whenever I visited I would wonder what the stable Elves had heard about me and when I was in the workshop, I would wonder what the workshop Elves were saying.

Had Dad really had a challenging start too? That didn't seem possible. Of course I'd only known him after he'd been doing the job for several hundred years. Anyone would get good at it after that long. Maybe even I would as well.

Except in my memories, KJ had never seemed to need much time to get a hang of any aspect of the job. He'd been that natural at it.

If there really had been a KJ. If I hadn't just made him up to cover my own inadequacies for the Santa Claus job.

I paused by Blitzen's stall and put a hand on his neck. His right ear swivelled toward me as he munched. His right eye blinked.

"I wish I was half as natural at it as KJ," I said.

Blitzen lifted his head and looked at me.

All sounds of munching stopped. All the reindeer had lifted their heads and turned toward me. From the first stall near the front, Rudolph's nose began to glow.

Every one of them were focused on me.

I swallowed. My heart began to pound.

"KJ?" I said.

Rudolph gave a snort and nodded his head, the red glow deepening and lighting up the stable at his end.

He recognized the name. They all did.

All the reindeer remembered KJ!

CHAPTER
ELEVEN

My mouth went dry. I had to be imagining it. The reindeer were just looking at me because I'd stepped out of the extra stall where all the extra food was stored.

But they'd been too busy eating to pay me any attention just a moment ago. It was only when I mentioned KJ that they reacted.

And they reacted because they knew the name.

Steady, I couldn't get all excited. It might not really mean anything. They may have just reacted to my tone. Reindeer were very intuitive. They had to be to follow Dad's instructions with split second timing as they travelled around the world when even a moment's hesitation could mean disaster. They would have heard distress in my voice. That's what they were responding to.

Maybe. Possibly. Probably.

Although I'd never seen Rudolph set his nose aglow at any other time of distress.

I stepped out into the middle of aisle. Every reindeer head moved as they tracked me. All munching sounds had stopped as they each swallowed their last mouthful of food. I knew none of them had finished their meal yet none of them bent toward their feed bag. Instead, they studied me.

I cleared my throat and turned in a slow circle to take in every reindeer. Even that troublemaker Donner had paused and was staring at me like the others.

"You remember KJ," I said. I wasn't asking a question.

Several of the reindeer snorted. A few nodded their heads. Even Rudolph lifted his chin as his nose glowed brighter.

My legs felt wobbly, like loose ribbon. I could have run and hugged each one of them. I had become convinced that I was hallucinating or imagining my memories, that I had lost my mind. But if they remembered KJ, I hadn't lost my mind. I hadn't made him up.

He'd been real. He *was* real.

And something had happened to pull him out of this reality. It was like I had originally thought.

"Do you have any idea what happened to him?"

It was a long shot asking the reindeer. Even if they somehow knew, it would be almost impossible for them to tell me. But they had a special connection to Dad, as Santa

Claus. If they couldn't tell me, they might be able to convey some of the information to Dad.

But as I glanced up and down the aisle, each of the reindeer shook their head. Even Rudolph bowed his head as if ashamed he couldn't help me.

I sighed. Disappointing but it had been a long shot. A very long shot.

But they remembered him and that was something. Something that grounded me again and gave me hope.

I wasn't sure why. I was no closer to knowing what had happened or what to do about it. Trying to gather my friends down in Toronto had been a bust and Venir wouldn't even talk to me any more. But still I felt hopeful.

I wasn't losing my mind. My brother was real.

And I was going to find him, to bring him back to his life.

So I could get back to mine.

BY THE TIME I REACHED THE HOUSE, MOTHER AND FATHER HAD already sat down to dinner. I made an excuse about checking in on the reindeer as I took my chair. Across the table was an empty spot. KJ's seat. It no longer disturbed me to see it. He'd be using it again.

Although we normally ate breakfast and lunch in the nook in the kitchen, mother insisted we eat dinner in the dining room. The walls were a light green colour, reflected in the darker green of table cloth that covered the long, mahogany table. The chairs were made from the same wood, in a clean, elegant design. As always, mother set the table with two simple, tapered white candles. She insisted we eat on the best China plates we had because what was the point of keeping them for special occasions when just being together was special enough.

I let the sound of my parent's conversation wash over me as I ate. Mother had made delicious roast ham, scalped potatoes, and steamed mixed vegetables tossed with various spices. She loved to experiment with different flavours. I was sure I tasted cumin.

"I really wish you would try to make a start on it this year," my mother said. "It's all your junk up there."

I bit into a piece of broccoli and focused in on the discussion.

"We're already starting to gear up," Dad said. "It might have to wait."

"You say that every year," she said. "It doesn't matter when I bring it up, you always put it off."

"I don't know why you're so keen to clean out the attic," Dad said. "We have plenty of space in the house."

"I'll start it," I said.

They both stopped. Dad blinked while mother's eyes widened. They looked like they'd forgotten I was there.

"I can start tidying up in there for you, mother," I said.

"You're thinking the front end, right? With the window that overlooks the village?"

"Yes, I think it would be nice to have that space cleared out," she said.

"It would make a nice office," I said.

A smile played across her face. "I think that's a lovely idea."

I knew she'd think so. She'd liked the idea when KJ had had it before I left.

I didn't know why but cleaning up that space felt like the right thing to do, another way to tap into that reality I was trying to retrieve.

"You'll be having your hands full with the workshop schedule," Dad said. "Along with everything else."

"I can squeeze in some time here and there," I said. "I'd be happy to."

Mother shot Dad a look of triumph, mixed with relief. Dad smiled back at her.

"Okay, since everything is on track for the moment. But once we get busy..."

"Don't worry about it," I said. "I'll make sure if doesn't interfere with anything."

"As long as you're sure," Dad said.

"Hush Kris, he's sure." Mother reached over and patted my hand. "A project of your own will do you some good."

I smiled at her.

I hoped so. I sure did hope so.

AFTER DINNER, I TOOK A LANTERN AND HEADED UP TO THE ATTIC. A set of collapsing stairs were built into the ceiling of an alcove off the main living room. A solid tug on the hanging rope bought them down in a smooth, easy motion. They didn't even squeak, just a click as they locked into place, the first step setting down with a gentle thud on the floor.

They seemed sturdy enough but the first thing I would look into would be to install a circular staircase that fit perfectly into the alcove. These collapsing stairs jutted out several feet into the hall. Too easy to get in the way.

So KJ had said when he had decided to install the new staircase.

I carried the lantern ahead of me as I made my way up to the attic. When I reached the top, I enchanted the lantern and set it adrift, directing it to rise to the highest point in the attic. With the light I was able to get a good look at the space.

The floor was a solid sheet of wood so at least I didn't have to worry about putting in a floor. The walls on either side sloped with the roof, allowing only a space about four feet in width along the centre were I could comfortably stand upright. On either side, the slope graduated downward until it finished at about knee height.

Tucked against the wall were cardboard boxes. They had

the look of age to them, the top ones sagging a little into the bottom ones. Writing on the sides was so faded I couldn't read them in the faint light from the lantern. I would have to open every box to see what was in them.

Dust tickled my nose as I turned in a slow circle to take in the entire area. Somehow KJ had managed to make this awkward room workable. He'd built shelving against the walls and a desk along the front beneath the window. A chair had given him more space to work with as it shrank his height so he could avoid bashing his head against the ceiling. He'd even installed recessed lights and put in a couple of sky lights to bring in more light and give a sense of space to the cramped area. A strong enough enchantment had kept the snow off the sky lights.

I could almost picture it.

Maybe...just maybe.

I closed my eyes and took a deep breath. I had never seen the office completely finished but I'd seen enough to get an idea of the space and how KJ had laid everything out. He'd painted the walls a light blue, so it looked like sky. The desk and shelves he'd made out of a light pine. Dark colours would only shrink the space, he'd told me.

Even so, many of his leather volumes had dark covers, but in the light shelves, they hadn't overpowered the look. In fact, they'd added depth and texture.

Even as he'd painted and varnished the floor, his slight odour of cinnamon could never be overpowered. If I concentrated, I could still catch a whiff.

I opened my eyes.

KJ's office spread out before me. His tan leather chair was slightly askew at the desk. Papers covered the surface, some in piles, others spread unevenly in front of the chair. On the right side of the desk, a white mug with a red handle rested on a Christmas wreath coaster. I recognized it as part of a set mother had given him for his birthday several years ago. Off to the right side of the desk, a pen rested across one sheet of paper, like KJ had just set it down before getting up from his chair.

My heart pounded and my mouth wet dry. I was afraid to move in case I disturbed this vision but I wanted to see what was on that paper. The way the pen was resting made it look like KJ had just written something down and stepped away. I had a distinct impression it was a piece of the puzzle to KJ's disappearance.

I inched forward one step, ready for the desk to vanish but it didn't. It seemed solid and real, as real as walking up those collapsing stairs had been. I glanced back behind me and spotted the metal railing of a spiral staircase.

This was more than a vision. Somehow I'd slipped sideways into the reality of it.

Turning back to the desk, I took another step forward then another. The desk stayed corporeal. I started to feel lightheaded and realized I'd forgotten to breathe. I sucked in air and let it out. My heart steadied although as I reached toward the chair, my hands were shaking.

The arm of the chair felt solid as I closed my fingers

around it. The wheels glided smoothly as I pulled the chair out from the desk. My legs felt like they were shaking now so I sat down. The padded leather seat gave a little, cushioning me. It may disappear in a moment, dumping me onto the floor, but for now it held.

I rolled closer to the desk to peruse the papers. With a shock I found many of them to be schedules for the Elves. Several were half started or crossed out. Graphs scribbled with notations that had a line drawn through them.

It reminded me of my own fumbling efforts to properly schedule the work and rotations. From the look of these scrapes of paper KJ had as much trouble as I had.

Was that possible? Had the appearance of his ease with the work been a ruse?

I picked the pen up off the sheet of paper on the right side of the desk. The sheet was unlined with only a few lines scribbled on it. I recognized KJ's looping style but as drew the paper closer to me, the ink began to fade. The words smeared, becoming unintelligible. But I caught a glimpse of the single word at the top of the page:

Noel.

And at the bottom, two initials.

KJ.

My brother had left me a note. One that was being magically destroyed as I looked at it.

A moment later, the ink vanished. The paper began to fade to translucence.

The edges of the desk blurred.

I jumped up just before the chair vanished and dumped me onto the floor.

Between one blink and the next, the room winked back to its original condition. Only the single lantern that hovered above me cast any light. The desk and chair were gone. The walls were back to their off-white, unfinished look. Old cardboard boxes sat where the shelves had been.

I felt something press into my left palm. I'd clenched my fists instinctively. Now I lifted them and opened them up.

A pen lay in my left palm.

KJ's pen.

It hadn't disappeared. Somehow being in my hand had protected it. If only the note had been protected as well.

The note from KJ to me.

He had been here, leaving me a note. Did he suspect something would happen to him? Had he been warned about it? Why hadn't he called me? Why leave a note?

I had more questions than ever but this time I wasn't going to stop looking for answers. Now I *knew* KJ was real. Nothing could convince me otherwise. The reindeer remembered him and I had experienced his workshop here in the attic. I had the pen in my hand to prove it.

This time I was going to find him.

But first I needed a few supplies.

CHAPTER

TWELVE

The lighting in the Supply Depot looked the same even though it was after hours. I didn't think there was a full shift working overnight, not yet. As the work geared up in the workshop, other areas would begin to run around the clock as well. Including the Supply Depot.

But for now, the long rows of metal shelving felt deserted.

I'd *winked* in a few rows over from the logging counter. As I moved along, the tapping of my steps on the white concrete seemed to echo, even with all the shelves. If any Elves were working here tonight they would surely come to investigate. I needed to get what I wanted and get out.

The only problem was I wasn't exactly sure of all the ingredients I would need for the spell I was thinking of.

Mother would know but I couldn't ask her. Couldn't let her suspect, couldn't let any of them suspect.

I was going to have to do this on my own.

I found paper and ink. Definitely candles and matches. After that, what? I wished I'd paid more attention to spell work but I'd always had my nose stuck in the latest mystery novel.

Okay, think. I was trying to draw out memory. So what else did I need for that?

Something precious, in payment for the magic. I hurried down another aisle. Found some gold dust. Loose gem stones. For good measure, I took three.

A bowl, some cinnamon. A couple of candy canes.

Good, yes, that seemed like enough.

The logical spot would be to return to the attic where I found the pen but I had a feeling I'd exhausted any residual memory of that place. If anything, it might impede the spell.

No, I was going to have to go somewhere that still had a trace of that other reality.

"What are you doing here?"

I jumped and spun around. The candles flew out of my hands. The gem stones slipped through my fingers. The candles landed with a crack and snapped in half. The gem stones rolled along the floor.

And came to a stop right in front of the curling toes of Venir's boots.

He stood at the end of the aisle, arms crossed over his leather apron. He wore the usual dark green outfit of the

Supply Depot. His curling white hair stuck out from his head but his ears poked up even higher. A frown creased his face and his brow was furled.

"I just came for a few things," I said. "I didn't mean to bother anyone."

He grunted and kicked at the stone at his feet. It was an emerald. It skittered toward me. I bent to pick it up.

"What's the spell?" he asked then put up a hand. "No, don't tell me. I don't really wanna know."

"You aren't going to tell anyone I was here?" I asked. I waved at the candle. The broken pieces floated toward me, pressing together and mending as they came.

"You asking me to lie?" He shook his head. "You are a lousy candidate for Santa Claus."

"That's because I'm not supposed to be and you know it," I said. I shifted the bundle of items until I cradled them in my left arm and then dug out the pen from my right pocket. I held it out to show the Elf.

"This pen was KJ's," I said. "I had a vision of his office in the attic of my parents' house. No, not a vision because you can't touch a vision. This was real. Before it vanished, this pen was lying on the desk on top of a note addressed to me. With the proper spell, I can recreate that note."

"I ain't listening to this." Venir backed up a few steps.

"Fine, don't." I struggled to keep the bitterness from my voice. Venir's disbelief hurt even though he wasn't really the Venir who was my friend. But for a brief time he had helped me, he had been willing to try.

That was over now.

"Just don't tell anyone I was here," I said.

Something softened in his face. He held out his hands toward me.

"Master Noel, don't do this again. I think you...I think you need some help. I'm sure if you asked Santa, even Mrs. Claus..."

"Don't you say a word to either of them, Venir."

The Elf scurried back until he was pressed up against a shelf. The box at his shoulder shifted.

I towered over him. I hadn't even realized I'd advanced. My knuckles holding the pen were white from gripping it and I held it like a talisman in front of me.

"I know you don't remember him and I know you don't believe me," I said. "But KJ is real and I know it. And so do the reindeer."

The concerned, apprehensive look on his face lessened. "What?"

"They recognized his name," I said.

Venir looked startled. "They did not."

"They did so," I said. "They recognized the name and they remember him. Now I know you don't and you think I'm crazy but I'm doing this spell and I'd rather you didn't upset my parents." I paused and took a breath. "Please."

He pressed his lips together, suddenly looking uncertain.

"Where are ya doin' it? The spell?" he asked.

If I told him he might tell my dad but if I didn't I knew he would for sure go to dad as soon as I left. Maybe if I took the chance and trusted him he would keep the secret. At least long enough for me to complete the spell.

"I'm going back to my office in Toronto," I said. "That's the place KJ visited me most often. It's the place I spent most of my time in. If there's anywhere I can pull off this spell it's there."

Venir wrinkled his nose. "Really? That place was kinda dumpy."

"That's where I have to do the spell," I said. "I wasn't asking you to come."

His expression softened. "You ain't?"

I gestured around me. "I've gotten you into enough trouble. I'll do this on my own." I pointed at him. "Just remember. I was never here."

He held up his hands in surrender. "Okay, okay, you was never here."

I made sure I had all the ingredients cradled in my arms. The pen was safely back in my pocket. I was as ready as I was ever going to be.

I gave Venir a final stern look. He swallowed and gave a quick nod.

Then I *winked*.

I landed in my office where my leather chair would have been. Instead I felt engulfed in a cloud of dust. I coughed and spat out the worst of it. Behind me, the window was unadorned with curtain or blinds. Pale light from the parking lot beyond shone yellow and revealed the floating dust that drifted around me.

Oddly, without the furniture squished into the room, it seemed even smaller than normal. I would have thought it would feel bigger when it was empty. I missed the vast expanse of the surface of my desk. It would be a lot easier to set up the spell.

I would have to make do with the floor.

Staying where I estimated my chair would be, I set four candles out at the four directional points. North, south, east, and west. Standing in the centre, I faced north and set the candle to light, then moved clockwise, breathing fire to light each candle. Soon it was stronger than the pale light from the window.

I set the bowl in the centre. In went the cinnamon, candy cane, and the pen. It was too long to fit completely inside the bowl but I shifted it so most of it stayed inside. I arranged the three gem stones in a triangle at the top end of the bowl and set the paper at the bottom end. A sprinkle of gold dust over the bowl and over the gem stones.

Ready. Or as ready as it would ever be.

I knelt in front of the paper, placing my hands flat against the floor on either side of the bowl. I closed my eyes and took a deep breath. Focused. I couldn't remember the words to the memory recall spell but I knew the feeling.

Hopefully that would be enough.

I focused on KJ, remembering him here in my office. The times he'd visited me, wearing his red flannel shirts. His hair slicked back from his head. His beard, longer than mine but shaped and neat. The times he would land in my chair behind my desk and put his feet up on the desktop, no matter how often I asked him not to do it. The way his eyebrows would arch at me when I talked about my cases. The countless times he would shake his head.

The few times he actually mentioned that he thought I was good at my job.

That didn't happen very often. KJ was not one for gushing. Not at me, anyway. Not even at children. But he had a strong, steady, calming presence and seemed genuinely interested in what they had to say. I'd seen how children responded to him at the Christmas in July promotion.

KJ would make a good Santa Claus. He may even make a great one.

If I got him back.

No. *When* I got him back.

I could feel the muscles along my back and shoulders tensing. Relax. Another deep breath. In and out. Another.

Focus.

Dust tickled my nose but I still smelled the cinnamon and candy canes. Cinnamon was the scent I most associated with KJ. He had always been a huge fan of mother's cinnamon sugar cookies. Once when we were children, he'd managed to knock over the bowl of dry ingredients all over himself. With a flick of his hands, he'd managed to stop everything from hitting him except for the cinnamon. It had covered him from head to toe. He'd started licking his hands and arms before my mother could stop him. His tongue had burned with the heat of the cinnamon but he'd loved it.

He hadn't loved it quite so much when mother whisked him into the shower, clothes and all.

I remembered.

I opened my eyes.

The inside of the bowl was glowing a golden bronze. The candles around me were flickering wildly, sending shadows dancing across the walls. I reached for the pen in the bowl. It felt warm as if someone had been holding it.

I pressed the tip to the paper before me.

"Show me what KJ wrote for me."

The pen quivered in my fingers. I willed it to move, to write, but the magic felt weak, unfocused.

My spell work wasn't good enough.

I pressed my lips tight together in frustration. Did I need more ingredients? Was not recalling my memories of KJ not enough? Was I going to need to find the words for the spell?

It would all take more time. Like I hadn't already been wasting enough time. Every moment I spent in this reality made it more and more real, made it more and more likely that I would never be able to get KJ back.

And I had to get him back. I had to.

I felt my hand squeezing the pen, pressing it down hard on the paper. That wasn't going to help. This was delicate magic. It needed a delicate touch. I couldn't force it.

I breathed and loosened my grip. Let the tip trace a line across the top of the paper, so lightly that it didn't even mark it.

Good. That was good.

A footstep sounded outside in the waiting room. Then another. Something stomped.

KJ?

Had I done it?

I dropped the pen and scrambled to my feet. As I dart to the door, I missed kicking the bowl by an inch. Burnt coals, wouldn't that have ruined the spell? But it wouldn't matter if KJ was here, if I'd done it.

Please let me have done it.

I leapt through the doorway and froze.

Venir stood in the centre of the room.

With a reindeer.

I recognized Blitzen from the small white patch on the right side of his nose. Even standing in the middle of a room, the reindeer had a regal bearing. His ears swivelled as he listened to the sounds of the building. He gave me a dignified nod.

"Venir, what are you and Blitzen doing here?" I asked.

Venir had his hands stuffed into the pockets of his parka. He'd left his leather apron behind but still wore the rest of his green uniform.

"I had ta know," he said, "so I went to the stables and talked to the reindeer. They confirmed that they remembered your brother and actually wanted to know where he was. They hadn't seen him in weeks."

I had always suspected that the Elves and the reindeer could communicate on some level. Rumour had it that the reindeer could read minds. I suspected Dad could communicate with them as well, probably part of the Santa Claus job.

"Why didn't they say anything about him before I mentioned him?" I asked. "Why haven't they said anything to Dad?"

Blitzen bowed his head. He took a few steps toward me and pressed his muzzle against my arm. He gave a loud snort.

"When I was talkin' to 'em they mentioned they thought somethin' had happened," Venir said. "They hadn't realized it until you mentioned KJ. They said they started thinkin' about it after you left."

"They only thought of it now?" I asked.

"Reindeer have a different sense of time than we do," Venir said. "They don't really pay attention until you focus 'em."

Blitzen rubbed his muzzle along my arm. I gave him a good scratch on the side of his face.

"So why is Blitzen here with you?" I asked.

"They feel guilty not realizing somethin' was up until now," the Elf said. He hunched his shoulders. "They ain't the only one."

Blitzen took a step closer and pressed his shoulder against me, almost knocking me over. He still thought he was the size of young calf with the same strength. I threw an arm around his neck.

"You came to help," I said. "Both of you. Thank you, Venir."

"Yeah, well." A blush turned Venir's cheeks almost as red as his parka. "You need it."

"I do," I said. "I'm having trouble with the memory spell. Maybe with the three of us we can get it to work."

I stepped back through the doorway into my office. Venir slipped in behind me while Blitzen filled the entryway. The tips of his antlers brushed the doorframe. His hooves clopped against the parquette floor.

The candles were still burning, sending flickering light and shadow across the walls. The bowl still sat in the centre with the gem stones in front and the paper behind.

I stepped closer, saw the cinnamon and candy canes covering the bottom of the bowl.

But no pen.

While I had gone to investigate the noises, the pen had vanished.

And with it, my hope of discovering the message KJ had left for me.

CHAPTER

THIRTEEN

Damn the halls!

"The pen's gone," I shouted.

"Where'd you put it?" Venir asked.

"I left it right there when I went to see who was in the waiting room." I pointed at the paper lying in the dust on the floor. Even in the flickering light you could see it was empty.

Venir leaned over, peering at the paper.

"You sure you left it there?"

"I'm sure," I said. I patted down my clothes, even turned out the pockets of my jeans. "See? No pen."

"Okay, okay. Maybe it rolled away somewheres. Let's look."

I pressed my lips tight together. There was no furniture in the room, nowhere the pen would have rolled and not been visible, even in the dim light from the four candles.

I knew the sound of someone humouring me. So much for him being here to help.

I was about to say something about it when Blitzen snorted and pawed at the floor. He took another step into the room, swinging his head wildly. The sharp tips of his antlers missed me by less than an inch. His shoulders brushed the sides of the doorframe as he tried to push forward. He let out a squeal as he stomped his foot.

"What's the matter with him?" I called to Venir.

"Don't know," Venir said. "He's upset about somethin'. Blitzen, slow down. What is it?"

The reindeer lowered his head. I found the antlers aiming right at my stomach. His eyes were wide, the whites glowing in the candle light. I watched the muscles ripple and bunch on the his shoulders.

Burnt coals, Blitzen was going to leap into the room.

And impale me in the process!

I send a wild look around me. Nowhere to go out of reach of those antlers. I was going to be skewered no matter what.

Blitzen gave out a snorting cry and lunged.

I braced for impact.

But instead of lunging forward. The reindeer flew upward. He ducked his head as his shoulders bumped the ceiling. Flakes of paint fluttered down like snow as Blitzen landed, square in the centre of my circle. With a grunt, he swept his feet backward across the floor, breaking the circle in several spots.

With a final snort, he lifted his head. The antlers swung upward, safely out of reach.

In the flickering candlelight, Blitzen's expression returned to one of calm. But he had been almost enraged just a moment ago.

A moment before he broke my circle.

But Venir had said the reindeer wanted to help me find KJ.

Unless the circle wasn't a way to find him, but a way to have me be found by... something or someone?

Someone who had taken the pen.

My heart was still hammering in my chest from the recent possibility of being impaled. I took a deep breath and let it out. Closed my eyes. This was my office. Even in this reality, it was a place I knew inside and out. Everything was familiar. I would notice anything out of place, anything different.

There. A tingling by the window.

The faintest hint of magic. I reached out toward it but it seemed to fade even as I focused on it. I moved my hand and touched the window frame. The bottom was slightly damp. Maybe it was leaking in this wet March but when I lifted my fingers away, I couldn't feel the moisture.

I brought them to my nose. Something sour, almost tangy. It reminded me of seaweed.

I opened my eyes and became aware of Venir's voice murmuring to Blitzen.

"Ask him if he saw who it was," I said.

"Who what was?" Venir asked.

"Who came in through the window and took the pen," I said. I turned toward them. Venir stood beside the reindeer, reaching his hand up above his head to pat Blitzen's shoulder. Blitzen stood with head high, facing me.

"The circle called to it," I said. "It must have felt the magic I was casting and came." I nodded to the reindeer. "Thanks for breaking the circle and stopping it. Who knows what it might have done if I'd tried again."

"Wait a minute," Venir said. "Are you sayin' something or somebody magical had something to do with your brother?"

I nodded. The thought solidified in my brain. It had to be an outside influence that had done it. Something or someone powerful enough to erase KJ from this reality.

I'd been spending so much time trying to convince others that I wasn't crazy, that KJ had existed, that I had not really even focused on what could have happened, what could have caused it.

Or who.

I felt myself straighten, not just physically but mentally as well. I'd been haltingly investigating but no more. Now I was all in.

I was going to find whoever had done this to KJ and, in the process, bring him back.

Time to start acting like a private detective again.

"Venir, see if you can detect the magic at the window. I need to identify who or what did that. If it's too far gone for you to detect, ask Blitzen if he can help you."

Venir took a step back. His eyes were wide as he gazed up at me.

"What's wrong?" I asked.

"You," he said. "You're all... I don't know. Different." He gestured with his hand. "In charge. Kinda reminds me of Santa."

I grinned. "This is *my* office," I said. "And I'm a private detective. I forgot that for a while but now I remember and we're going to detect."

I jerked my thumb at the window. "Check it out."

He nodded and hurried over.

I bent to gather the scattered bits of my circle. It wouldn't be good to leave it here, not just in case the landlord decided to check out the space. Any lingering magic could cause trouble. I drew the candles together and set them floating up toward the ceiling. Light bounced off the beige walls and brightened the room just a little. Enough to see the cracks in the paint and the flecks from the ceiling that covered the floor.

Some had landed on the paper. I picked up the note pad and shook it off. The flecks of paint drifted to the floor. They really did fall like snow, the great fluffy kind on a day with no wind. The only problem with the fluffy kind was that it wasn't any good for building forts. Which, on the positive side, meant it wasn't any good for snowballs either.

When we were kids, it had always been a toss up, whether we would end up building forts together or KJ would ambush me with snowballs.

Okay, maybe he wasn't the only one doing the ambushing.

I smiled to myself as I bent to retrieve the bowl.

Glanced at the note pad.

And froze.

Faint, barely visible writing had appeared on the paper. In the dim light, it was impossible to read but I tried anyway, squinting and bringing the paper closer to my face. I could almost make out the top word.

Noel.

My heart hammered in my chest. My mouth filled with saliva, tasting sour. A sudden flash of heat swept my body, like I was wrapped in a moist, wet blanket filled with boiling water. The stench filled my nostrils, bitter, wet, like rotting garbage, all fishy and spoiling.

I gagged, dropped the note pad. Bent over, hands on knees, gagging and retching.

I felt like I had been smothered.

No, drowned.

I became aware of hands on my back, patting me. A warm head pressed against my right shoulder. Venir and Blitzen trying to help me.

"Easy, kiddo, take it easy."

Venir's words coalesced in my ears. I became aware that he had been speaking for some time.

"Easy, you're all right," he said.

I gave a final cough and wiped my mouth with the back of my hand. Straightening took a little effort. My body trembled from what I could only think of as a psychic assault. I steadied my breath, trying to slow my galloping heart beat.

Blitzen presented his shoulder to me as I pushed myself to my feet. I leaned against him. The hard, powerful muscles of the reindeer felt as steady as a rock.

"You okay?" Venir asked.

I managed a nod and waved at the note pad lying on the floor.

"There was writing on it," I said, "before I was attacked."

Venir stooped to reach for the pad. His fingers stopped a few inches from it as he glanced back at me.

"Attacked? You was havin' a coughin' fit."

"No, I wasn't," I said. "Something was wrapping around me, something wet and boiling, trying to smother me. It felt like I was drowning."

Venir scooped up the note pad. A frown played across his face.

"You sure? I didn't feel nothin', no hint of magic in the room. Nothin' even on the window sill."

He turned the note pad over and glanced at it. He shook his head.

"Nothing here."

Of course there wouldn't be. Whoever or whatever was trying to stop me had distracted me from reading it before the writing faded. My spell had worked more than I'd realized, until it was interfered with. And it was powerful enough to target its magic specifically while masking it.

I glanced over at Blitzen. His nostrils flared as he puffed

breaths out. His eyes were keen and alert as he swept his gaze over the office.

Maybe the magic hadn't been masked from everyone.

"Ask Blizten if he felt anything," I said to Venir.

The Elf frowned. "If there was somethin' that he felt, I woulda felt it too."

"Not if someone was trying to cover it up," I said.

Venir looked skeptical but he tilted his head toward the reindeer. Blitzen swung his head toward the Elf, pinning him with a steady gaze.

The skeptical look faded into surprise.

"He did feel somethin'," Venir said. "Tingling around you. Really focused."

I nodded. I felt steadier now. I gave Blitzen's shoulder a pat as I straightened away from him.

"Like I thought, targeted," I said. "Check the pad. There's no writing now, is there?"

Venir flipped the pad over. Shook his head.

"What does it mean?" he asked.

I grinned at him.

"It means whatever caused this, whatever took KJ, is scared," I said. "It knows I'm coming and that I won't stop."

"So whadda we do?"

I noticed the 'we'. He was starting to sound more and more like the Venir I knew.

"We're going to hunt it down," I said. "I want you to find out who or what can use magic like that, hidden, but stinking, sour and fishy, with a feeling of smothering or drowning."

Uncertainty crinkled Venir's face. He wasn't quite the same Elf although he was trying. I gave him a reassuring nod.

"You can do it," I said. "You know people in the Magical Realms. Just be casual, ask over drinks."

"Okay," he said. He still looked a little skeptical. "What are you and Blitzen gonna do?"

"Don't worry about that," I said. "Meet me back here in an hour."

He gave a slight frown then shrugged. A moment later he was gone. I couldn't feel any residual of a portal so he had probably *winked* somewhere where he could open one safely.

I turned to see the reindeer regarding me with alert and interested eyes.

"Okay, Blitzen, it's you and me," I said. "Let's see if we can find a trace of this creature."

Blitzen lowered his head and gave an affirmative snort.

<h1 style="text-align:center">CHAPTER
FOURTEEN</h1>

The first thing to do would be to mask Blitzen. I couldn't wander around the city with a reindeer on my heels without attracting unwanted attention. But I didn't want to send him back to the North Pole, even if he would go which I knew he wouldn't. Reindeer could be quite stubborn when they wanted to be.

I stroked the smooth fur on the side of his neck.

"I'm going to mask you, big guy," I told him. "People around here will think it strange to see a reindeer wandering around. Is that okay with you?"

I couldn't understand reindeer the way an Elf could but I recognized an affirmative nod when I saw one.

Keeping one hand on his neck, I slid my other hand down along his large flank. Even at rest, I could feel the power in his muscles, coiled and waiting to be used. While the flying part of the reindeer's job was more magic than brawn, they definitely needed strength for the constant landing and take-offs. I remembered Dad telling me how the very first Santa Claus had had to search through many herds of reindeer to find ten strong enough to withstand the pressure of the magic and the physical demands.

There had originally been ten, but the tenth reindeer, Cloister, had faltered early on and never been replaced.

I wondered if the other reindeer missed him or even remembered he was gone.

No way for me to ask.

I took deep, regular breaths. Tuning into the North Pole magic that emanated from the reindeer was easy. We had both been there recently and both of us were on the same wavelength, magically speaking. I knew it wouldn't be so much a spell or even me doing the masking, it was more of me nudging Blitzen to mask himself.

I just had to encourage him to do it.

The tingling started in my toes and spread through my body to my fingers. Within moments, it was almost impossible to tell where my hands ended and the powerful body of the reindeer began. Our resonance matched so completely.

Another breath centred me. I focused, envisioning Blitzen fading within the room.

Blitzen gave a snort of disapproval, shifting on his hooves.

"Easy, boy," I said. In my mind's eye, I brought the image of Blitzen back, but fainter, more of an outline.

"You're still here," I said. "But you're hiding. Like hide and go seek."

I knew he would understand the reference. KJ and I had played the game often as boys. We'd even included the reindeer at times. That was when I learned how easily they could mask themselves while still being there.

Blitzen blew through his lips and tossed his head. Was that a nod? I couldn't be sure.

Until the cream coloured fur faded before my eyes.

And I found myself alone in the room. At least it looked like it.

I could still feel Blitzen's body under my hands. I gave his neck a solid pat.

"Good boy."

A velvet nose pressed against the side of my face, breathing warm against my skin.

"Okay, boy, let's see if we can find a trace of this creature," I said. "It came through the window so maybe there's something outside that can give us a direction."

A soft snort answered. It almost felt like 'lead the way.'

I turned and led the invisible reindeer out of the room.

Outside it took a moment for me to figure out which window was mine on the floors above. I positioned myself underneath and focused upward. The cold night air tingled on my cheeks but if there was any magic, it was too faint for me to detect.

I had to get closer.

Fortunately I had something that could fly.

"Blitzen," I called, almost in a whisper. "Are you here, boy?"

I felt a warm nose press against the left side of my face. I reached up and patted his muzzle.

"I need to get up there to the window," I said. "Will you carry me up there?"

The reindeer gave a snort and I felt the head pull away. Although they were used to drawing the sleigh, no one rode them very often. Sometimes when KJ and I had been boys we would beg a ride on their backs, but usually they didn't allow it.

I was hoping this time would be an exception.

"I need to get closer to the window to see if I can detect the magic," I said. "That would give us an idea of where to go."

I waited. With Blitzen now invisible I couldn't be sure he was even close enough to hear my whisper. Or even if he'd stuck around at all. He may have decided to return to the North Pole, leaving me standing behind a building at night, talking to myself.

But the reindeer had remembered KJ. I couldn't imagine any of them would leave while I was looking for him.

Especially honourable Blitzen.

I felt something press against my shoulder. I reached up a hand and felt Blitzen's shoulder. As I touched it, I felt it moved down, in a jerking motion. Forward and then back. Blitzen was kneeling for me, lowering himself so I could climb onto his back.

He was on my left, not the right side for this, but I managed to swing one leg over him and pull myself up onto his back. As my legs stretched around his thick body and I grasped onto the fur on his neck, I realized I couldn't see anything underneath me except the snowy ground. As the body jerked under me, I saw hoof prints appear, first the front hooves and then the back as Blitzen stood up.

A wave of dizziness washed over me. Sitting on top of a reindeer was impressive enough without the reindeer being invisible. I could feel my heart begin to pound.

I sucked in a deep breath, drawing cold air into my lungs. It was a jolt, like a splash of water on the face, just enough to stop me from panicking. I forced my gaze upward, looking at the building instead of the invisible reindeer beneath me. As long as I couldn't not see him, it felt like I was sitting astride Blitzen.

Just don't look down.

Even more important to think about when I felt the muscles underneath me bunch and leap into the air.

We soared upward. Instantly I knew we were going to

overshoot. I leaned forward, hoping I was close enough to Blitzen's ear.

"Don't go over the roof," I said. "That window there. The second down from the top."

In a moment, our forward momentum slowed to nothing. We hovered, floating in the air but still about five feet from the window.

I tugged on Blitzen's neck. "Can we get closer?"

I felt the slightest movement under me, as if the reindeer gave a kick with his back legs. We floated toward the window.

Three feet away. Now two feet.

At one foot, I reached out and touched the side of the window pane. The jagged smoothness of ice scraped my fingers. Was that a tingling of magic I felt or just the tingle of cold?

I needed some time to focus if Blitzen could hold his position for a few minutes. I touched the side of his neck.

"Right here, boy. Hold it right here."

I heard an answering snort.

We were close enough that I could rest the palm of my left hand against the window. Cold made my fingers almost curl but I forced them flat against the glass. The cold was deep enough to burn but maybe it wasn't just the cold. I could feel something underneath it, something sour.

Focus. If I could distinguish the magic from the surroundings I would be able to follow a trace of it...

I felt it lash out at me, like the slap of an ocean wave. The night sky spiralled around me. Cold wind swept across my face. I heard a shrieking call.

Blitzen!

It wasn't the night sky spiralling, we were falling!

I felt the reindeer bucking and shuddering underneath me. He bleated in panic. The ground was racing to meet us.

I threw my arms around his neck. Pressed my face to invisible fur.

"Blitzen! Slow down! We're crashing, pull up! Pull up!"

My words were drowned out in the roaring wind but Blitzen must have heard them. I felt the body beneath me settle down. Stop struggling.

The ground was still rushing to meet us.

But I felt the solid thump of hooves sinking into snow. Blitzen's head went down and I felt his legs bow with the impact. Then he straightened and I heard ragged panting.

I stayed where I was, clinging to the back of an invisible reindeer as I glanced up toward the window.

It should be ablaze in menacing light, a warning of the threatening magic still lingering but there was nothing. No visible difference between my window and any of the others.

But I could feel it, the sour burn ready to lash out again with an overpowering effect.

And this was just the residual trace.

How would I be able to fight back against a full on blast of that?

Whatever had taken KJ was more powerful than I'd imagined. Of course it would have to be. It had changed the time line, erasing KJ from the world. That wasn't some nickle and dime magic. It was elemental.

Something overwhelming. Overpowering.

All I had was a reindeer, an Elf, my own North Pole magic, and a stubborn refusal to give up my brother.

Easy as wrapping a plain box for Christmas, right?

Damn the halls, how could I fight that?

I slid off Blitzen's back. Snow crunched under my feet. After the shakiness of the flight, it was nice to feel solid ground beneath me. I shook my head. First things first. I had to find it, then I could have my rump handed to me. No sense getting ahead of myself.

I felt my heart rate steady as I took another deep breath of the cold air. Funny that I could still taste the sourness. It seemed to coat the back of my throat, as if I had swallowed it.

Wait, sourness. That was the trace!

Another deep breath and I lowered my defences just a little. There, I could feel it in the air, the sourness and a tingling sensation.

Leading away from the building.

I was supposed to meet Venir back here in an hour. A quick check of my watch showed me I still had almost forty minutes left. I could wait around and tell him about the window or I could try to see where the trace led.

I reached out to where I thought Blitzen was standing and felt the soft fur on his side. I gave him a good pat.

"What do you think?" I asked. "Should we see what's on the other end of that magic?"

Blitzen gave a snort that might have sounded dubious.

"We aren't going to try to interfere with it," I assured him. "I just want to see where it leads to."

Would he agree? Even remembering KJ might not overpower the reindeer's urge for self-preservation. After all, it was probably smarter than I was.

But then I felt his body shift downward. Letting me climb onto him again.

Seemed like Blitzen was just as smart as I was after all.

Or maybe he thought I could actually do this.

I swallowed around a sudden lump in my throat.

"Thanks, boy," I said and climbed onto the reindeer's back.

He stood and I again forced my gaze upward to stop the vertigo that tried to whirl in my head. I didn't think I'd ever get used to seeing nothing underneath me.

"Let's head up but not too close," I said. "I can feel the sourness. Let's see where it leads."

Blitzen gave a snort and leapt into the air.

I hung on for dear life.

Soaring in the cold night air gave me a brief taste of what it might be like for Dad on Christmas Eve as he raced around the world to deliver presents.

However, he at least had a nice sleigh to ride in, even if it was stuffed full of presents most of the night.

He didn't have to cling to the back of an invisible reindeer as he raced across the night sky.

Nor did he have a sour tingling crawling across his body.

Cold air bit at my nose and ears as we raced along. I could feel shifting air currents moving past us, bringing moisture and dryness in different measures as we passed through clear patches and clouds. In the darkness, the clouds were impossible to see except as a deeper darkness that blotted out the stars above me.

Below me, the city spread out full of twinkling lights. We were high enough up that I could see most of it spreading out in either direction, with a dark band of blackness directly ahead.

Lake Ontario.

And the sour tingling seemed to be drawing me closer to it.

As we approached it, I could almost sense the moisture in the air. Reflected light from the city sparkled along the edges, glistening and shimmering on the waves. Even in the most bitter cold, I knew this lake didn't freeze and the black curtain of its surface seemed to rise and fall beneath me.

Not too far out into the lake were the small Toronto islands. I remembered first meeting Venir on Centre Island when he'd warned me about someone planning to kill Dad. That had led me into the Magical Realms to stop a rogue fairie who had been bent on destroying the peace Dad had negotiated between the Winter and Summer Fae. I never would have known about it without Venir.

Was that still a threat in this strange time? Would Venir learn about it and tell me or would this be how I gained the job of Santa Claus?

The thought made me shudder.

Blitzen banked toward the left, turning in a wide sweep. As he turned, we dropped lower and lower. I could feel cold, wet spray from the lake dot my face. The sour tingling still burned in my gut but where was the reindeer going? He was turning back toward shore, wasn't it leading us away?

I tugged on Blitzen's fur.

"Where are you going?" I shouted but my voice was lost in the frigid air.

We dropped lower and lower. I could hear the rustling of the water beneath us, almost hissing in the cold.

I tightened my grip on Blitzen's neck and blinked at the water beading on my face and eyes. Was he going to dump us into the water? My heart pounded. I gulped in air, getting ready to *wink* away.

Then the spray of water was gone. I felt the reindeer's body shift under me. Forward momentum slowed and we dropped down. I felt the jolt of Blitzen's legs hitting ground.

We'd landed.

I clung to his back. Around us, the darkness took on a

different layer. It wasn't the solid blackness of the water. We'd landed on one of the islands but it wasn't Centre Island. That one I knew. It had to be one of the others, Ward's Island or Hanlan's Point.

"What are we doing here?" I asked.

Right. As if the reindeer could answer me.

I felt Blitzen shake his head. My hands gripping his neck slipped. I got the impression he wanted me off.

I slid down off his left side, landing on a beach. Sand felt gritty under my boots. The air felt cold and damp against my face. As I took in a breath I detected a sickly sweet odour in the air. Sour and stale. It was an odour I never liked smelling and somehow it was here again.

I reached out and felt Blitzen's neck. "Did you know?"

He gave a snort that I interpreted as yes.

The darkness didn't see quite so thick or my eyes were adjusting. I could make out a bank of rocks ahead of me and a row of bushes looking forlorn without leaves. There didn't seem to be any snow here, even in March. Probably the spray of the water kept it at bay.

I moved forward, heading toward a path that seemed to lead between the rocks and the bushes. Shadows deepened as the stench thickened. It wasn't just the sickly sweet smell now, there was something kind of...mossy about it. I took shallow breaths, feeling my stomach tighten.

As my boots crunched on frozen grass, the smell intensified. I stopped as I cleared the rocks. Behind me, Blitzen snorted again. I felt his presence over my shoulder.

I didn't want to look but I knew I had to.

With a sigh, I brought my hands together. A few murmured words and I felt the stirring of my North Pole magic. I opened my hands and a sparkling glow floated there. I cast it upward. It floated above my head, one foot, two feet, three, casting golden light around me.

Bright enough to show the body lying splayed on the grass before me.

CHAPTER

FIFTEEN

Even with the glow from my sparkling light it was difficult to see a lot of detail on the body. Plus I didn't really want to get that close. But I was a detective, or at least I was supposed to be, and here was a body. I had to at least take a look.

I stepped forward until I was about a foot away then crouched to get a better look. It lay on its side, face toward me, but one arm was throw over its face as if to ward off the killer. It wore dark pants and a darkish shirt with white splotches. No, that wasn't right. The shirt was white but something was covering it.

Something with that mossy, seaweed stench.

I gestured toward the light and it floated down. The brightness increased, giving me a better view, enough that I could tell it was a man.

What was he doing here in the middle of the night without a winter coat? How had he come to have this mossy stuff all over him?

And what, if anything, did this have to do with KJ?

Something inside me was afraid to know. Was I going to find KJ in much the same position, sprawled in a heap, covered with this sickly seaweed, mossy stuff? How could that be?

How could any of this be?

I could feel my heart start to pound as anxiety rose within me. The cold air felt too confining, freezing my lungs, making it difficult to draw breath.

I pushed myself up to a standing position but my legs felt unsteady. I took a step back from the body, then another. The stench of seaweed coated the air. I felt it invade my nostrils, smear the inside of my mouth.

Bile rose, burned the back of my throat. My mouth flooded with saliva. I felt like I was going to throw up.

A snort sounded behind me. A powerful shoulder shoved me. I staggered but stayed upright. My legs held me. I felt the soft, warm breath as a velvety nose pressed against my cheek. I reached up to pat his neck, cling to his neck.

"Okay, 'm okay," I managed to murmur to the reindeer comforting me.

My heart rate slowed. The panicky feeling lessened. The air didn't feel quite so suffocating now. I took steady breaths.

Easy now. Easy.

I didn't usually have panic attacks, even when

confronting a body. Mind you, I hadn't expected it but when did I ever expect to find a body? If it was going to make me panicky, wouldn't it have done so before?

What was it about this body?

Was it because KJ was missing? Did I fear he would be the next one I found?

My stomach tightened at the thought but it didn't send me into a blind panic. I had a hold of myself now.

Therefore it had to be something else.

Something outside me.

Something caused me to panic.

Something I wasn't quite aware of.

I gripped Blitzen's neck.

"There's something here, isn't there, boy?" I said. "More than just that body. That's what drew you here."

The reindeer snorted and once again I wished I had the same rapport with the reindeer that a Christmas Elf would have with him. Would Venir have known what Blitzen meant?

No sense worrying about it since the Elf wasn't here. I would have to make do on my own.

So what to do about this body?

There was only one thing I could think of although I wasn't sure of the reception I would get.

Time to make a call.

STAN MALLORY STEPPED OUT OF THE WATER TAXI, CLOTHED IN A beige trench coat completely inadequate for the cold and a scowl on his face. As he paid the driver, he flashed his badge and gave a stern warning for the man to stay put. The driver gave a vigorous nod as Mallory turned and stalked across the dock toward me.

It hadn't been as difficult to stir his memory as I had expected. Dad had placed everything back to the way it had been but hadn't wiped Mallory's memories as much as made them fuzzy and unimportant. My call had brought them back into sharp relief although Mallory didn't look too pleased to see me.

I also didn't see any other officers with him.

Did that mean he didn't believe me?

Mallory stopped in front of me. The scowl still marred his expression. Dark circles hung from his eyes and a scruffy beard dotted his cheeks.

"Where's this body?" he asked.

So much for pleasantries.

I led him across the island, sticking to the main path as much as I could. Only a few lights were lit on the island but I kept the glowing sparkle hovering around us. Mallory barely grunted at it.

When we reached the spot where the body had been lying, Mallory gave another grunt.

"So, where is it?"

I had stayed a few steps back, letting Mallory take the lead. But now he turned to me, the scowl marking deeper lines on his face.

"What?" I asked, like an idiot.

"The body." He gestured behind him. "Where is it?"

I hurried up to stand beside him and waved the sparkle glow forward. It illuminated the ground before us.

A patch of empty brownish grass lay before us.

No sign of a body.

No, that wasn't right. The grass showed the depression of where the body had lain. I crouched. There was still a hint of decay in the air.

"It was here," I said. "You can see where the depression is in the ground and I can still smell it."

Mallory crossed his arms, tugging the trench coat tighter around him. A gust of wind made the edges flap around his legs.

"So where is it? Did it get up and walk away?"

His anger simmered in his voice, ready to spill over and engulf me. I had to find a way to short circuit it and focus on the case.

I grabbed his arm and yanked him down. He stumbled and put out a hand to catch himself.

It landed smack in the middle of where the body had lain.

He let out a cry of disgust and lurched back. When he lifted his hand I saw a film of something greenish on it. He yanked out a tissue and began scrubbing his hand.

"Tell me you don't smell anything," I said. "Tell me whatever you touched is normal for the ground here."

"I don't know what's normal for the ground here," he said, still scrubbing. "And I don't smell...."

He took a sniff. His forehead wrinkled as his brows drew down.

He sniffed again.

"That smells like death," he said.

I put out my hands, as is presenting a gift.

He took another sniff. "Smells recent."

"Recent like it was just here," I said.

He frowned at me as he balled up the tissue and stuffed it in his pocket.

"So where's the body now?"

Good question. It wasn't like it could have gotten up and walked away.

"And what are you doing here? I thought you were back at the North Pole."

I stood up and my knees cracked.

"I'm looking for my brother," I said.

"I thought your father didn't believe that," he said.

"He doesn't remember KJ," I said. "No human other than me seems to. But the reindeer do."

At that moment, a loud snort sounded on Mallory's right. He jumped and then his head yanked back.

"What the...?"

"That's Blitzen," I said. "I covered him in an invisibility spell because he wouldn't go home and it would look a little odd to have a reindeer following me around."

"Odd," Mallory repeated. He had a wild look in his eye. "Like none of this is odd."

His voice gave a squeak at the end, a hint of hysteria. After everything, he probably thought he was imagining hearing the snort of a reindeer, the feel of Blitzen bumping him.

The last thing I needed was a hysterical Stan Mallory.

"I'm going to break the mask," I said to Blitzen. "Mallory needs to see you, boy."

I heard an affirmative snort right in front of me. I reached out and felt the side of Blitzen's flank. One steadying breath and I tuned into the spell I had used to mask him. The tingle of it warmed my fingers and spread through my body. I waited until it flowed down to my toes, then I gripped the magic and yanked.

The spell shattered.

Blitzen appeared in front of me, blocking Mallory from view.

"Holy shit!" Mallory said.

Blitzen turned his head to give Mallory a quizzical look. I peered around Blitzen's massive chest.

"This is Blitzen," I said. "Blitzen, this is Stan Mallory."

The reindeer gave a snort of greeting. He clomped forward a few paces and stuck his nose toward Mallory.

Mallory stood staring wide-eyed.

"He wants you to rub his nose," I said.

Mallory reached up and gave a tentative rub. Blitzen wiggled his head a little and pressed his nose into the palm of Mallory's hand.

"Soft," Mallory said. He gave a firmer rub. Blitzen's eyes half closed in pleasure.

Mallory reached up and scratched Blitzen's cheek, running his hand toward the reindeer's neck. Blitzen took another step forward to get closer to the petting. A rumble of pleasure sounded from deep in his chest.

"This is really Blitzen?" Mallory asked. "One of the flying reindeer? Like, he can really fly?"

Mallory's eyes were still wide but this time from wonder. Even with the scruff of beard on his face and the grey in his hair, he looked decades younger. His usual cynicism dropped away, leaving him looking at Blitzen with delight.

It was a nice moment but seeing that a body had recently been here and now it wasn't, I knew I was going to have to break it.

"He can really fly," I said. "He brought me here and we found the body together. Then I called you."

I could see the child-like wonder fade from Mallory's face. The hand that petted Blitzen's soft neck slowed.

"Right," he said. "Tell me what you remember about the body."

I described the look of it, the arm hiding the face, the clothes covered with some kind of moss-like material.

Mallory nodded. He had stopped petting Blitzen completely but his hand still rested on the reindeer's neck.

"What else did you see around the area?" he asked.

I described the scene, the lack of footprints, no other changes in the area around the body. With every word, Mallory's expression grew darker, more frustrated.

I knew the feeling.

"So what'd you bring me out here for?" he snapped. "I can't do anything without a body."

"I didn't exactly know it would disappear," I said. I sighed and rubbed a hand over my forehead. What had felt like progress now felt more like spinning my wheels. Nothing about this made sense. Was this man's death even connected to KJ's disappearance? The only thing that linked them was the strange sour stench, like rotting vegetation or moss. But I still had no idea who or what left that behind.

"I have to go and check in with Venir," I said. I glanced my watch. My hour was up. I was already late.

"Wait a minute," Mallory said. "You drag me all the way out here and now you're leaving."

"I'm sorry, Stan," I said. "I didn't know the body would disappear." I gestured behind us. "I'll pay for the water taxi."

"I don't give a damn about the water taxi, dammit."

Blitzen snorted and jerked his head, away from Mallory's resting hand. His antlers flashed and in the glowing sparkle, I saw the reindeer's eyes widen in fear.

Then I felt a tingle of malevolent magic against my skin. The stench of wet, rotting moss thickened.

A deep rumble started.

The anger twisting Mallory's face faded into puzzlement. "What the...?"

"C'mon!" I raced toward him, grabbing his arm and pushing him forward.

We both took off running.

The rumble deepened, a slight hiss sounding as it grew louder.

And closer.

Mallory ran on my right. Blitzen kept up on my left. I glanced over at the reindeer and he caught my look.

He bounded ahead of us. Then stopped, presenting his left flank.

Would he be able to carry two of us? Would the weight be too much? I knew it was North Pole magic that gave Blitzen the ability to fly but there was a limit to everything. Sure he helped pull a sleigh filled with toys, a weight that was probably hundreds and hundreds of pounds, but he only helped. He didn't do it all on his own.

But there was no one else here now.

I shoved Mallory ahead of me toward the reindeer.

"Get on!"

Mallory didn't need to be told twice. He scrambled up the side of the reindeer.

I risked a glance behind us.

At first all I could see was darkness. A thick, liquid darkness that seemed to undulate and shimmer as it drew closer. Over the roar rumble, I heard the sound of trees snapping like twigs under a heavy boot. I sent the glowing sparkle higher in the air. And that's when I saw it.

The wave of water bearing down on us.

It rose up, stretching into the night sky, ten feet, twenty feet above my head. Steadily reaching higher. Racing toward me, ready to swat me down.

My heart pounded. I turned and leapt onto Blitzen's back. Mallory sat in front of me, holding onto the reindeer's neck. Blitzen's eyes were wide with terror.

"Up!" I yelled and slapped the reindeer's flank.

Blitzen shuffled a few steps. I felt his legs shaking. His nostrils quivered. He was staring at the wall of water as it raced toward us.

I slapped his flank again, focused my magic on him.

"Up!"

The water roared.

Blitzen leapt into the air.

I felt the rush of cold air tugging at me, trying to drag me off the reindeer's back. With Mallory in front of me, hanging onto Blitzen's neck, I had no handhold's. I gripped the reindeer's body with my thighs and hunched over, pressing my hands on Blitzen's rump behind me.

Not the most steady position.

The rumble roared around me. I felt cold water spray my face.

Even as we soared upward, I saw water reaching for us. Tendrils of water swirling, stretching, reaching.

Like fingers or a lasso.

I felt Blitzen straining for speed. Even without an Elf's rapport, I could tell the reindeer was labouring. Any second he would reach his limit.

Then what?

I sucked in a deep, frigid breath. The taste of rotting moss filled my mouth. I spat it out. Focused.

Calling to the North Pole.

I felt the cold calm descend on me. I drew it in and channelled it toward Blitzen.

Muscles shivered under me then I felt a burst of speed.

We shot higher, faster.

We were going to make it!

I opened my eyes just in time to see a gigantic tentacle rise up from the top of the wave.

It lashed out.

A sharp, burning pain hit my left side.

I felt myself falling to the right.

Falling...

Wind howled in my ears as I thought I heard Mallory's voice calling, "Noel!"

Then everything went black.

CHAPTER

SIXTEEN

My body ached all over. My left side felt like a gigantic bruise from my shoulder to my thigh. My throat felt raspy and my lungs were sore.

Considering I should probably be dead after falling from a height of several hundred feet, I was doing better than I expected.

Although where was a good question.

I let out a groan as I opened my eyes. The air around me seemed to glow with a greenish light. Dim and almost undulating. Barely enough that I could see a few feet around me. Beyond that, the darkness seemed thick and heavy.

But it didn't feel like the darkness of night, not quite. Instead it felt like the darkness of some interior place, unlit.

As I pushed myself up into a sitting position, the

greenish glow brightened, as if responding to my movements. Just ahead of me, I could see where it came from. Some kind of glowing moss on the wall in front of me. But the wall was uneven, not the false straightness of a built wall, this was a natural formation.

I looked up above me. Still darkness, but I could hear a slight, echoy drip-dripping of water.

A cave.

For some reason, it felt like it was deep underground.

Or deep under something.

I put my hands on the ground and felt a soft, cushiness. More moss. Pushing against it, I managed to force myself to my feet. My legs shook a little but held me. The rest of my body protested this movement but I could already feel myself starting to stiffen. If I waited too long to move, I'd barely be able to move at all.

The air smelled of moisture and that mossy scent, similar but not exactly like what I had smelled in my office or on the body I'd found. The sound of the drip-dripping seemed to come from all around me, an effect of the cavern. I didn't want to get near it but not being clear where it came from, I just had to pick a direction.

That way.

I kept the wall I could see on my right and started to move forward. Or shuffle. I couldn't exactly move quickly.

Muscles ached and complained, letting me know in no uncertain terms that they were very displeased to be moving like this. They would have preferred a nice hot bath. With Epson salts. And massive quantities of pain killers. Maybe even a massage.

Why did I expect them to be moving after falling off a reindeer flying up in the sky?

No, not falling. Knocked off.

By a tentacle.

The memory flooded back to me.

I remembered the greenish, bluish scales glinting in the dim light. The shivering of the suckers on the underside, aiming at me like I had a target on my back. The coiling muscle of the tentacle as it reared back to strike. The feel of it like a steel cable whipping against my left side as it hit me.

Then the feeling of falling.

From that height I should definitely feel more than muscle soreness.

So how had I ended up here. Wherever here was?

That was the question of the hour, followed closely by how do I get out of here?

As I shuffled along I noted the irregularity of the wall beside me and the floor under my boots. Somewhere along the way I had misplaced my red parka. Fortunately I still had my boots. The rest of my clothing, dark pants, red flannel shirt, were intact. So not only was I stuck in some underground cave, I'd lost my coat as well.

This was shaping up to be a lousy day.

The wall on my right began to curve toward me. I was reaching the end of the cave. Damn the halls, if this was a dead end I would have to back track and my muscles didn't feel too happy as it was.

It could have been worse. I had a feeling that if those suckers had latched onto me, the tentacle could have smashed me to a pulp. Or dragged me into the water.

I froze.

Maybe it had. Didn't this cavern feel like it was underground? Maybe it was underwater?

How *had* I gotten here?

Swirling snow, how was I going to get out?

I started shuffling forward again. The cavern wall curved in front of me, blocking me from going further. But it wasn't the dead end I expected.

Not with the closed door blocking the way.

It looked like it was made out of iron, turned green from the moisture in the air and the moss that had grown around it. It was windowless, with a large round metal wheel in the centre, the kind on the doors in a submarine. The metal felt cool and solid in my hands when I gripped it but no amount of tugging in either direction would get it to budge.

Then I felt it, the same kind of sourness that crept along my spine as before.

It wasn't just disuse and decay that kept this door closed.

I took a deep breath, focusing on the coldness of the metal. It reminded me of snow drifts at the North Pole, chilly against my skin. Blazing fires, warm sugar cookies, and frothy hot chocolate could combat that kind of chill. All of it helped connect me to my North Pole magic.

Soon I felt it tingling along my nerves, bringing a whiff of cinnamon that overpowered the stale, sour smell.

The way I would overpower the magic that keep this door closed.

I tightened my grip, felt the bite of metal against my skin. Cold like snow, not like the depths of the ocean. I felt the stirring of water around me. It reminded me of the gigantic wall of water rising up from the lake, barrelling down on me.

My hands shook. The spell enchanting the door was fighting back, drawing on the ocean, on the sourness, on the wall of water. It would flood over me...

Except the cold would turn that water to ice and snow, swirl it up into the air, as light as flakes. Hardened into a frozen shield that could be climbed over.

This spell may be tough, but my North Pole magic was tougher.

Even as I shivered from the blast of cold racing through me, I felt sweat pour down my body from the exertion of calling on my magic. How much longer would I be able to focus? Most of my practice had been with quick spells. Maintaining a sustained effort was more than I could handle.

Then I felt the wheel shift under my hands. Just a smidge. I grunted and pushed at the wheel. The metal let out a loud grating groan. The wheel jerked, then began to turn.

I puffed with effort. I could almost feel the grooves grinding as the metal wheel pushed through them. But it turned, slow and steady, until a final click made the meal wheel shudder in my hands.

I tugged on the door.

The hinges made a shrieking sound as the door began to open.

Just as it began to inch wide, the thought occurred to me: what if the ocean was going to blast through from the other side and flood this chamber?

Too late to worry about that now.

The door creaked and groaned as it opened but no water flooded in, not even a trickle. I was safe from drowning.

For the moment.

Pale light spilled through the opening, brightening the area around the door, revealing even more moss than I had originally thought. I gave another tug. The door grated again and opened another few inches. Still not quite enough for me to get through.

I pulled harder, muscles straining. The door creaked.

And flew open, knocking me back.

I landed on my rump, palms scraping on the ground. I winced at the sting but when I lifted my hands I found the skin was still intact. Just more bruising.

Why not? Collect the set.

I lurched to my feet and shuffled toward the open door. Compared to the light in the cave, the dim light was still strong enough to make me squint. I moved to the right side and peered around the corner.

Another corridor that appeared to be carved out of rock, but this one looked cleaner. No moss covered the white-washed wall although it seemed to glow with a dim light, like a firefly. Even the floor looked more level. No nasty protrusions or dips to spill me on my rump.

I waited a moment to see if anyone came along, not that I knew who to expect. I couldn't see anything that resembled cameras either. Not that I expected to see those either. This didn't seem like a technological place, not the way the corridor seemed carved out of rock.

I wasn't quite sure what kind of place it was and I wasn't going to learn any more just standing here.

I stepped through the doorway and headed down the corridor.

The light cast an even glow through the entire length. It seemed to run about thirty feet before ending in a T junction. As I moved, I noticed closed doors on either side of the corridor. Instead of door handles, a hand hold had been carved into the door but I didn't see any lock. None of the doors had the round wheel in the centre like the door I'd opened.

Why was that? What was beyond those doors?

Since I was here, I might as well take a look.

The hand hold was large for my hand but the door pushed open easily. No creaking or groaning, no resistance. Inside, huge round bowls covered the floor, filled with green plants. Fern-like leaves seemed to quiver in the air. Vines stretched long, thin tendrils up the walls. The air smelled sweet and clean, even with the hint of mossiness. I breathed in deeply.

I noticed a sign on the wall to the left of the door. The script was flowing like water but not in any language I knew.

Just from looking at the greenery I imagined it said something like oxygen room.

One more deep breath. I could feel my muscles relaxing, energy flowing through me again. Breathing that clean air was almost as refreshing as a nap.

A final breath and I retreated from the room, closing the door behind me.

The next room was more of the same, more ferns, more vines. Even the sign appeared similar.

Maybe I had come out on a maintenance level of wherever I was.

I reached the end of the corridor and hit the T junction. The corridor spread out to the right and left, both sides looking similar to where I'd come from. They each stretched off into the distance, neither appearing to lead to an exit.

I just had to choose which way to go, with nothing to indicate which was the best way.

So, right or left?

I sniffed the air, nothing different in either direction. Nothing to draw me this way or that.

Burnt coals.

I turned left.

I would go as far as I could in this direction and if I didn't find anything, I could always turn around and take the right branch. I didn't like the idea of back tracking but if I couldn't find a way out or answers along this way, I would have to do it.

The first door I can across on the left was the same kind

of hand hold carved into the door. I pushed it open, expecting to see the same ferns but the room was empty. From the door, I could see that it wasn't in a usual square shape. The edges were more rounded, more natural looking.

Another indication that this space, whatever it was, had been carved out of rock, following some natural formation.

I pulled the door closed and continued on.

The next door on the left had another hand hold but this time when I tried to open the door, it stayed shut. Strange. I couldn't feel the slight give before opening either.

A locked door?

My heart rate increased. I stood a little straighter. Maybe there was some kind of answer behind this door. Even if there wasn't, a locked door was just begging to be opened.

And I was going to open it.

I tightened my grip on the hand hold, feeling it pitch against my fingers. I pushed again but it didn't budge, not even a centimetre. I relaxed and took a deep breath. Breathing out, I focused on my hand, sending a tingle of magic along the pads of my fingers.

I didn't have to expend nearly as much magic as I had trying to turn the wheel. After a moment, I felt the click through my fingers and the door swung open.

It wasn't plants or an empty room this time.

Thick, coloured tapestries of blue and green lay on the floor and hung on the walls. A large, thick mattress lay on the ground directly across from the door. And lounging on top of it, lay a man in a loose white shirt and black pants. His feet were bare. He held a book in front of his face. He lowered it, a grin lighting up his face.

"Ligeia?"

The grin turned to a frown when he saw me.

"Who the devil are you?" he asked.

"I could ask you the same question," I said. "Why were you locked in this room?"

The frown deepened into a look of petulance. His lower lip stuck out. He had long black hair that hung in waves to his shoulders and a black beard covered his chin and thin cheeks. Brown eyes looked at me warily.

"She tire of him already?" he said. "I knew he would last no longer than a year or two. She be back to me soon enough." He gave a once over look from head to toes. "You ain't lasting longer than a month, I reckon."

"And you've lasted longer?" I asked. Anything to keep him talking until I could figure out what he meant.

He closed the book and tossed it onto the mattress. He swung his legs over the side and stood up, moving in a smooth, fluid manner. But once standing, he seemed to sway just the tiniest bit from side to side.

"Aye, I lasted hundreds of years because I know her, I know what she likes. She's got a pirate's heart, lookin' to conquer. I talk her language." He made a throwaway gesture at me. "You're just a pretty boy. She'll tire 'a ya soon enough and come back ta me."

I cocked an eyebrow at him. "So she's keeping you safe," I said. "That's why she locked you in this room."

His lips thinned as he squeezed them shut. I could sense the restrained violence in the man. Maybe I shouldn't antagonize him too much.

"Who is she?" I asked, then I remembered the name he had called out when I opened the door. "Ligeia?"

Puzzlement furled his brow then he stood up straighter.

"She didn't bring you here. You didn't hear her call."

"No, I didn't," I said. "I got here by accident."

The man shook his head. "No accidents here, lad. If she didn't bring you for fun then you was brought for sacrifice."

Sacrifice. The word sent a chill through my body.

He chuckled. "The sea beast brought ya. A tasty morsel for her. Must be somethin' special about ya for it to bring you here rather than devour you itself."

Sea beast. The tentacled creature that had swiped me off Blitzen's back. It was aligned with this Ligeia. Was Ligeia the source of the sour magic?

I had to know more.

"Who is Ligeia?" I asked.

The smile that lit the man's face had an edge of malice to it.

"You'll be findin' out soon enough."

He wasn't going to give me anything, not voluntarily or at least not out of friendship. He didn't strike as a friendly person. I was going to have to play to his weaknesses.

I shrugged. "Never mind, I'm sure I'll find out. Even if I didn't hear her she might decide I'm worth keeping around. Longer than you anyway. Enjoy your time in here."

I stepped back through the doorway. As I started to pull it shut, the man darted forward, grabbing the edge.

"I don't think so, mate," he said. "I'm thinking you should be shut up in this room."

He lunged, grabbing my shoulder. I allowed him to pull me several steps inside the room but I could tell as soon as he touched me he didn't have any magic.

It wasn't exactly going to be a fair fight.

I caught a glimpse of his left hand balled into a fist, aiming for my face.

I breathed out, sending North Pole magic through my breath.

His hand stopped three inches from my face. The skin turned blue. Icicles hung from his knuckles. The fabric of his white sleeve crackled like dry paper.

The man yelped and jerked his hand away. He cradled it against his chest, rubbing the skin. His teeth chattered as the cold rippled through him. After a few moments, flesh on his hand turned from blue to a light pink. He grimaced and I imagined the pins and needles feeling of his hand warming up was quite annoying.

"How about we start again?" I said. "You tell me who you are, what you're doing here and who Ligeia is and I'll tell you who I am."

He clenched his teeth, still rubbing his hand. The flesh was pinking up quite nicely. He hissed out a breath.

"Fine," he said. "I'm Jack Avery and I followed a call in the sea. Ligeia's the one who called me. Now who're you?"

"I'm Noel Kringle," I said. "Youngest son of Kris Kringle."

The belligerent expression on Jack's face shifted to puzzlement. "Kringle? Why do I know that name? Ya weren't a sailor, were ya?"

I shook my head. "It's the given name of Santa Claus."

"Santa…" Jack's eyes widened and he let out a loud belly laugh. "Oh, ya had me goin'. Son of Santa Claus. That would make me Bluebeard rather than ol' pirate Jack Avery." He laughed again.

"How do you think I froze your hand?" I asked quietly.

His laughter trailed off. He wiped tears from his eyes, let out another guffaw. Then stopped and stared at me.

"You ain't kidding?"

I shook my head.

"You mean it, you really are him, the Santa son?" Jack asked. He glanced down at his hand. The skin looked normal again. He flexed it, wincing as the fingers moved a little slower than they should. Another minute or so and the muscles and tendons would recover completely. I hadn't cast a strong spell.

Jack lifted his gaze back up to me.

"I guess that means the other guy was tellin' the truth too," he said.

A pounding echo filled the room but Jack stood staring at me after pronouncing those words. Words I felt drop into the pit of my stomach. How could he not hear that pounding? How could he not wonder where it was coming from and why?

Then I realized it was just my heart thundering in my ears as it took my brain just another moment to fully process Jack's words.

The other guy.

KJ!

CHAPTER
SEVENTEEN

Suddenly Jack was gagging in my face. His fingernails dug into my hands. I felt the soft cotton of his shirt fabric in my palms.

Burnt coals, what was I doing?

I'd grabbed Jack's shirt at the neck and dragged him up on his toes. His pale skin turned red.

I loosened my fingers enough so he could breathe but still held onto the shirt. It was the only thing stopping them from shaking.

"Who...who is the other guy?" I asked.

Jack shoved my hands away then staggered back. His legs hit the edge of the mattress and he sat down hard, bouncing once. He coughed and cleared his throat, his hands rubbing at his neck.

"Blast and damn you, I'm not tellin' you nothing," he said. His lips pulled back from his teeth in a snarl.

I raised my hands in surrender.

"I'm sorry," I said. "But I think this other guy you're talking about is my brother. He's vanished and I've been searching for him." I told him the story with just enough detail to be convincing but not enough to overwhelm. Besides, I wasn't convinced I could trust this Jack Avery.

Fortunately, he appeared to listen. The snarl faded from his face. He rubbed his neck almost absentmindedly. When I finished, he pursed his lips.

"So a tentacled beast swiped you off the back of that reindeer," he said. "A flying one at that." He shook his head. "Sounds fantastic."

"Which part, the flying reindeer or the gigantic tentacle?"

He laughed. His voice sounded a bit harsh. I winced at the sound of it. I hadn't meant to hurt him. Hearing about KJ got me anxious.

Finally Jack's laughter petered off.

"Aye, so this other guy, full of bluster, came swaggerin' in, sayin' he was the son of Santa. Was all angry at bein' locked up but a few visits with Ligeia settled him down." He chuckled. "She can be quite persuasive when she wants ta be."

I felt that chill again, tingling along my skin like shards of ice.

"Do you know what room he's in?" I asked.

Jack tilted his head. "Maybe. What's in it for me?"

My stomach tightened. This man was a pirate, or had been. He was used to taking what he wanted by force or at least by strong persuasion. And what did I have to offer? What did he want? I could offer to take him out with us.

I studied him for a moment. When I'd first come in he'd been annoyed to find someone new here. Hadn't he talked about her getting tired of me fast?

Maybe leaving wasn't what he wanted.

But I could at least give him the choice.

"You can escape with us or stay here with her," I said. "When I take my brother out of here, you'd have her all to yourself."

Greed flashed across his face, evident in the glint of his eye and clench of his teeth. He gave me a smile that had more than a hint of teeth.

"Now you're talkin'," he said. "But you know she'll be a might annoyed when you go. It's a big risk for me ta help you and have to face her after."

I sighed. "What do you want?"

"You're the son of Santa which means you can get lots of presents," he said. "That's what I want. As many presents as I want and I want 'em to be gold and jewels."

I raised an eyebrow. He still wanted gold and jewels, even if they didn't do him any good in this place. Had he even aged a day since he'd gotten here? I had a feeling he'd been here for decades, maybe even hundreds of years. What use did he have of such riches?

Probably none but it didn't matter. He wanted them and I could tell from the gleam in his eye he wouldn't take no for an answer. Not that it would be a problem. When I returned to the North Pole, I should be able to easily conjure up enough gold and jewels to satisfy him.

But I had to get there first.

"Fine," I said. "I'll shower you in gold and jewels. Just help me get my brother out of here."

He studied me for a moment, probably trying to tell if I was lying. I worked on keeping a sincere look on my face, although I didn't quite know what look would persuade him. After a moment, he gave a nod.

I must have convinced him.

"All right, lad, I'll show ye where your brother is."

He pushed past me, heading for the door. He yanked it open and stuck his head out. Checking the passageway, he gestured back to me.

"You comin', lad?"

I followed.

He turned left, following the way I had been heading. I felt relief that at least I'd been going the right way.

We reached the end of the hall and Jack turned right, heading down another corridor. As we moved along, I noticed that the walls started to seem a little rougher, like we were walking through an older section. The glow from the walls seemed even dimmer, the uneven texture creating shadows that blurred the edges of the walls, the floor and the ceiling. More and more it felt like I was travelling down the gullet of some great beast.

Maybe a beast with tentacles.

"What can you tell me about Ligeia?" I asked Jack. "Who is she?"

In the dimness, I saw his shoulders shrug. He didn't bother to look back at me. His face was lost in shadow.

"She is who she is," he said. "Not much to tell."

Or maybe he didn't want to tell me. I sensed more than just simple reluctance from him. This man wasn't a friend. He would act only in his self interest and for now it aligned with mine but I had to be prepared for the time when it would shift.

As I knew it would.

Just as long as I found KJ and we could get out of here. Wherever here was.

However we could get out.

I didn't really have an idea about that quite yet. But something would occur to me.

I hoped.

About three quarters of the way to another junction, Jack stopped in the centre of the hall. He turned to the wall on his left. It was deep in shadow but I could barely make out the outline of a door. Instead of reaching for the hand hold to open it, Jack pressed his hands against its surface. I heard him mumble under his breath, then he pushed.

I caught a whiff of sourness and the door slid open.

A spell on the door, one he'd broken.

Did Jack have some magic of his own? I hadn't sensed it on him. Maybe he only knew the incantation to break the spell holding the door locked. I hoped he didn't know the incantation to set it again.

Maybe I should make sure he came into the room with me.

As the door opened, he turned toward me. I held out my hand in an 'after you' gesture.

In the dim light, I caught a twist to his lips. Was that a smirk? He inclined his head and stepped through the door.

I followed.

The room was not as nicely furnished as Jack's. The glow in the room wasn't much brighter than the hall but it allowed me to see the bareness of the floor to the edge of a thin mattress. The walls were unadorned rock, looking jagged and unfinished. Other than the mattress there didn't seem to be another other furnishings, no chair or dresser.

On the mattress, sprawled the form of a man.

My stomach tightened. KJ? I couldn't tell. The face was turned away. The figure was lying on its stomach. Ragged clothes adorned the limbs, sleeves ending in torn fabric just below the elbow, pants shredded to the knee. I couldn't see any injury but the light was possibly too dim for that.

I took a step closer, aware that Jack Avery now stood closer to the door. How easy would it be for him to dart out and lock me inside?

But I had to know if this was KJ.

Before I could move, Jack strode forward and grabbed the arm of the figure on the bed. He shook it, forcing the form to roll onto its back.

"Hey, wake up. Wake up already."

The man flopped onto his back. His head lolled toward me. I recognized the beard, now grown out and unkempt. The long white hair, looking greasy and dishevelled. His cheeks were thin, sunken. Dark circles deepened around his eyes as his eyelids fluttered. He let out a groan.

KJ.

I found myself kneeling by the mattress, holding his hand, his fingers thin and skeletal in my palm. This close I could smell the stale sourness that emanated from him.

"KJ," I murmured, keeping my voice low as he seemed to wince at the noise.

His head turned toward me. His eyes were half open now but his expression was slack, unaware.

He just needed some time to wake up, some time to recover. Once I had him away from here, he would be all right. He had to be.

I didn't know what I would do if he didn't recover.

But recover from what?

I glanced over at Jack who stood on the other side of the bed.

"What happened to him?" I asked.

He gave me a disdainful look. "What do you think?" he said. "Ligeia's been paying him attention."

"You keep mentioning her without ever explaining what she is," I said. "Damn the halls, tell me."

Jack opened his mouth but it was KJ who answered me.

"Monster." His voice was rough and low. He coughed. I grabbed his shoulder and turned him toward me. After a moment, the coughing fit stopped. He lifted a shaking hand to his mouth and wiped his lips.

"She calls so sweet." KJ's voice was quiet but seemed to fill the room. "I heard her over and over on a practice run. I had to follow the song."

"Song," I repeated. Something was tickling the back of my mind. The sour wet smell, the seaweed, the tentacle.

"A Siren," I breathed.

Jack shivered. On the bed, KJ trembled.

"Couldn't resist," KJ said. "Didn't want to. She promised...promised..."

"Whatever you wanted," I said.

"That's how she gets ya," Jack said. "She promises everything your heart desires."

My mouth felt dry. My heart hammered in my chest.

"And this place," I said. "It's her lair."

"Right in the thick of it," Jack said.

I had no idea how I'd gotten here after the tentacle had swept me off Blitzen's back and I didn't want to know. I just knew I had to get out. Now.

We had to. KJ and I.

I tightened my grip on his shoulder and pulled him to a sitting position. It was like moving a rag doll.

"Come on, KJ, we have to go."

I tugged on his arm, gestured for him to swing his legs over the mattress. He obeyed but he seemed to have little strength. When he tried to stand, his legs shook. I had to let him lean on me until he stood upright. Even then he swayed a little from side to side.

"Where we going?" he asked.

"Out of here," I said. "Home to the North Pole. As far away as possible."

As I'd spoken, I'd started to lead KJ toward the door but as soon as I said 'North Pole' he stopped, planting his feet on the ground.

"No, I'm not leaving," he said. This time his voice was solid and clear.

Over his shoulder, I saw Jack smirk.

"KJ, you have to come," I said. "Whatever she's doing is killing you. You have to get away from her."

He shook his head, sending straggling white hair wavering across his face.

"No, not going. Not leaving Ligeia. I love her."

"KJ, she's a Siren. You said yourself she's a monster. She's sucking the life out of you."

"I never said monster," KJ said. "You said it."

Jack let out a harsh laugh.

"You won't convince him," he said. "He's deep in her thrall. I seen it before. She'll drain every drop."

Of course, and KJ would be more potent than most because of his link to the North Pole. And in order to entrap him completely, she'd used whatever power she had to rewrite reality, completely erase him from existence so no one would know he was missing.

Then how had I remembered him?

It didn't matter now. I had and I was here to get him. If the Siren kept draining him, I had no idea if she would be able to tap into the power within the North Pole, slowing draining it from the world.

If that happened it would be a disaster.

Literally.

The North Pole wasn't just the place where Santa Claus lived and built toys to deliver to all the girls and boys at Christmas, it was the first line of magical defense, holding the Normal Realm safe and separate from the Magical Realms. Draining the North Pole of its magic would lay the Normal Realm unprotected.

And those few magical entities I had been chasing down over the last few years would be like a mere trickle compared to the flood that would envelope the world.

I couldn't let that happen and I knew KJ, in his right mind, would never let that happen either.

Too bad my brother wasn't in his right mind.

I could tell from the set of his jaw that he wasn't going to be budged by any argument I could come up with so I was going to have to go about this another way.

And I knew just the way.

"So Ligeia is special," I said.

KJ's tense form relaxed a little. His shoulders dropped a

centimetre. A faraway look came into his eye as he gazed past me.

"She's amazing," he said.

"Sounds like it," I said. "I assume you'll want to introduce her to mom and dad before you marry her. You are going to marry her, aren't you?"

Uncertainty shifted across KJ's features. "I don't know."

"Well, she can't be all that special then."

"She is," he insisted.

"Okay, then you'll have to bring her home to meet the folks. You'll have to get yourself cleaned up and get everything ready for her arrival. You'll want it to be perfect for her, right?"

"Yes," KJ said. "Perfect."

"Then we have to get you cleaned up." I tugged on KJ's arm. He shuffled forward one step, two.

"We'll make it perfect for her."

"Perfect," KJ repeated.

Three steps, four. We reached the doorway. Just another few steps and we'd be in the hall.

"Perfect," I said. "We'll make it perfect."

"Yes, perfect." KJ shuffled forward. His steps increased in speed. Fifth steps, sixth, and we were through the doorway.

"Jack, which way...," I started.

The door slammed shut behind KJ. Pounding started on the door. I heard Jack yelling for him to let him out.

Then a screaming shriek filled the air, drowning out the sound of Jack's pounding.

KJ lifted his head toward the ceiling. His mouth dropped open in awe then his lips moved but I couldn't hear him over the wailing shriek.

"What?" I yelled and yanked KJ closer. His lips stopped close to my ear.

"She's coming," he said. "Ligeia is coming."

Oh, just perfect.

CHAPTER

EIGHTEEN

I grabbed KJ's hand and pulled. Even though he was bigger than I was, it felt like dragging a feather behind me as I raced down the hall. I had to keep glancing back to make sure he was still behind me.

I hit the junction where Jack had brought me and turned right. My shoes slapped the floor.

The shriek echoed behind us, getting louder.

Closer.

I pumped my left arm, clenching KJ with my right.

My lungs burned. The sour scent thickened. It had to be the precursor to her appearance. I must have come close to seeing her multiple times or had just missed her.

I was hoping to miss her again.

Another junction. Another right turn.

I felt KJ tugging back, fighting my grip. I glanced back.

His head was turned away, looking behind us. Even as I ran, dragging him forward, he was trying to lean back, return to that shriek.

To the Siren's call.

I was damned if I was going to let him.

I tightened my grip on his forearm, feeling the bones grind under my palm. KJ yelped. Pain flashed across his face and for a moment, his expression cleared. His eyes brightened. Confusion crinkled his brow.

"Noel, what...?" he shouted.

"Run!" I yelled.

Jagged rocks walls flashed past us. I recognized the doors I'd opened. Then at the end, I spotted the door with the metal ring.

I increased my speed.

My lungs were on fire. The sour, seaweed stench filled the air.

My legs burned.

Behind me, KJ stumbled and staggered, trying to keep up.

The shrieking increased in volume. I felt it like a wave flooding toward us through the tunnel. Ready to drown us.

We reached the door. I shoved KJ through first. As I jumped through, I grabbed the metal ring and pulled. The door swung as if in slow motion.

I leaned back, pulling harder. As the door inched closed, I glanced back down the hall.

A wall of water rushed forward, swirling and flowing like smoke. In the centre, a figure writhed and undulated, as if swimming toward us. Hands reaching, fingers curved like claws. A mouth opened, shrieking.

I felt KJ move up beside me. Damn the halls, he was going to make a run for it.

But instead he reached forward, grabbed hold of the metal ring and pulled with me.

The door jerked, and slammed shut with a bang. The volume of the shrieking cut in half but I could still feel it crawling along my skin.

I tightened my grip on the metal wheel and turned it. It creaked but turned several inches before stopping. I hoped it was enough.

Enough to stall her. Enough to give us more time.

To get where?

Somehow I had ended up here after being knocked off Blitzen's back. I remembered falling through the cold air. Water and ice swirling around me. I must have been drawing on my North Pole magic, trying to ward off the water from swamping me.

"Noel." KJ's weak voice interrupted my thoughts. "What now?"

He was sagging against the wall, clearly exhausted, but there was more life in his eyes.

"Now we keep going," I said.

I grabbed his arm and tugged him along. We managed five paces before the banging started on the door behind us.

I could feel it reverberate through the ground. Further ahead in the darkness, I heard the tinkle of falling pebbles.

It wasn't going to take her long to get through that door.

Even with the greenish glow emanating from the walls, I couldn't move very fast in the dimness. The ground was too uneven. Sudden dips and bulges made running hazardous.

As I dragged KJ, I was acutely aware of the door behind us and the steady banging against it.

Any moment now she would break through.

How could I fight her?

The cavern seemed to angle to the left. I felt the drag of gravity get heavier. The floor of the cavern was rising, forcing us to climb. I puffed, trying to keep a steady pace. KJ's ragged breath sounded loud beside me.

"KJ, what can you tell me about her?" I asked. "Does she have any weaknesses?"

He shook his head, his lanky hair waving in front of his face.

"Can't talk about her," he wheezed.

"Anything," I said. "Does she hate sunlight? Silver? Bad opera?"

"Can't," he said. "Too close."

His eyes were wide with fear. I got it then. She was too close. Any mention of her might pull him back into her thrall.

He'd managed to come out of it, at least a little.

Now wasn't that interesting.

I filed that thought away for another time as the cavern floor angled steeply upward.

I pushed with my knees. Grooves worn into the ground were almost like shallow steps. Our speed dropped as I helped KJ scramble upward. Behind us, the banging increased in volume.

Either she was getting more frantic or she was just about through.

I dragged KJ up over a lip of rock and found myself standing on some kind of landing that was only three feet wide. A wall of solid rock was in front of us, almost black in the dimness. I felt empty air above our heads although I couldn't see higher than a few feet. Then I noticed something glint in the rock face. I stepped closer.

Rungs. Leading upward.

I grabbed KJ's arm and dragged him forward. I placed his hand on the rung.

"Up," I said.

Without a word, he reached up and grabbed the next rung and started hauling himself upward.

I followed.

As we climbed, the darkness closed in around us. The pale, greenish glow from the cavern faded away. In moments, I couldn't even see the rungs in front of me. The only way I knew KJ was still there was the ragged breathing above me.

I took a deep breath and drew on my magic. Hanging on in mid air, I dug my right hand into the rung to free my left hand. I clenched it into a fist and blew on it. I felt the coolness of North Pole magic tingle along my palm. I opened my hand and a tiny spark of light floated upward. It created a silverish glow as it floated above me, revealing KJ hanging onto the rungs above. I thought I caught a glimpse of relief on his face.

"Keep climbing," I called.

He headed upward with the tiny spark floating at pace.

In its soft light, I couldn't see an end above us. Was there an end? Would we have to keep climbing forever? And what happened if we got too tired. I knew KJ didn't have a lot of reserve left. Already I could see his limbs shaking as he pulled himself up rung by rung. If he fell, he would take me down with him and maybe we would fall forever.

Stop. I was just unnerved by the Siren behind us. Even though she hadn't aimed her full song at me I could almost feel it creeping along my skin like slime. We had to keep going. That was all. We just had to keep going.

"Noel, there's a ledge up here." KJ's voice floated down to me.

I lifted my gaze in time to see him scramble over the lip of a ledge. The tiny spark cast dark, sharp shadows across his face as KJ leaned back over to look down at me. He held out a hand.

"Hurry up," he said with an edge of impatience was so close to his normal self that I almost felt tears prickle at the back of my eyes.

"On my way," I said.

My arms and legs ached as I pulled myself up. Each rung

felt a little shallower, a little harder to dig my toes into. Dirt dug deep under my fingernails.

Just a few more rungs.

KJ stretched his arm another few inches. Reaching.

One more rung. I could almost grab his hand.

A solid bang echoed through the cavern. A wailing shriek sounded.

Ligeia had broken through the door.

I lunged upward and grabbed KJ's hand. For a moment, his face looked slack in the pale light from the spark, then the shadows sharpened as he bared his teeth. I felt his hand tighten around mine and he pulled.

Adrenaline flashed through me. Energy flooded my limbs and I felt my legs pump hard on the rungs as I climbed upward. I scrambled to my feet and found myself on the ledge KJ had mentioned.

The first thing I noticed was it wasn't a natural outcropping. The surface was concrete. I waved the spark closer. Its pale light revealed the back wall.

With a metal door set into it.

And of course it was locked.

The wailing shriek sounded again. The acoustics of the chamber made it echo weirdly. It was hard to tell if she was any closer but I was sure she was on her way.

KJ clutched my arm.

"Noel, we have to get out of here," he said. "If she comes, when she calls me. I'll have to..." He trailed off.

"We're getting out of here," I said. "Don't worry. I can get us through this door."

I turned to peer at the lock.

I sure hoped I could get us through this door.

In my other, private detective, life, I had practised with lock picks so I didn't have to try to use magic all the time. Opening a lock with magic was a delicate procedure. Using lock picks was much easier but unfortunately, I didn't have any on me.

Magic it would have to be.

If I could focus enough with the shrieking getting closer and closer.

I pressed my hand to the metal above the key hole. It felt cold and hard and smooth. After all the rocky textures of the cavern, it felt foreign. Steady deep breaths and I focused on the lock, allowed my magic to tingle in my hand. Through my palm and fingers.

Gentle now. Just gentle.

I visualized the lock, felt its components settled into lock mode. Just a little twitch, a slight movement, and it would unlock. Easy. Just breathe.

The shrieking jumped in pitch, making me flinch.

Damn the halls.

Breathe. Just breathe. Focus on the lock. Never mind the horrible Siren coming to get us.

Steady on heart. Slow down. There.

I focused on the lock again. Felt it inside the door. Moved my fingers, the slightest motion.

I felt the click more than heard it.

Relief almost made me sag to the ground. Instead I grabbed the handle and pulled.

The door swung open.

A weary smile burst over KJ's face.

Behind him, a bluish-greenish hand slapped onto the concrete landing from below. The shriek intensified.

I grabbed KJ's arm and yanked him through the door.

My heart thudded in my ears as I jumped after him. Behind me, a second hand slapped onto the landing. A figure pressed itself up, rising above the concrete. Head bowed, long, lanky, black hair streaming down, hiding the face. Skin rippled as it rose up, as if the creature were seen through water.

As it lifted its head, I slammed the door in its face.

Darkness enveloped me as I staggered back. The air tingled and crackled with energy around me. I felt it shivering against my skin. Clammy hands touched my shoulders. I yelped.

"Hey, it's just me," KJ said. "Where are we?"

I shook my head then realized in the darkness KJ couldn't see me.

"I don't know," I said. "But we've got to get moving. That door won't hold."

I fumbled around on the wall beside the door, feeling for a light switch. If I had to, I'd use magic but I wanted to hold off if I could. I had a feeling I was going to need it against the Siren.

I couldn't feel a light switch but I felt something like a pipe that unclipped from the wall. I ran my fingers along the surface and felt a button. I pressed it.

Light sprang from the front of the flash light. In the yellowish, light I saw KJ squint.

"Let's go," I said.

I swung the light around. It was definitely a man-made tunnel. Rounded concrete arched above our heads. Our boots echoed as we hurried along, slapping on the concrete. Was this some kind of drainage tunnel? It seemed perfectly dry but the walls were unadorned with no doors leading off.

It definitely felt like a drainage tunnel.

I hoped we wouldn't end up in some kind of pool or the lake. I had a feeling the Siren had definite advantages when it came to water.

Banging echoed behind us. Ligeia had reached the door. This one probably wouldn't hold her off for long either.

She was gaining on us.

I reached back and grabbed KJ's arm. I increased my speed. His steps echoed as he staggered behind. The light danced crazily as I pumped my arm. My breath felt as ragged as KJ's sounded.

How much longer would he be able to keep up? How much longer would I be able to?

The light bounced across rungs set up in the concrete. I stopped, gasping for air. KJ stumbled to a stop against me. He sagged against the wall.

The rungs led upward to a round manhole cover. It had another, smaller, round wheel in the centre.

I tugged on KJ's arm.

"Up we go," I said.

This time I went first. My legs shook as I pushed myself up the rungs. At the top, I had to hold on with one hand while trying to turn the wheel with the other. Fortunately, it moved easily. Good for us. Not so good with Ligeia on our heels.

Maybe there was a way to block it on the other side.

A click sounded and the round door began to lift. Then a hand grabbed it and yanked it out of my grasp. A face appeared above me, mostly in shadow, but enough that I recognized the square jaw and squarish head.

"Stan!"

"What the hell, Kringle," he said as he grabbed my shoulder and started hauling me up.

I scrambled to my feet as KJ poked his head up from the hole in the floor.

"I found my brother," I said as KJ climbed out. He turned and grabbed the steel door and slammed it down.

"Does this lock?" KJ said. "She's right behind us."

"Ligeia," I said. "She's a…"

"Siren." Venir's voice called out from the shadows.

I glanced around. We were in a dimly lit alcove. Just over Mallory's shoulder, I saw a doorway that opened into a room that seemed as large as an auditorium.

Venir stepped forward, followed by a familiar clip-clop.

Blitzen's head leaned over Venir, first taking me in before swinging toward KJ. In an instant, the reindeer leapt toward my brother, presenting a nose to be rubbed, shielding his body with its larger self. KJ grimaced as he threw an arm around Blitzen's neck. I couldn't be sure in the dim light but I thought I saw tears in his eyes.

I turned back to Venir.

"That's right," I said. "And she's right behind us. We have to block this entrance or deflect her or something."

"I'm on it." Venir hurried over to the manhole cover in the floor and knelt down. He began to whisper, moving his hands in intricate motions.

I found myself standing next to Mallory.

"How did you end up here?" I asked. "Where is here?"

"It's the Riddle's Astounding Aquarium under the CN Tower," Mallory said. "After you got swatted off behind me, the reindeer carried me all the way here. As soon as we landed, your little Elf friend showed up."

That made sense. Blitzen would have honed in on Venir's presence as soon as Venir revealed himself. He must have returned from the Magical Realms where he'd learned about the Siren.

I was going to have to ask him about that, but not quite yet.

"Why here?" I asked.

"Damned if I know," Mallory said. "This place is creepy at night." He gestured to the right.

A wall of black took up the entire side of the auditorium.

On the left, I could see rows of seats angling upward into the dimness but the right was completely black.

But not empty.

I could sense something there, something that seemed to move just beyond the edges of my perception.

Something slapped against the black wall. I thought I heard a gurgle.

Aquarium. Of course. It was some kind of tank with some sea creature inside.

I hoped it didn't have tentacles.

I turned away from the wall as Venir approached. His white hair was damp with effort, his cheeks red as he puffed out a breath. His hand shook a little as he pushed his hair back off his forehead.

"That'll hold for a bit," he said. "But we gotta get out fast. Where to, boss?"

I opened my mouth to speak when I spotted a photo hung on the wall behind Venir's head. I pushed past him to get a better look.

A man and a woman standing out in front of a building that looked almost like a wave. The sign Riddle's Astounding Aquarium was to the woman's left. Both of them wore white shirts and black pants, smiling and waving at the camera.

The man had the same shape as the body I had found on the island.

"Ah, if you're done site-seeing," Mallory said.

I pointed at the photo. "That's the body I found. The one that disappeared. The man."

Mallory peered over my shoulder. "Okay, Malcolm Croswell with Lacie Trent. Got it. Let's go."

"But who are they?" I asked.

"We'll figure it out. Away from here."

Of course, he was right. We had to get out. I knew that. My mind felt sluggish. I shook my head.

"So where we goin'?" Venir asked.

"Where else?" I said. "My office."

CHAPTER

NINETEEN

Between Venir, myself, and Blitzen, travelling back to my office took almost no time at all. I didn't kid myself that the Siren wouldn't be able to reach us there but maybe it was a little more difficult than right by open water.

The empty rooms were almost as familiar now as my regular office with furniture although I did miss having a place to sit. KJ was still so exhausted that he sank down onto the floor, leaning against the wall to stop from falling over. Weariness was etched in deep lines in his face. His white hair, usually so luxurious and full, hung limp and flat against his skull, making him look old.

Blitzen hunkered down beside him, resting his head on KJ's lap. KJ slowly stroked the reindeer's neck, staring off into space.

Venir, Mallory and I stood against the far wall, near the half bath. Venir stood with his hands stuffed into the pockets of his red parka. He glanced over his shoulder at KJ. He frowned.

"So that's him? Your brother?" he asked.

"Yes," I said. I waited for any sign of recognition but Venir just looked doubtful. Even KJ's physical presence didn't break the spell of Venir's forgetting him.

Unless there was no spell.

But something or someone had changed things, starting with KJ's capture by the Siren. But was this how Sirens worked, rewriting the history of the one they focused on?

I turned to Venir.

"How did you figure out it was a Siren?" I asked.

The Elf turned his attention away from KJ. He gave a cough and then cleared his throat. I noticed he wouldn't look at me, but stared at the floor between himself and Mallory.

"Venir," I said. "How did you figure it out?"

A flush brightened his cheeks.

"I went ta this faerie bar," he mumbled. "Asked around. Mentioned the smell and the water. They all thought I was joking that I didn't know what it was."

"A faerie bar?" Mallory said. He raised an eyebrow at me.

I waved away his implied question and focused on Venir.

"They thought it was obvious," I said.

The Elf nodded. "Even the Gnomes knew and they don't know nothing about nothing, except brewing Gellers."

"Did they tell you how to stop her?" I asked.

Venir cleared his throat. "Not exactly."

"Why not?"

He pressed his lips tight together. His shoulders hunched under his coat. From the way his hands rested in his pockets, I could tell he'd clenched them into fists.

"Venir," I said. "Did they tell you how to stop her?"

"I didn't ask, okay?" he blurted. "They kept laughin' at me. I just left."

"You just left."

The Elf jutted out his chin. "I ain't puttin' up with being laughed at."

I could feel my own face growing warm. My breath came faster.

"It didn't occur to you that we would need to know how to stop it?" I asked.

Venir hunched his shoulders.

"Okay, that's enough." Mallory held up his hands between us. "Arguing about it isn't going to fix this. We need to figure out a next step."

I let my breath out slowly. My anger had spiked, throbbing in my temples with my heart beat but it wasn't doing any good. I wasn't even sure any more what I was angry about. Yes, Venir should have gotten more information but I was also angry that finding KJ hadn't magically fixed everything. My life still didn't feel like my own and I was starting to wonder if I'd ever get it back.

But at least I had found my brother. That was something. I could build from there. I had to.

As long as I could avoid the Siren.

So first things first.

"Okay," I said. "Let's find out how to stop her."

"You can't."

KJ's voice was quiet and flat yet still seemed to fill the room. Every part of him sagged against the wall, even his hand that lay unmoving on Blitzen's neck.

"You can't fight her," he said. "When she calls you, you have to answer. You have to go to her. There is no fighting it."

I crossed to him and crouched in front of him. His eyes stared past me.

"KJ, do you remember your life before that? Do you remember leaving me a note?"

A frown creased his face.

"In your attic office, on your desk. You wrote a note to me. Do you remember what it said?"

His frown deepened, creating lines between his brows and narrowing his cheeks. Sweat started to bead along his hair line. I could almost feel the effort in his concentration.

"I...wrote...," he said. His voice sounded wane and out of breath.

"That's right," I said. "It said 'Noel' at the top and 'KJ' at the bottom. What did you write in the middle?"

The veins in his temples throbbed. His neck muscles stood out. He was trying so hard to remember but he couldn't.

Or something was preventing him.

I grabbed his hand on Blitzen's neck.

Pain flashed up my arm, tingling along my nerve endings. I felt myself gasp before I sank into it. It felt like a wave rolling over me. But something felt hollow about it, not real.

A spell.

A spell on KJ to stop him from talking.

I had to break it, to free him.

But breaking a spell from the inside was almost impossible. While I was being affected by it, it was difficult to see the workings of it, the boundaries that I could use to pry it apart.

There had to be another way.

Most spells were specifically aimed, tailored to a particular person or place. That concentrated the power and prevented it from dissipating over time. Since this spell had been cast on KJ, it had been tailored to him. Dragging me down had to be putting a strain on it but not enough of one. I had to put more pressure on the spell, stretch it so I could break the bounds of it.

I tried to turn my head but my muscles felt frozen. I could feel them straining with effort, ready to tear themselves apart. I couldn't even open my mouth to call to Venir for help.

There was only one thing to do. And I hated doing it.

I shifted my hand half off of KJ's hand, felt the soft fur of Blitzen's neck.

Sorry about this.

I yanked the reindeer into the spell along with me.

Blitzen's entire body jerked. I heard a bellow thunder up

from his chest and out of his mouth. I could almost make out the edges of the spell.

Just another moment...

The reindeer jerked, stomping his feet on the floor and propelling his body upward. He stood swinging his head from side to side, snorting. His rapid motion had broken my hold on KJ's hand and knocked me onto my butt. I sat blinking stupidly as Blitzen lowered his face, tipping his antlers toward me. I may not be able to communicate with reindeer the way a Christmas Elf could but I knew pissed off when I saw it.

"Blitzen, stop."

KJ's voice sounded weak and thin.

Blitzen's gaze flicked back toward KJ then returned to me. He didn't look any less pissed. Instead he appeared to wonder how fast he could gore me.

"I'm sorry, Blitzen," I said. "I had to break the spell. I wish I could have warned you but I couldn't speak."

The reindeer snorted again. He still looked mad as hell, although maybe a little less stompy.

"So you were talking about this note," Mallory said. "KJ, do you remember it now?"

The police detective spoke with a certain blandness, disinterest flattening his face. Of course, he couldn't see the spell, couldn't tell its affects but I had a feeling this was a performance.

KJ's attention jerked toward the detective. For a moment, I saw a familiar flash of annoyance cross my brother's features. He hated being interrogated. It was the first real hint of him coming back to himself.

Relief almost made me sag and I almost missed KJ's response.

"I think so." KJ's voice came a little louder, a little stronger. He was sitting up against the wall now, no longer slouching against it. I sensed energy in him, still not strong but stronger than it had been.

That spell keeping him quiet had been draining him as well.

"What did you write?" Mallory said.

KJ's brow crinkled as he concentrated. I saw the exact moment that awareness shifted to stubbornness on his face.

"I'd like to tell Noel alone," he said.

Mallory opened his mouth to rebutt but I beat him to it.

"It's better if you tell all of us, KJ," I said. "I wish we could respect your privacy but we don't have time. Not with the Siren out there."

My brother huffed out a breath and nodded. He pushed himself up off the floor until he was standing. He swayed a little and leaned back, butt against the wall, for support. Already he had better colour in his cheeks and his eyes flashed with personality.

Knowing KJ, it might make him more difficult to deal with but it was a relief to see him more like himself again.

"I met someone," he said. "Mother has been pestering me for eons. You know that. Integrity of the family business and all. So this time, I let her fix me up with a friend of a friend of a friend's daughter. We went out a few times." He shrugged and a blush brightened his cheeks.

"She was nice, funny," he said. "We had some good times. Then she started acting strange, after this new exhibit came to her work. I tried to talk to her about it but she denied anything was wrong. Then she stopped talking to me. I had to try one more time to see her. I left you the note, asking you to look into it if something happened to me."

"And something happened," I said.

He gave a slow nod. "I don't really remember what. I went to her work. Then it's just...snatches. The song..." He shuddered.

"Okay," I said. "That's okay. Tell me more about the woman. What was her name?"

"Lacie Trent," KJ said. "She works at an aquarium."

I felt my mouth drop open.

"What?" KJ said. He looked from me over to Mallory. Mallory looked grim.

"I found the body of her colleague," I said. "At least I think it was. It was hard to identify."

I gave him a quick rundown of finding the pen, trying the spell in the office, splitting up with Venir, then finding the body on the island. KJ's expression became more and more concerned.

"You think the Siren killed Lacie too?" he asked.

"Maybe," I said. I caught a glimpse of Venir opening his mouth. I gave a slight head shake. He shut up.

I didn't want to hit KJ with my suspicion that Lacie was the Siren. Not yet anyway.

"You mentioned some exhibit," I said. "Tell me more about it."

"I never saw it," KJ said. "I don't think it was open yet. They were getting it settled in."

"She didn't tell you what it was?" Mallory asked.

KJ shook his head.

At his side, Blitzen lifted his head and gave a snort. He stomped one hoof and glared at me.

If only I could speak reindeer. But I didn't need to, Venir was right here.

Blitzen wagged his head from side to side, flashing his antlers in the air but careful not to hit any of us.

The waving antlers reminded me of something.

And I didn't need Venir to tell me what it was.

The tentacle. Whatever had tentacles that large had to be the creature from the aquarium. But no aquarium could contain something that large.

Maybe it hadn't started out that way.

Was it the same sea beast Jack had mentioned? If so, the creature had to be hundreds of years old, possibly thousands. Yet it still didn't explain the size discrepancy.

Unless the creature had magic of its own.

Maybe the Siren wasn't the worst thing we were dealing with.

"It was probably related to the sea beast that knocked me

off Blitzen's back," I said. "It must be aligned to the Siren. We have to assume it has magical properties as well."

"Have to?" Mallory said.

I nodded. "To shrink itself to get into the aquarium and then to get out again. Plus the change to the time line isn't something a single magical entity could do on its own. This is massive magic. A fundamental shift in reality."

"We've only got your word on that," Mallory said.

I gestured toward KJ. "Here's my brother as proof. Besides, you know I'm not lying."

I looked him straight in the eye. Mallory dropped his gaze first and gave a brief nod. His expression looked pained, like he didn't want to admit it but had to.

I knew the feeling.

"How do we stop it?" Venir asked. "Is it even possible? It was bad enough with one thing, now yer tellin' us there's two."

The Elf shook his head and it struck me again that although he was Venir he wasn't *my* Venir. My Venir would have jumped right in without question, maybe because he knew we'd beaten things back before. This Venir didn't know that.

I had to remember that. No matter how much things looked similar here, they were not the same.

Not the same.

The thought tugged at me but I didn't know why. There was something there, something I could use, but my subconscious didn't want to surrender it yet.

"So, how do we stop them?" Mallory's voice broke my concentration.

"I'm still thinking," I said. "In the meantime, I want to get KJ to safety."

"Do you mean...?" Venir started.

"That's right, we're taking him back to the North Pole."

Mallory shoved his hands into the pockets of his trench coat.

"So you guys are making a break for it and what, I get to wait here for this Siren and the tentacle beast?"

"Nope," I said. "You're coming with us. Time for you to meet the folks."

CHAPTER

TWENTY

Mallory chuckled then it faded as he caught sight of my expression.

"You can't be serious," he said.

"I am," I said. "You said it, we can't leave you here. The Siren will find you. Don't worry, it won't be for long. We just need to regroup and then we'll be back to stop her."

"You're going to come up with an idea just like that?" he said.

I grinned. "I always do."

I gestured to Venir. The Elf stepped forward and grabbed the edge of Mallory's trench coat.

"The stables," I said.

Venir nodded and *winked*. Mallory disappeared at the same moment, a surprised look on his face.

I turned to KJ. "Grab hold of Blitzen. He and I will carry you."

"I can *wink* myself," he said. He sounded cranky. The complaint loosened another tight band around my heart. He was sounding more and more like himself again and, although he could be annoying, I was happy to have him back.

"Just hold on," I said. "Quit whining."

He pressed his lips together and glared at me but still put a hand on Blitzen's neck.

I grabbed KJ's shoulder and put my other hand on Blitzen's neck, near KJ's hand. The circle was complete now. Blitzen lifted his head and gave a snort. I nodded to him.

And the three of us *winked.*

THE STABLE AIR TASTED FRESH AND CHILLY. STOMPS AND THUMPS against wood doors greeted us. Blitzen let out a loud snort and tossed his head. From behind me, I saw a flare of red. Rudolph's nose was aglow.

Mallory stood before me beside Venir. His eyes were wide as he looked around the insides of the stable, at the rows of stalls and the reindeer heads poking over the tops of doors. He froze as he looked past me and I knew he'd spotted

Rudolph. In a moment, the lines on Mallory's face dropped away and he looked like a young boy again.

"Is that really him?" he asked.

"It is," I said. "Do you want to meet him?"

Before Mallory could respond, a creak sounded as the door behind us opened. The stomp of boots sounded as several Christmas Elves hurried in.

"What's all this here noise?" Felric said.

I turned as Felric stopped. The two other Elves flanking him stumbled to a stop as well.

We all stood in the centre of the aisle staring at each other. Finally Blitzen gave another snort.

"Master Noel?" Felric said.

My stomach twisted at the sight of him. I remembered hearing him talk about how disappointing I was as the heir to the Santa Claus title. I took a deep breath and let it out. I wasn't going to have to worry about that again, not with KJ back.

At least I hoped not.

"What time is it?" I said. "We need some full size snow gear out here for me and my friends. We're heading up to the house. As well, I want the tower put on alert. Any strange magic must be reported at once."

My urgent tone must have gotten through the surprise of seeing us in the middle of the stables. Felric gave an quick nod, his hand coming up in a half wave, half salute. He turned to the other Elves and shooed them away. The two of them took off running, booted feet pounding on the packed snow as they raced for the front door.

"We was wonderin' where Blizten got up to," Felric said. He stepped toward the reindeer. When he spotted Venir, he frowned.

"I needed him," I said. "But it should be all right now." I patted the reindeer's neck. Blitzen swung his head to look at me. I could almost read concern in his eyes.

"Go on home, boy," I said.

Blitzen gave a snort that almost sounded like a sigh. His hooves clopped on the ground as he stepped toward his stall. When Felric still stood looking uncertain at all of us, the reindeer snorted loudly and kicked out, hitting the door to his stall.

Felric jumped, then hurried over to open it. Blitzen strolled inside.

By the time he finished securing the door, the two other Elves had returned, carrying armloads of coats and boots.

In short order, everyone who wasn't bundled was soon bundled up, including Mallory who looked only slightly ridiculous with a red parka over top of his beige trench coat. The dark green, knitted cap looked especially fetching and I told him so.

He managed to glare at me before returning to looking around with wonder.

I led the way out of the stables. The night air was crisp and cool. The ever present sunlight glowed on the horizon. Mallory looked startled as we stepped outside.

"It's the North Pole," I said. "Sunlight for six months and darkness for six months."

"Right," he said.

We moved on, at a slower pace than I would have preferred. KJ still moved with less assurance than before but he shrugged off any of my offered assistance. He seemed steadier, if slower. The confusion had faded from his face. With every shuffling step, he looked more and more like himself.

Yet the Elves in the stables hadn't recognized him. That meant whatever magic had restructured the world was still at play.

"KJ, I have to tell you something before we reach the house," I said.

He puffed as he took another step. He was trying more to lift his feet than shuffle.

"Yeah, what?" he said.

"Mother and dad," I said. "They might not remember you."

He stopped. "What?"

"The Siren or the tentacle beast, or maybe both of them," I said. "They've messed up the world. No one remembers you. They think I'm the heir to Santa Claus."

Laughter burst from my brother's lips. Colour flushed his cheeks and for a moment he looked exactly like KJ on his best days, eyes bright and full of sparkle. Then the laughter faded, first to a chuckle, and then a final snort.

"Hey, you aren't kidding."

I shook my head. "I wish I was. I think they tried to change the time line so they could keep you prisoner."

"So how did you remember?"

I shrugged, feeling the parka shift on my shoulders. "I just did."

"What about your friends in Toronto? Didn't they complain?"

"They didn't remember anything either," I said. "I never went down there in this time line."

KJ glanced back at Mallory who stood behind him, listening to our conversation.

"So you never solved any of the cases, did any of the things you did," KJ said.

I took a breath. "Right."

He looked back at me and I could feel him studying me. "Are you sure I wasn't the only one they were trying to control?"

My heart pounded. I'd been trying to convince myself that this whole situation had been all about KJ but something else inside of me wondered. Maybe it really had been about sidelining both of us, first taking KJ out of the equation and second, putting me into a place where I would mess up.

"Let's go," I said. My voice sounded hoarse to my ears.

We headed for the house.

As the sight of white house with red trim appeared over the rise, I heard Mallory gasp behind me. The front door opened and a figure in a red parka stepped out onto the porch. White, wavy hair brushed back. Beard neatly trimmed along his jaw line. Even with the puffiness of the parka, Dad looked thinner than his usual Christmas weight. But there was still some undefinable something that made him Santa Claus.

Until he frowned and worry lines creased the sides of his mouth.

We reached the bottom of the porch.

"Noel, what's going on?" he asked. His deep voice filled the air even as he spoke quietly.

"Let's go inside and talk," I said. "Both you and mother need to hear this."

As we all filed past him into the front foyer, I watched his expression carefully. As KJ moved by, Dad gave no notice of recognition, nothing but polite interest, the same way he looked at Mallory.

Whatever magic had done all of this, it was still in full effect here at the North Pole.

That couldn't be good.

Inside, we shed coats and boots before Dad ushered us into the front parlour. White carpeting covered the floor leading to a large, overstuffed dark green sofa that stretched across the front window on the left. Just across was the fireplace with the huge white mantle. Family pictures lined the top.

None of them included KJ.

My brother gave them a quick glance, then he stopped and looked again. Slower. With more care. He moved down the entire length of the mantle, studying each photo one at a time. Finally he reached the end and turned to face me.

His expression was closed. Lips pressed tight together in a thin line. Fine wrinkles showing at the outside edges of his eyes, the only indication of stress. But I didn't need to see him wailing to know how much it hurt him. He'd managed to escape from the Siren only to return home to find no one remembered him.

Being trapped in that cavern room wasn't the worst thing done to him.

I wanted to say something but nothing I said would make it better. Not until it was fixed.

And I was going to fix this. Damn the halls, I was.

The door leading to the kitchen creaked as it opened. Mother appeared in the doorway, wearing a light green dress. Her crisp white apron with the red ties looked immaculate, the way it always did. At the sight of me, her eyes widened and a smile burst over her face.

"Noel, dear, I've been so worried."

She hurried forward and embraced me, smelling of candy canes and nutmeg. I hugged her back. Over her shoulder, KJ's face grew even stonier.

When Mother drew back, she noticed the others with me. A courteous smile brightened her face.

"I didn't realize you'd brought guests," she said. "Please sit, all of you."

She gestured to the sofa and a set of matching armchairs

that had appeared on either side of the coffee table in front of the sofa.

Before the others could move, I took Mother's arm by the elbow.

"I think you should sit down," I said. "You and dad. I have something I need to tell you."

Dad already stood at the far end of the sofa. He gave a slight shrug and sat down. He patted the cushion beside him. Mother gave another pleasant smile to Venir and Mallory. Venir blushed and dropped his gaze. Mallory had regained that wide-eyed kid look from inside the stables.

I studied Mother carefully as her gaze swept across KJ.

No hint of recognition.

KJ looked more and more like a block of ice.

My heart ached for him. We didn't always get along but I would never have wished this on him. Not even during our worst fights.

"Are you going to introduce your friends?" Dad asked. "Besides Venir, of course." He tapped a finger on his chin. "That one looks familiar."

He was looking at Mallory.

"He should," I said. "You found me with him with you the last time you brought me back from Toronto. This is Stan Mallory, he's a police detective. And this..."

I held out a hand toward KJ. He stepped away from the mantle. His movement was stilted, rigid, proclaiming how hard he held himself under control.

"This is KJ," I said. "My brother."

Mother looked puzzled and Dad frowned again.

"KJ was in thrall to a Siren," I said. "I barely managed to break him out of her caverns and bring him home."

"There's no Sirens here," Dad said. "Not in this realm."

"There shouldn't be," I said. "But things have been leaking through from the Magical Realms for some time now. I've dealt with several of them. Or I did in my version of this time line." I held up my hand as Mother opened her mouth to speak.

"I know you don't remember," I said. "I know nobody else does and I can't explain why I remember the differences but I do. And finding KJ proves that something has changed our world. It has to be fixed."

Uncertainty creased Mother's face. She glanced over at Dad. He rubbed his chin, his fingers brushing the strands of his beard. I could feel the weight of his regard as he looked first at me. His gaze then shifted to KJ.

"There is something about this young man," he said. "Can you see it, Mary?"

"No, I..." She paused. Her eyes narrowed as she studied KJ. "I...I don't know. He does have your chin."

Dad grunted. "How could a simple Siren do all this, if what you say is true? They don't have that kind of power."

"I don't know," I said. "There is this tentacled creature..."

Bells began ringing, musical and joyful sounding even at a high volume.

Everyone froze, startled. The urgency of the melody increased. A moment later, I could feel the crackle of magical energies on my skin, prickling like pins and needles.

Venir gasped. "Incoming!"

I raced for the door. Pounding footsteps behind me told me everyone else followed. I threw open the front door and hurried out onto the porch. Before I hit the stairs leading down to the path in the snow, I glanced up.

And froze.

The air crackled and sparked above us. In the sparkling sunlight, I caught sight of a massive wave of water rushing across the land. As it moved toward us, the snow at its base melted, joining the wave.

Hurdling toward the house.

And hovering at the crest of the wave, riding it, I spotted the Siren.

She opened her mouth wide to blast forth her song but the peels of the bells drowned her out.

Dad stepped past me and headed down the stairs. At the base he stopped and lifted his arms.

"The North is under attack. Stations everyone. Defend the Pole!"

Even as the wave drew closer, I felt the sparking and power around us increase. The air seemed to shimmer. From the hill that the house stood on, I could see down into the village proper. Elves appeared outside the buildings, raising their arms.

The air crackled with the scent of ozone. It took a silvery shimmer that seemed to blanket the house and the village in a magical dome. A moment later, I spotted reindeer shooting up into the sky, one after the other, like tiny fighter bombers.

They headed for the wave of water.

Besides me, I felt KJ stiffen. I knew what he was thinking. He'd been trained his entire life to take over as Santa Claus and one of the duties was defense of the North Pole. He seemed to vibrate with the need to help.

Then the wave smashed against the magical dome.

I could feel the impact wash over me. On my left, I heard Mallory gasp. His hands pressed to the sides of his head. Blood dribbled from his nose.

The wave of water seemed to slosh over the dome, cutting off the sunlight and plunging us into a strange, glistening twilight. A rumbling roar started to drown out the musical chimes of the bells. And I could hear the howl of the Siren start to break through.

"They won't be able to hold her back for long," KJ said.

I shook my head. "But it's just a Siren."

"Does that look like just a Siren?"

The water flowed over the dome and then past it. Then it shifted direction and began to rise into a wave again. Higher and higher. Aiming for the dome.

Aiming to crack it wide open and sweep the North Pole away.

KJ was right. This wasn't just a Siren attack.

The bells still rang out but they were no longer completely obscuring the sound of the Siren's call. I could hear the shrieking song starting to seep in. How long would it be before she broke the masking effects of the bells completely? How long would the Elves be able to withstand her thrall then?

If she had been able to capture KJ, there was a chance she could capture the attention of everyone here.

Including Dad.

Including me.

There had to be a way to stop her.

And I had the beginnings of a tremendously stupid idea.

CHAPTER

TWENTY-ONE

I grabbed KJ's arm.

"We have to go back to the aquarium."

"That's nuts." Mallory's voice sounded over my left shoulder. "We just came from there."

"Right, and we have to go back."

"Why?"

"That's where it all started," KJ said. "Lacie worked there. It's where we met. Where the new exhibit is."

I nodded. "Where the tentacled creature is and I think it's giving power to the Siren."

"Okay," KJ said. "We go back and stop the tentacled creature, disrupt its power transfer to the Siren. Any idea of how to do that?"

"Not a clue," I said. "I'll think of something when we get there."

"That is the most half-assed…," Mallory started.

"Would you rather stay here and wait for her to break through?" I said.

The muscles along his jaw twitched as he clenched his teeth.

"Ah hell," he said. "Fine. I'm in."

I glanced at Venir. "If you want to stay here, you can."

Venir swept his gaze down to the village, taking in the rush of the wave as the Siren launched her attack again. Again the dome held as the water sloshed over it. But the water rose up again, ready for another strike.

And the shrieking of the Siren was getting louder, even as the bells continued to ring.

"Even if I stayed I wouldn't do much here," Venir said. "If I can help stop her, I will."

"Okay. Let's get ready to go…"

The crunch of snow behind me distracted me. A snort sounded behind me.

Blitzen stuck his head over my shoulder.

"You have to stay here, boy," I said.

He shook his head. Then behind KJ, Comet landed with a thud. Beside him, Vixen alighted on the snow. Then Donner crashed down and pulled his lips back from large teeth, as if grinning. Then Dancer and Prancer and Dasher, all landed in a row behind Mallory.

Finally Rudolph landed beside KJ. A soft glow brightened his nose.

"All of you? You can't…"

I felt a hand squeeze my shoulder.

"Take them," Dad said. His face was pale. Stress lines etched into his forehead and around his mouth. His skin glistened with sweat.

"They can't do much against the water," he continued. "Maybe they can help you. We'll hold on here."

Over his shoulder I could see Mother nodding. Her hands were clenched into fists at her side. The air filled with the scent of cinnamon. I could feel her warmth radiating out, washing over us. With that little half smile, she was telling me she believed I could do it. She knew we would prevail. She wished us speed.

I breathed in her gift.

And gave Dad a nod.

"Hold the Pole," I said. "We'll slay the beast."

He gave my shoulder another squeeze then he turned to KJ.

"Watch out for your little brother," he said.

KJ looked startled. It was plain Dad still didn't remember him but it was his usual command to KJ. KJ swallowed and blinked several times. His eyes looked watery. He gave a quick nod.

Dad stepped back. He gave me a final grim smile before he turned back to face the village. The wave was starting to crash over the dome again.

I put a hand on Blitzen's neck.

"To the aquarium."

THE AIR SMELLED OF EXHAUST AND SEAWEED AS WE LANDED ON THE sidewalk outside the aquarium. After the sunshine of the North Pole, the darkness of night in Toronto was disorienting. I had no idea what time it was or even what day it was any more.

Seemed rather fitting considering everything.

Venir, KJ, and Mallory stood before me. The reindeer gathered around us, forming a protective circle. Their ears twitched as they turned their heads from side to side, scanning the area. The sidewalk was empty. Good thing as a cluster of reindeer standing on the sidewalk in the March snow would surely attract attention.

Mallory looked pale and nauseated. His hands shook a little as he tugged at the zipper on his parka.

KJ still looked pale too, but better. He stood a little straighter and he had a familiar gleam in his eye.

Venir stood with his shoulders hunched, sweeping his gaze around us like the reindeer.

"So genius private detective, what do we do now?" KJ said.

Yep, he was definitely feeling more and more like himself.

Which also tickled something inside my mind. I felt like another little puzzle piece was dropping into place. I just wish I knew what the picture was going to be. It might help with everything.

"You mentioned Lacie told you about a new exhibit," I said. "We'll go inside and take a look."

"And?" KJ said.

"Annnnddd see what's there," I said.

"You have no idea what you're doing, do you," he said.

"Sure I do," I lied. "I'm just not ready to share it yet."

Mallory coughed. I thought I heard him say 'bullshit' in between coughs.

I pushed past them and approached the aquarium. The double glass doors were locked but as I bent to deal with it, I felt Dasher and Comet move up. A solid tingling shimmered through the air. The doors clicked and swung open.

The nine reindeer had a solid base of magic. I hoped it was enough.

Inside we moved past the empty ticket booth and a darkened concession stand. Pale red emergency lights glowed every five feet as we moved deeper into the building. KJ had taken the lead, moving with a steady assurance.

Despite his stronger appearance I knew he was putting on an act that he was fully recovered. Maybe he thought I'd pull him out if he wasn't up to it but the fact was I needed all the help I could get.

Besides, KJ never needed to prove anything to me.

As we reached a familiar looking floor I moved to KJ's side. "I'll take point," I said. "You come in from the side."

I could almost feel KJ bristle.

"You think I'm too weak to lead?"

"I think you've worked with the reindeer more and can deploy them faster than me," I said.

He huffed. "Okay."

In front of me was the right door to the auditorium. KJ moved toward the left one. I shooed Venir after him and waved Mallory toward me.

"Stay close," I said.

At the left door, KJ gave a nod. All I could see was the outline of his white beard as he moved his head. I waved my hand and then pushed the door open.

The rows of seats were empty, angling downward toward the huge tank at the front of the stage. The red emergency lights gave everything an eerie glow. The thin carpetting muffled our steps as we moved down the aisles toward the tank. Inside it looked murky, like someone or something had stirred up the sediment at the bottom of the tank, swirling it until it was impossible to see inside.

As I passed the last row of seats before the empty floor in front of the tank, I started to feel a tingle of magic along my skin. It felt slippery, almost slimy, like water thickened with gelatin. The stench of seaweed grew.

Beside me, Mallory grimaced.

"What the hell is that?" he said.

He pointed at the tank.

Something moved inside. The water shifted, swirled, as something large seemed to pass by, moving from left to right. I could almost make out a long limb as it moved before me but it disappeared deeper into the tank before I could be sure.

I glanced over. KJ and Venir stood at the left end of the tank. Just over KJ's head, I spotted the frame on the wall that held the photo of the aquarium attendants. KJ's girl, Lacie, was there but KJ kept his back to the photo. I could tell from the stiffness in his body that he had seen it. It was obvious even from a distance.

KJ gave a motion with his hand and the reindeer lined up in front of the final row of seats, facing the tank. When they finished deploying, he gave me a nod.

Time for my plan.

Whatever that was.

I had to come up with something. Immediately. So what did I know?

There was a Siren who had enthralled KJ and locked him in her cavern. There was a tentacled monster that seemed to be in league with the Siren. Somehow one or both had managed to change reality to erase KJ from existence. To prevent him from being rescued? Then why hadn't it worked on me?

Too many questions that I didn't have the answers for, and they were too distracting. Stick to what I knew.

Somehow the creature and the Siren were connected to this tank. The magic that tingled along my skin confirmed it. If we could disrupt the connection, maybe we could stop the Siren's attack on the North Pole.

Maybe we could even right the disruption to reality.

The big question was how to do it.

Suddenly I felt myself grinning. What could two sons of Santa, a Christmas Elf, and all the reindeer do with a tank full of water?

After all, we lived surrounded by water at the North Pole, except that water was in the form of ice and snow.

"Zip up," I said to Mallory. "It's about to get cold in here."

I signalled to KJ and Venir.

"Freeze the water. Turn it to ice and snow. The Siren scooped up the snow at the North Pole to make her wave, let's give this creature a taste of its own medicine in reverse."

Venir clapped his hands. KJ grinned.

As one, we all turned toward the tank.

I felt magic swirling around me. Behind me, the reindeer stomped and snorted. I felt cold air waft forward in a wave, falling from the ceiling to almost pool on the floor. I glanced back. All the reindeer had leapt into the air and now hovered near the ceiling. Rudolph's nose glowed bright red, casting light on the water's surface at the top of the tank.

The water started to swirl and almost bubble. Whatever was inside was getting agitated. It didn't like what we were doing.

Good.

I turned back to the tank. I lifted my hands and focused my own magic, calling on the cold of the North Pole, channelling it.

Come forth, come forth, and bring the cold and desolation of winter. The sleep of snow, the peace of ice.

I felt the cold pouring off me, flowing from me like an invisible flood of ice, crawling on the floor toward the tank.

"Jez, it's freezing," Mallory said. He was shivering beside me. His breath puffed out in a white cloud of cold. His teeth started to chatter.

I wanted to tell him to hold on but I couldn't spare the breath.

I had to stay focused.

The glass surface of the tank began to frost up, an intricate lace-like effect crystalizing across the surface, moving faster and faster. The water within moved sluggishly, thickening as it began to freeze.

A bang sounded from inside the tank. A tentacle slapped at the glass.

For a moment, the suckers adhered to the glass, pulsing, then the tentacle slid back into the depths.

Then another bang. The tentacle smashed at the glass.

A crack appeared in the ice.

I waved Mallory away but kept my attention on the tank. The cold was piercing now and I needed my full concentration to keep up the effort. I thought I heard footsteps moving away, the carpeting crackling underneath boots.

A tentacle shot up from the top of the tank. I heard ice crack as it burst through the surface of the water. The tentacle slammed into the ceiling then whipped forward.

The reindeer scattered, fleeing across the room to avoid the sweep of the tentacle. It caught one of Cupid's legs, sending the reindeer spinning into the wall. The reindeer let out a wail as it hit and plummeted toward the seats below. Just before it landed, Cupid righted himself and shot across the room toward the back, barely avoiding another sweep of the tentacle.

With the reindeer scattered, their efforts distracted, I could already feel the cold begin to wane. I took in a deep breath and let it out, watching the air puff out like white smoke. I drew deeper on my magical connection to the North Pole, channelling the cold.

After a moment, I felt it pouring off me. The tips of my fingers turned numb. I couldn't feel my cheeks or my nose. None of that mattered. Only the cold mattered.

Sending the cold into that tank.

Ice thickened on the glass, turning white and obscuring my vision of whatever dwelt inside. I could imagine the water freezing solid into a tank-sized block of ice. The tentacled creature would be trapped inside, its power cut off from the Siren. Dad could then dispatch the Siren and come here to help us destroy the tentacled creature for good.

It would work. We would do it.

I could almost feel the muscles in my face contracting into a smile.

A shrieking wail sounded. The stench of rotting seaweed billowed from the top of the tank and several tentacles slammed against the ice coating.

It shattered.

Shards of ice exploded outward. They rained down. Flecks of ice and snow wet my cheeks.

A mass of tentacles smashed the ceiling. Cracked appeared, spreading like cracks in ice.

Another slam against the ceiling.

Chunks of plaster began to fall.

Over the shrieks, I thought I heard KJ yelling.

"Keep focusing," I yelled.

I drew in a deep breath and blasted out cold.

The tentacle writhed above the tank. The shrieking increased. Icicles dripped from the suckers on the bottom end of the tentacles.

Then one darted forward.

Aiming for me.

CHAPTER

TWENTY-TWO

Before I could jump back, the tentacle whipped around me. The stench of rotting seaweed made me gag. A wet, slimy muscle wrapped around me. I felt the suckers pressed against me.

I struggled, but my arms were trapped at my sides.

It was the worst full body hug I'd ever had.

I opened my mouth to cast a spell but I was yanked off my feet.

The room spun around me. I caught sight of KJ yelling, his arms raised up. Venir's mouth open in shock and horror. A glimpse of Mallory running back down the aisle toward me.

The hooves and antlers of the reindeer as they flew around me. Their legs kicked out, trying to hit the tentacle but miss me.

It all flashed by in seconds.

Then I plunged into the frigid water.

The shock of cold made me gasp. Water invaded my mouth. I gagged, tried not to breathe it in. My lungs ached. I hadn't managed a deep breath before hitting the water.

I struggled but the tentacle held firm. It squeezed even tighter, pressing out what little air I had out of my lungs.

It felt like it was going to be a tossup whether I died of drowning or being crushed.

A feeling of mocking laughter wash over me. I squinted, trying to see through the murky depths. If I was going to die, I wanted to at least see what was killing me.

All I could see was the suggestion of something huge writhing in the darkness. More and more tentacles waved and flowed through the thickening water. The temperature was still dropping. Even if I was going to die in here, KJ would freeze this beast out. We would still stop the Siren and save the North Pole.

See? You aren't going to win.

I felt myself yanked down again. My lungs burned. I squeezed my mouth shut, fighting against instinct to open it, to suck in air. There was no air here, only water. Only drowning. It was a fight I couldn't win but I'd fight it as long as I could.

Grainy sediment flashed past my vision, clouding the water further. The temperature of the water seemed to be rising. Maybe from the creature agitating, its body heat radiating into the water.

Good. The more it bled out body heat the faster it would freeze.

C'mon KJ, hurry up.

I kept being dragged down. It seemed impossibly far. How deep was this tank?

The pressure in my lungs and head grew. I couldn't hold out much longer. I was going to try to breathe. That would be the beginning of the end.

Then the tentacle whipped me upward. My head broke the surface of the water. I gasped in air. Water dripped in my eyes. I felt warm, dry air on my skin.

I shook my head, sending my wet hair off my forehead.

The interior of the auditorium was gone, replaced by an underground cavern.

Around me, the water gave off a sickly, green-blue glow that shimmered on the walls of the cavern, giving it an underwater look. The cavern was a rough circular shape with only a small ledge of ground sloping into the water at one end. In the shimmering light, I could almost make out rough-looking steps carved into the rock, leading from an opening in the rock wall at the top of the cavern. The steps angled down to the ground where a figure stood at the water's edge.

Ligeia?

No, it couldn't be. She was leading the attack on the North Pole. I couldn't see her breaking that off.

Unless she had won.

No, I would know that. I would feel it in my bones. In my soul. Even though it was fighting for its life, the North Pole still stood.

For the moment.

So who was that figure?

I tried to squirm in the tentacle's grip but it squeezed tighter. I groaned. My organs felt like they were being squeezed hard enough to burst. I took fast, shallow breaths, trying to ignore the pain of breathing.

Burnt coals, if it was going to squeeze me to death, why was I here?

The figure waved an arm and gave a shout.

The tentacle loosed its grip, enough that I could draw a deeper breath. Then it lifted me higher and whipped me toward the open ground.

It slammed me down. I rolled, feeling wet sand grind into my skin. I ended up on my back, panting, trying not to move. My entire body felt like a giant bruise, first from being crushed and then from the impact of my landing.

The air stank of a fishy, sour stench that I could taste even as I breathed through my mouth but I didn't care. The feel of oxygen in my lungs was wonderful even as my chest muscles ached from drawing air in and out. I just lay there and breathed for a moment.

A shadow passed over my face, blocking out the shimmering from the water.

"Back again are ya?"

The sneering voice sounded familiar. As my eyes adjusted to the dim light, I recognized the thin angle of the face, the wavy hair.

Jack Avery!

I pushed up against the ground and managed to sit up. My arms shook like jello. I rested my hands in my lap.

"Jack," I said. "You got out of the room."

"That seems obvious," he said. He tilted his head. "Don't know why the beast ain't killed you yet. Must be somethin' special to ya. Must be wantin' Ligeia to deal with ya."

The chill that made me shiver wasn't from the water evaporating from my skin. I rolled onto my knees and struggled to push myself to my feet.

A hand grabbed my arm and helped me.

I managed to stand and not sway too much. My entire body trembled from fatigue. I would have loved a nap, one that lasted for a decade or more.

I didn't think Ligeia would accommodate me.

I turned to Jack who was looking at me with amusement.

"She's attacking the North Pole," I said. "Do you understand what that means? If she destroys it, the world will be overrun by monsters."

Jack shrugged. "Why should I care? The world ain't done nothin' fer me, lad."

"If the North Pole falls, I won't be able to get you your reward."

That sparked a glint of interest in his eyes.

"So, you remember your bargain," he said.

"I do. But I can't fulfill it if the North Pole falls."

Jack scratched his bearded chin.

"What do ya think I can do about it?"

"Call her back," I said. "Tell her I'm here, that the sea beast brought me for her. She'll come."

Jack's eyes narrowed in suspicion.

"So what if she does? If she comes, she'll be killin' ya and then where'll my reward be?"

"You'll still get it," I said. "I left word there about it. It'll be delivered to you regardless."

I kept my gaze on him steady and open, hoping he wouldn't see through the lie. He was enough of a liar himself that I was sure he didn't take anything at face value but I was also counting on his lust for gold and jewels. In the struggle between his suspicion and greed, I hoped greed would win out.

"How can you be sure?" he said.

"I'm an honourable man," I said. "I stand by my oaths."

That, at least, was the truth.

Jack chewed the inside of his cheek. For a moment, I thought he was going to scoff at me and then drag me back into the Siren's lair proper and lock me in one of the rooms. In the state I was in I wouldn't be able to resist him. My muscles still throbbed and trembled from being crushed and slammed into the ground.

So exactly how was I going to defeat the Siren?

It didn't much matter if I knew or not if Jack didn't believe me.

Then Jack nodded.

"All right but the price is now doubled," he said.

"One and a half times," I said.

His eyes narrowed and he scowled at me, but I knew I couldn't just give in to him. He would suspect a trap. If I tried to negotiate he was more likely to keep believing me.

"Doubled," he insisted.

I let out a big sigh and allowed my shoulders to droop even lower.

"Okay, double."

A triumphant grin lit up Jack's face. He waved me toward the rock wall with the steps dug into it.

"C'mon then," he said. "We'll get outta here."

"But you're to call Ligeia."

"I will, don't be so impatient."

"Look, if the North Pole falls...," I started.

"I heard ya," he said. "If it falls, blah blah blah. Got it. But I can't be callin' her from here. This is the sea beast's lair. We need to go to Ligeia's room."

He headed up the steps, moving fast. I followed, trying to keep pace and failing miserably. Leg muscles screamed as I began to climb the steps. I grabbed hold of the rock wall with my right hand and my arm muscles trembled. Each step felt like agony.

Hunching over to grab for the next step, I ended up practically crawling. A moldy, dirty stench of earth mingled with the sourness of the water. I tried to breathe through my mouth but it seemed to coat my tongue.

But the time I reached the top, I was gagging and coughing. I had to hold onto the rock wall to steady myself as I cleared my throat, trying to stop the cough. My body swayed on the last step. Just what I needed, to fall backwards all the way down.

But Jack grabbed my arm and yanked me through the doorway.

I stumbled after him. The hallway seemed to shimmer before me. I couldn't tell how far we walked before he opened a set of double doors and dragged me through.

I stood swaying just inside the door. A room about thirty feet wide stretched out before me. The floor seemed to be made of glass with water flowing underneath it. The walls shimmered with blue-green light rippling and sparkling over it. At the far end of the room was a huge, ornate chair that rested on a pedestal that rose up out of the floor. The curves of the chair legs and the back made me think of tentacles. The fabric in the seat and on the back looked like scales. The way the light shimmered on the steps leading up the pedestal to the chair reminded me of water lapping.

From the ceiling, huge stalactites hung down, almost like gigantic icicles. Just one of them looked large enough to slice me in half if it fell.

Jack shoved me forward. Although the floor looked like it was slippery, I didn't slide. I stumbled but managed to stay on my feet. When we reached the middle of the room, Jack yanked me to a stop. Then he pressed a hand to my shoulder, pushing down.

"On your knees," he said. "Ligeia demands obedience."

I was about to ask about him when he dropped to his knees beside me.

"Double," he said. "You agreed."

I nodded. "I did."

"All right. We'll be callin' her then."

He pulled out a blade from sheaf at his waist. In one movement, he sliced open his left palm. Blood welled up. He pressed his palm to the floor and smeared the blood. At first it only looked like a mess but then I noticed how he moved his hand up and down, adding a curl to the top of the smear.

Waves. He was drawing waves in blood.

He completed a row right in front of him, then he grabbed my left arm. He clamped it between his body and his elbow. I felt the warmth of his blood against the back of my hand as he forced my hand open with his left hand. I yelled as he sliced my palm open.

Pain seared my palm. Blood welled up.

He slapped my left hand onto the floor and forced it across the surface. The smearing image of waves looked messier than his as he pushed my hand along.

Finally he released me. I clenched my left fist, trying to stop the bleeding as he lifted his arms to the ceiling.

"Ligeia, I call to you," he cried. "Hear me, Jack Avery, your faithful servant. I present to you one who would give you power, one who would give you the world. Hear my call ripple through the waters of the world. Answer my plea."

He slapped his hands down on the floor, underneath the bloody waves. For a moment, nothing happened, then the ragged lines of blood began to ripple. It looked like waves rippling forward and back. Then the shimmering under the floor began to ripple like waves. The lights on the walls undulated.

Even the pedestal leading to the chair looked like it was flowing like waves.

The air filled with a salty, sour stench. I had to breathe through my mouth to minimize it.

A rumbling sounded from behind us, quickly filling the room. I glanced up nervously at the stalactites hanging above us.

Wouldn't it be just my luck for one to fall and crush me just as I was getting ready to confront Ligeia?

Maybe one would crush her too.

No, even with North Pole magic, my luck wasn't that good.

The rumbling increased in volume, now sounding like the roar of waves. The howl of a great storm at sea. I almost expected to feel salt water splash my face.

Then a loud crack sounded and I did feel a spray of mist on my cheeks. A watery fog bellowed forth from the huge chair, billowing down the pedestal steps and engulfing us in a grey mist. The salty, sour stench filled my mouth and nose, the mist prickled along my skin and made my eyes water.

It lasted for a few seconds then the cloud flowed away, like a wind at sea blowing it off. I wiped the tears from my eyes. Coughed out the worst of the salt.

Glanced up.

Ligeia stood in front of her chair at the top of the pedestal, staring down at me.

CHAPTER

TWENTY-THREE

Ligeia tilted her head, regarding me from the top of her pedestal. I regarded her right back.

She still looked similar to Lacie Trent from the photograph I'd seen in the Riddle's Astounding Aquarium. But instead of the white shirt and black pants, scales of blue-green shimmered on her skin, curving down her body like a body suit. They pooled at her feet, making her legs look like a single appendage, and I knew where the image of a mermaid came from. Her hair, no longer the light brown from the photo, was slicked back from her head. It was a dark, brackish green. Her skin was slightly grey, like a dead body that had been too long in the water.

"Is that how you lured my brother?" I asked. My voice echoed in the chamber. "You stole the body of the woman he loved?"

A smile twisted her lips. As she opened her mouth to speak, I tried to steel myself. This was a Siren who used her voice to entrance people. I didn't want to be one of them.

"I was invited," she said. Her voice trickled through the room. Musical and soothing, like the hiss of waves from a seashell.

I felt my heart pounding. My body trembled. Suggestion, just suggestion. Part of it had to do with kneeling in front of her. It made it feel like I was supplicating myself.

Noel Kringle, second son of Kris and Mary Kringle, in line to the Santa Claus dynasty, didn't supplicate himself for anyone.

I pushed myself to my feet. Beside me, Jack hissed and grabbed at my arm. I stepped to the right, out of reach.

"Lacie Trent invited you," I said. "Why was that? What did you promise her?"

Ligeia laughed. The sound teased at me. I clenched my hands into fists until I felt my nails bite into my palms. Pain distracted me.

Good to know.

"Did Lacie know you would kill her work colleague?" I asked.

I was taking a chance letting her know I knew about Malcolm Crosswell's death. She might not be pleased about it.

And she didn't look pleased. The smile dropped from her face. She looked down at me impassively. No part of her moved. It was as if she had turned to stone. An outcropping of her elaborate chair.

I risked a glance at Jack. He remained on his knees, gazing up at her. All trace of sarcasm or taunting had been wiped from his face. He stared up at Ligeia, his expression as blank as hers.

Was he even still in there? Had he even been since I'd first stumbled into his room? Was he some kind of puppet shell that the Siren used?

Was the body of Lacie Trent, changed as it was, the same kind of thing?

Was this some kind of elaborate shell game, flashing fancy answers at me while the real creature who had set this all in motion hid safely away? Was it all some kind of intricate ruse? If so, what was the end game?

What exactly *was* that sea beast?

Now a smile twisted on Ligeia's face, as if she read my doubts on my face.

"You are a clever one," she said. "Like I've been told."

"Told by who?"

I blurted it out. I couldn't help myself.

But she only smiled again. Then before I could speak again, she opened her mouth and began to sing.

The song filled the cavern room, flowing and flickering like the light that played across the walls. The stalactites broke up the sound but instead of ruining it, it seemed to echo and change, reverberating through the room.

It was lovely and horrible and painful all mixed together

in a way that seemed to vibrate through my skin and bones. My head pulsed and ached with it.

With effort, I forced my head to turn away. Jack had fallen backwards onto his back and lay writhing on the floor. His eyes were rolled up in his head. As I watched his body convulsed. A trickle of blood dribbled from his ears.

The volume of the song increased. I felt it pounding at my skull, trying to drive away my thoughts. I clenched my teeth, felt my jaw begin to ache.

Resist. I had to resist her.

But what good would it do if I didn't do something to stop her?

What good would it do at all?

Why fight so hard anyway?

It wasn't like it would do any good. Look at Jack.

There was no escape. Even KJ hadn't escaped. Not really. One more burst of song and he would come racing back.

There was no escape.

There was no resistance.

There was only the song.

Relax and let it in....

No!

I bit the inside of my mouth. Pain sliced through the fog of my thoughts. The hot iron taste of blood simmered on my tongue. I felt the words, the pressure dissipate. I shook my head.

No, she wasn't going to get me with that song.

The song shifted, from a call and lure to a cry of outrage.

Ligeia stood at the top of her pedestal, hands curled into claws, mouth open in a snarl. Her song was now full of fury and rage. The greenish-blue light swirled around the walls like flames. The stalactites shivered and shook above me.

I resisted. And boy, did that piss her off.

I took a stumbling step back, past Jack who still writhed on the floor, but instead of wriggling in ecstasy, he jerked in pain.

Another step. My legs shook. The song battered at me, tearing with notes that felt like hooks in my flesh. I felt wetness dribbling down the sides of my neck. My own ears were bleeding. But I still managed another step back.

As my weight settled back onto my left leg and I shifted my right foot back, it suddenly occurred to me to wonder how.

How was I still moving away from her?

A Siren's call was supposed to be irresistible. Yet I had rejected her, and even now as she shrieked at me in anger, I still managed to move away from her.

How?

How was I doing it? Not even KJ had been able to resist her and he'd always been stronger with magic than me.

How was I able to resist?

It didn't make any sense.

None of this made any sense. How was I the only one who had remembered KJ at all? Remembered my old life, my friends, my cases, the way it should be?

Not even the Council had remembered KJ.

The Council...

Thinking of them brought something they had said back to me.

There is only one child born in the Kringle family per generation, one child to carry on the Santa Claus position.

Even my mother had mentioned that once, that usually there was only one child born to the Kringles.

Until there was me.

A second son. Upsetting the balance.

Was that enough?

I knew how delicate magic could be. For all its strength, it depended on precision. Change a variable, even slightly, like an extra pinch of salt, and everything could go out of whack. It might explain my resistance to the Siren.

I was an unnatural event in the universe.

So in an unnatural event, maybe I had some ability to resist that no one else had, enough to remember the past, to remember KJ.

And even to resist the Siren's call.

The shriek around me reached a higher pitch. Rumbling sounded through the room, coming from the door behind me. Even over her scream, I heard something battering along the hall.

She wasn't just shrieking in anger after all. She was calling something else.

Maybe something with long, slimy tentacles.

Burnt coals.

My chest started to ache in sympathetic remembrance. I

so did not want to be crushed. I suspected this time the tentacle wouldn't stop until I popped like a Christmas cracker.

There was only one thing to do.

Answer her call.

But maybe not in the way she desired.

I stopped my backwards lurching and began to shuffle toward the pedestal. I kept my eyes fixed on the rocky steps, avoiding the Siren's gaze. Her shriek reverberated around me, still pounding against me, feeling like a physical force against my flesh. My body seemed to ache in rhythm to the shriek. My heart began to pound to the beat.

Blood from my wounded inner cheek still dribbled onto my tongue. I swallowed but the iron taste still coated my mouth. I turned my head and spat it out. Red spittle glistened on the floor, seemed to pick up the flickering, flowing light. Seemed to be calling me.

Maybe giving in to her wouldn't be so bad.

No, stop, I had to keep concentrating. Even as I moved toward her. I focused on the feel of my boots hitting the ground. I couldn't hear it but I imagined each step would click down on the hard surface. Soon I was passing Jack again.

He now lay still on the floor. His eyes were rolled back in his head. Blood smeared on the sides of his head and pooled on the floor, matting his wavy hair. But his chest was still rising and falling. He was still breathing, still alive.

Such as it was.

I couldn't help him, not now, so I kept moving. With every step, her song shifted, becoming more alluring again. By the time I reached the bottom of her pedestal, she was practically cooing at me. A sweet-sour scent of salt and seaweed wafted over me, but instead of turning my stomach, it attracted me.

Before I realized it, I was halfway up the pedestal steps to her.

Swirling snow. My resistance wasn't as strong as I'd thought. The closer I got to her, the stronger the pull, and the weaker my resolve.

This was not good. Not good at all.

My plan, such as it was, had been to get close enough to muzzle her. I still had my scarf around my neck which could gag her and blind her. I even had tissues in my parka pocket, courtesy of my mother, who always kept a stock of tissues in the pockets of every coat in the house. The cold weather of the North Pole always caused runny noses and my mother believed in being prepared. A large enough wad of tissue could stop up the Siren's ears.

Blind, deafened, and struck dumb, maybe then there would be a way to help Lacie. If she was still in there.

But how was I going to do it if I couldn't control myself?

The iron taste of blood still lingered on my tongue. My inner cheek no longer throbbed.

Time to wake it up.

I stabbed my tongue at the sore spot in my cheek. Pain flared again, shooting tendrils along my jaw and up to my temple. The fogginess of my thoughts seemed to clear, even as the song swirled around me.

Closer I climbed. Another few steps. The Siren opened her arms. The stench of sour seaweed thickened as I moved upward. Her song battered at me, urged me onward, promised soothing warmth and burning passion.

I tasted the blood in my mouth.

My hands twitched.

One final step.

She reached for me.

I had the scarf in my hands. Her song shifted to alarm. Then outrage.

I swung the scarf around her head.

Her nails clawed at me. Scraping my parka.

Lifted higher. She scratched at my face.

I jerked back, losing my grip on the scarf. She grabbed at it.

I caught one end. Stuffed it into her mouth.

The song muffled.

Her eyes bulged. Burning with rage. Hatred. The scarf barely muffled her shriek.

Without the song overpowering everything, the rumble from the hall filled the room. Something slammed into the door. Once, twice.

The door swung open.

A tentacle burst through.

It surged into the room, whipping from side to side, as if

searching for me. I could almost feel it squeezing me again, crushing the life out of me.

I darted behind the Siren. Grabbed the other end of the scarf and wound it around her head. Then wrapped my arms around her, pinning her arms to her sides.

The tentacle snapped to the right. The tip grazed Jack's legs. Instantly the tentacle froze. Then it flashed around his body, lifting it high into the air. Jack's head lolled to the side, his eyes still closed. Then I saw his chest rise and fall.

He was still alive!

I cried out but the tentacle was already squeezing. The thick muscle rippled as it compressed tighter and tighter. Jack jerked, even unconscious, trying to escape. His face reddened.

The image shimmered as tears filled my eyes. I wanted to look away. Couldn't. Couldn't stop it.

Jack snapped under the pressure. His limbs hung loose and floppy. The tentacle continued to curl around it, squeezing even more. After a moment, Jack disappeared under the seething muscles and quivering suckers.

The tentacle snapped back through the door, dragging Jack with it. The last I saw of him was a booted foot flopping against the floor.

Where was the sea beast taking him?

I didn't want to know.

But I had a feeling it would be back once it realized Jack wasn't me. It had come specifically to get me, to protect the

Siren, and when it learned it had grabbed the wrong person...

Well, I didn't want to be around for that.

But where could I go? Return to the aquarium? That would put everyone there at risk. Maybe KJ and Venir could escape but Mallory would be defenseless. Not to mention all the people nearby. Even on a cold March night, there were too many possibilities for people to get hurt.

I had to find somewhere else, somewhere deserted.

And then what? How was I going to stop this tentacled sea beast?

I had no idea. But I would think of something.

I hoped.

CHAPTER
TWENTY-FOUR

It took some doing, but I managed to tie one end of the scarf around Ligeia's head and the other end around her wrists behind her back. At least it allowed me to step away from her, from the fishy, sour stench of her.

Through the scarf, her voice was muffled but I knew it wouldn't last for long. Already I could feel a tingling in the air. Her voice wasn't the only magical thing about her although it was probably her strongest weapon. If she managed to cast a spell, it might incapacitate me long enough for the tentacled sea beast to return.

I wasn't going to be here when that happened.

And neither was Ligeia.

At least this form of her, using the body of Lacie Trent. I didn't think the woman was still inside there. When I'd held her back, locking her arms to her sides, I hadn't felt any trace of human left in her. I should have. Any magical possession I'd heard of couldn't extinguish the spark of humanity so completely unless the person was dead.

Lacie Trent, whomever she had been, was gone even as her body remained, a slave to the Siren.

And, by extension, to the sea beast.

First things first though. We had to get out of here. I considered *winking* but I wasn't sure if the Siren's influence would cause issues. There was only one other thing I could think of.

Although they hadn't been much help.

With one hand clenched tight on her arm, I closed my eyes and focused. Instead of the hard rock under my feet, I felt the shifting of dust. Instead of the watery, sour smell, I breathed in dry, flat air. Instead of the shimmering, watery blue light on the walls, there was darkness with only a dim light to illuminate the area around me.

I felt the Siren struggle against me. Her voice, still muffled by the scarf, gurgled out a few notes.

My heart pounded. Steady. I breathed. Focus again, don't let her distract me. Feel the dust and the dirt. See the darkness of the cavern around me.

Cool, dry air brushed my cheeks. Dust tickled my nostrils. I opened my eyes.

Dimness with the sense of a yawning cavern around us.

Beside me, the Siren growled.

A pool of light brightened around us. The familiar torches burned at four corners, mapping out a square space.

Beyond the reach of the light, I sensed the greater depths of this cavern, the rock walls, the uneven stone floor, the mountain rising high above us, a protection, a shelter for this chamber.

For the Council.

They hadn't remembered KJ before but maybe they would know how to stop a Siren and a sea beast.

"What is this?" a voice called out from behind me.

I felt them now, closer in the dimness than they'd ever been before. I sensed them standing just beyond the reach of the torches' light.

"This is the Siren," I said. "She caused the time shift, the change in reality. She seduced my brother KJ and wiped him from the world. I need to destroy her or send her back to set things right."

I felt rather than heard murmurs around me. They were having one of their conversations that they didn't want me to hear. Impatience made me tap my boot on the uneven stone underneath me. For a Council that was supposed to be all knowing and all powerful, they didn't seem that impressive. I was getting a little tired of their inability to help.

"Hey, how about talking to me?" I said. "You guys are supposed to be taking care of the balance between Realms. I'm only on retainer and I seem to be doing a better job than you are."

Silence.

Not even the sense of an unheard conversation around me.

Uh oh.

Beside me, the Siren chuckled.

I swallowed with a suddenly dry throat. Had I overstepped?

The silence lengthened, stretching my nerves even farther. I strained to see beyond the light of the torches but it seemed to blend into deep darkness beyond. I listened but only the occasional gurgles from the Siren broke the silence. Each gurgle was a little louder, a little clearer. Soon she would burst forth with song again and then what?

Could I shove my parka in her mouth?

A pebble skittered across the light in front of me. A hooded shape appeared at the edge, still more shadow than solid form.

"She did not change the world," a voice said from deep in the hood.

I cleared my throat. "She did," I said. "She seduced my brother."

The hood gave a single nod. "She did accomplish this but she did no other."

I frowned. What did that mean?

"We changed the world, shifted the reality," the voice said, in answer to my unasked question. "It was the only way to prevent destabilization of the Kringle dynasty and the Santa Claus legacy. We shifted the reality to remove KJ from the lineage to prevent the Siren and her accomplices from gaining direct access to the North Pole magic."

"You did that?" My shout echoed back to me from the cavernous space around me. "You left my brother to rot?"

"We removed him from succession," the voice said. "Until such time as he could be retrieved."

"Oh really?" Anger made my whole body tremble. I wanted to step forward and confront that hooded figure directly but that would have meant letting go of the Siren. No way was I doing that. I had to settle for sarcasm.

"You were retrieving him, were you?" I asked. "You didn't seem to be doing a very good job."

"Indeed," the voice intoned. "We sent you."

The words pressed against me. Huh?

"Swirling snow, you didn't even remember him," I said.

"Didn't we?" Amusement tinged the voice.

They'd lied to me.

Why?

To stop me from leaning on them for help. I saw it now. They weren't going to come to my rescue. Ever. Whatever I did or whatever happened to me, I wasn't high enough up on the chain for them to care.

Then why remove KJ from succession? Why put me in the line of fire but then refuse to help me?

Normally I thought I could understand or parse out the motivation for most magical creatures but this Council was beyond me. I sensed layers that I would never fathom.

I let out the breath that I felt like I'd been holding for days. My shoulders sagged. So they had remembered KJ but denied it in order to...what? Keep me in the succession for

Santa Claus or force me to go after KJ on my own? I suspected either worked for them.

"Fine," I said. "I retrieved him and I caught the Siren. Now you have to help me get rid of her. Her and the sea beast."

I felt a ripple through the air, like the murmur of voices. The torches, which normally just sent out light, seemed to radiate heat. I felt sweat pool on my collarbone. The space between my shoulder blades itched.

In front of me, the hooded figure took a step closer. Its form became almost solid. Darkness filled the space under the hood but I sensed a face inside. If I had to guess, I imagined it was staring at me intently.

"What sea beast?" it asked.

"Oh no, don't start that again," I said. "You know very well what sea beast. The one that's been working with the Siren." I glanced over at her, standing still beside me. Under the edge of my scarf, the corner of her mouth seemed to twitch in a grin.

I didn't like the look of that.

"We do not know this sea beast," the figure insisted. "This is the truth. We only saw the Siren."

Even with the heat from the torches, I felt a chill tighten my muscles. I gripped the Siren's arm harder even though she stood silent and still. It still felt like she was going to make a break for it and I wanted to be ready.

"Let me get this straight," I said. "You lied when you said you didn't remember KJ but now you're saying you don't know this sea beast and that's the truth. You expect me to believe you?"

Lying. They had to be lying. I wanted them to be lying, for whatever strange, unknowable reason only know to them. Please let them be lying.

Please.

The hooded figure nodded.

"We speak the truth to you now, Noel Kringle. We do not know this sea beast you speak of."

Damn the halls.

If they didn't know, if they really didn't know, if they hadn't even seen it, then the danger was greater than even they could handle. Whatever was breaking through from the Magical Realms was overpowering. Impossible to stop.

And I was standing smack in the middle of the way.

Beside me, the Siren chuckled.

A hideous screech filled the air. The form in front of me jerked. Then was yanked away. Cries of alarm and panic mingled with the screeching. I heard and felt entities fleeing. Dust clouds puffed into the air, creating an almost foggy appearance and diffusing the light. Through the twilight, I saw another figure in a hooded cloak hurrying away. Something lashed out and grabbed it, yanking it deeper into darkness.

A tentacle.

Burnt coals, somehow it had followed me here.

No, it had followed the Siren.

She still had that curled lip, almost like a smile, as she

tried to chew on my scarf. There had to be some kind of psychic link between her and the sea beast.

That meant no matter where I took her, the beast would follow.

Okay, then, sucker, you're it.

I grabbed the Siren's arm and yanked. As she stumbled, trying to regain her footing, I focused and *winked.*

The moment seemed to stretch, like a note being held long past expiration. It was the Siren, fighting against my magic. But even as she fought, I felt the cold, calmness of the North Pole, centring me. As long as I had that connection, I knew she wouldn't be able to resist.

We landed on the tile in front of the huge aquarium, facing the row of seats that stretched up in the auditorium.

"Noel, watch out!"

KJ's shout made me turn. Beside me, the Siren had wiggled free of the bonds holding her hands. She tugged the scarf from her lips. Opened her mouth.

KJ landed a slap on her face. The shock of it made her turn toward him.

I grabbed the end of the scarf and stuffed it into her mouth again.

KJ held her arms as she struggled against me. I tied the scarf tight around her head but after wrapping it several times, the ends were too short to tie her hands.

"Use this."

Mallory held out the cloth belt from his trench coat.

KJ spun her to face away from me and I secured her hands behind her back.

"We thought that...thing had killed you," KJ said. His expression was grim.

"Not yet," I said. "But I expect it'll be here soon to try to finish the job."

I told them about finding myself back at the Siren's lair, Jack's death, and escaping to the Council, only to have the sea beast follow us.

"So you weren't kidding about things being wrong here," Mallory said.

I shook my head.

KJ's expression had gone from grim to blank.

"They abandoned me," he said. "They pulled me out of succession."

I didn't like the look on his face.

"Only until I could rescue you," I said. "As soon as we stop the Siren and the sea beast, I'm sure everything will go back to normal. You'll have your place again."

"And just how are we gonna do that?" Mallory asked.

Good question. The combined might of KJ, Venir, myself and the reindeer had barely managed to hold the sea beast off. Then it had taken on the Council. Had they been destroyed? No way to know unless I went back and I wasn't going to do that.

"KJ, can you remember anything about your captivity?" I asked. "Anything that might help us stop the beast or sever the tie between it and the Siren?"

Venir coughed and cleared his throat. "Um, the reindeer might be able to help with that."

I turned to face him. The Christmas Elf stood near the first row of chairs. The reindeer clustered around him, some head turning from him toward me, others scouting the air above us, as if looking for trouble. Donner gave a snort and stomped his foot as he glared at the Siren. Beside him, Blitzen nudged him as if to get him to pay attention.

"How?" I asked.

Venir glanced at the reindeer that clustered around him. His white curls stuck out from his head in disarray. A smudge of dirt was smeared along the right side of his jaw. Dark circles hung from his eyes. He looked tired and almost done in.

I glanced around the rest of the group. They didn't look much better, even Mallory who wasn't really equipped to deal with this kind of magical battle.

But KJ looked the worst.

I had tried not to notice, but after seeing the fatigue on Venir, it was impossible to ignore it on KJ. He had never even started to recover from his captivity in the Siren's lair. It was only by sheer force of his stubborn will that he stood upright without swaying. That and maybe a little bit of North Pole magic. But it still didn't wipe out the gaunt look on his face or the way his shoulders seemed to droop.

But all of that paled to the missing gleam in his eyes. That confident, assured glint was missing in KJ's eyes and I didn't know how to get it back.

I would find a way though. Assuming the sea beast didn't kill us all first.

I turned back to Venir.

"So how can the reindeer help?"

Venir cleared his throat again. "Well, ya know how Elves can talk to the reindeer. We hear'em too but it's not vocal, not in our ears. We hear'em in our head."

A psychic link. I gazed over the reindeer. They were all looking back at me and although I couldn't hear it, I could almost imagine their thoughts flowing at me.

I was starting to catch on to Venir's idea.

And it was giving me an even better one.

"Can they tune into the link between the Siren and the sea beast?" I asked.

Venir glanced around him. Blitzen lowered his head to gaze at Venir, then snorted.

"They can try but it may be too strong for them to break," he said.

"I don't want them to break it," I said. "I want them to intercept it." I grinned. "I want to send the sea beast somewhere the Siren isn't. Divide and conquer."

"You have a plan," Mallory said.

I nodded. "I have a plan."

CHAPTER
TWENTY-FIVE

"Great," Mallory said. "What's the plan?"

"I can't tell you," I said.

Mallory cocked his head. From the diffuse lighting coming from the embedded lights in the auditorium ceiling, I noticed stubble dotting Mallory's cheeks. It looked more grey than brown.

"You don't really have a plan, do you," he said.

"I do," I said. "But I really can't talk about it."

I gave a meaningful glance toward the Siren.

Saying anything out loud would get back to the sea beast.

After a moment, Mallory caught the look and nodded.

"Keep an eye on her, will you?" I said. I moved over to KJ and took his arm. It only took a slight tug to get him to follow me. Although he stood a couple of inches taller than me, he seemed to have shrunk, his head bowed, his shoulders hunched. His feet dragged on the floor as he walked.

I led him a quarter of the way up the aisle, far enough that I gauged Ligeia couldn't hear us. I made sure our backs were turned; I didn't want the Siren to even see our lips move, just in case. I gave a quick glance back to make sure both Mallory and Venir were casing her. Even the reindeer had spread out to encircle her.

I turned back to KJ.

"I can't imagine what you went through," I said. "But I need you to tell me anything you think might help us stop her, stop that sea beast."

He shrugged. Weariness and apathy seemed to have settled on his shoulders like Dad's cloak. It wasn't a look that suited him.

"KJ..."

"What do you want me to say, Noel?" he said. "You want blow by blow details? You want to know what it's like to have someone you cared about turn out to be something evil? You want to know what it's like to have your life stolen away and no one even remembers you?"

His voice grew louder in anguish.

"I remember," I said. I kept my voice low. KJ pressed his lips tight together and turned away. He stared up the aisle toward the back of the auditorium where the shadows were thickest.

"I remember the snow forts we used to build when we were kids," I said. "That time we built that one wall so high I thought it was higher than the reindeer barn. It even soared over your head. I remember you boosting me on your shoulders so I could pack snow on the top and I accidentally dumped a handful of snow down your neck."

A muscle on KJ's jaw jumped and I knew he was suppressing either a grin or a scowl. At the time, he'd yelped and almost danced a jig trying to get the snow out of his coat, but he'd never dropped me.

Although after he'd put me down, he did dump snow down my pants.

"I remember when we tried to bake that cake for mother's birthday," I said. "And you thought baking soda was the same thing as baking powder."

The jaw muscle jumped again as KJ clenched his teeth.

"I told you it wasn't the same," I said, "but you didn't listen to me. It even smelled kinda funny while it was baking but you said it was fine. And it was fine right up until mom took a bite. Yuck!" I stuck out of my tongue.

KJ whirled on me.

"That was you. You handed me the baking soda."

He jabbed a finger into the front of my parka. His hand was clenched so tight his knuckles had bleached white.

At least it was a reaction.

"The Siren," I said.

He yanked his hand back as though my words burned him. He glared at me but at least this time he didn't turn away.

"I thought you were going to have reindeer send the sea

beast away," he said. "Why do you need to know about my captivity then?"

"Every piece of information is vital," I said. "This is part of a pattern of menace trying to bleed into the Human Realm. It's been happening for years and it's escalating. This sea beast might just be the thing that breaks the membrane between the realms wide open. The only thing standing in the way is Dad and the North Pole."

KJ sighed. His shoulders drooped even lower. All energy seemed to drain down his body into the carpeted steps we stood on.

"I don't remember much," he said. "Every time she came into the room she began to sing and when she sang it was like my mind went away. All I have left are fragments."

I frowned. That didn't sound at all like Jack's experience.

Maybe the Siren hadn't lured KJ as a mate after all.

The Council had pulled him out of succession.

My stomach clenched. The Siren had been trying to break KJ. How far had she gotten? From his state... No, I couldn't even speculate. I wouldn't speculate.

I cleared my throat. "Tell me about the fragments."

"Christmas," KJ said. "I seem to remember her asking about Christmas. About how the Kringles had got the Santa Claus appointment. How the transition happened."

I shivered. Had this been why the Council had pulled KJ out of the succession? Had he been permanently compromised?

No, I couldn't believe that.

"Anything else?" I asked.

His brow furled. He stared at the shadows in the far end of the auditorium. His face looked gaunt and troubled. Haunted. Finally he shook his head.

"Nothing, even when she kept playing Jingle Bells over and over."

Jingle Bells. That had always been one of KJ's favourite carols, although he'd taken to denying it in recent years. How would the Siren know that? I couldn't imagine it would come up in conversation with Lacie Trent. Would it?

"Did you mention that song to Lacie?"

KJ shook his head.

How had she known? Could she read his mind? But wouldn't he have to be thinking about the song for her to catch it? It wouldn't be something that KJ thought about often, especially in March.

Unless someone who knew him told her.

It suddenly felt like gravity was weighing heavier on me. All my muscles wanted to sag, to spill me onto the floor in a puddle.

Had someone who knew KJ betrayed him? Who could it be?

As far as I knew, the only people he knew outside of the North Pole were the people I'd introduced him to, like Mallory and Shirl.

That left only people at the North Pole.

An Elf.

No, that couldn't be.

Could it?

I remembered how KJ had sneered at Venir before, had played a part in his demotion. Had there been other Elves that KJ had cracked down on? For the most part, Elves obeyed the rules but there were still the occasional slacker. Like any group, there were the rebels.

Had KJ made enemies who resented him enough to try to break the power of the North Pole? Did they even know that was what they were doing?

Maybe it had started out as just a prank, a way to get back at KJ.

And it had turned into something world-threatening.

"KJ, when you were doing the workshop schedules for Dad, were there any Elves you were having trouble with? Any who seemed to be late for shifts or ran below quota?"

A startled look crossed his face.

"What does that have to do with anything?"

"Maybe nothing," I said. "But every detail matters."

He shook his head and sighed with exasperation.

"Fine, fine. Let's see. Most of them just needed reminding to stay focused, not get distracted by singing carols or raiding the candy cane stash. A few weren't suited for the workshop. A couple asked for reassignment. A few I had to reassign myself."

"Who were they?" I asked. "The ones you had to reassign?"

"I still don't see what this has to do with it," he said. "They were Stalistar, Felric, and Belogan. Stalistar went to packaging, Felric to the stables, and Belogan to maintenance. They all seemed happier in their new assignments."

His tone sounded defensive, like I was accusing him of pushing them out of the workshop positions on purpose. All the Christmas Elves coveted working in the workshop building toys because it seemed so glamorous but it wasn't for everyone. It took focus, discipline, dexterity, and ingenuity, not to mention a particular kind of Christmas magic to build so many toys in so short a time. The pressure was enormous. Not every Elf could or wanted to handle it.

But what if one of those Elves had been disappointed by their transfer?

Or worse, what if they had been fine with it and somehow betrayed confidences by accident?

I thought back on each of the Elves. I didn't know Stalistar or Belogan personally but I'd seen glowing reports of their work. I couldn't imagine they would say anything.

But Felric.

The stables. I remembered him. He'd been one of the Elves talking about how much of a disaster I was as an heir to the Santa Claus title.

They certainly weren't wrong.

But as I thought back about it, he hadn't been malicious in his comments. He'd shown me great compassion, saying I still had a long time to get a hang of the job.

I couldn't believe he would betray KJ or I on purpose.

But it might just have been inadvertent.

And still as damaging.

The tiniest wedge that could bring the North Pole to its knees, and destroy the protection it afforded against the Magical Realms.

From KJ's expression I knew he blamed himself, no matter how ridiculous it was. It wouldn't matter to him that he had been trapped and enthralled on purpose, he would still see it as his responsibility, his failing to protect the North Pole, to protect the Santa Claus legacy.

"I think you weren't the only one fooled by the Siren," I said. "I think it, or whatever is behind it, has been planning this for a long time. You were just one more step toward destroying the North Pole. You couldn't know or suspected. Why would you? Nothing you did caused this but you can help me stop it."

KJ's shoulders still slumped but he stood a little straighter.

"How?" he asked.

"You have a great bond with the reindeer. You're going to instruct them on interrupting the link between Ligeia and the sea beast. Have them send it to the South Pole. Then we'll take her back to the North Pole."

"Are you crazy? That's exactly where she wants to go and it won't be long before that creature comes after her."

I nodded. "I know. And we'll be waiting."

KJ gaped at me and then shook his head. "You really are crazy if you think we'll be able to contain her and that thing. If she gets loose even for a moment, she'll even enthrall Dad."

"She won't get loose," I said.

"You can't guarantee it."

"You have to trust me, KJ. I know what I'm doing."

He stared at me and I did the best I could to look competent. Kept a serious look on my face. Had no spinach in my teeth.

He had to listen to me. This was the only way. Only at the North Pole, with full access to my Christmas magic, would I be able to pull this off.

Of course, it could also end in disaster and the destruction of the North Pole.

But there wasn't any other way to stop this. Any other action was just a holding response, and it wouldn't hold back the sea beast forever. I had to stop it at the core. And there was only one place to do it.

But I needed KJ's help. If he would only trust me.

For once.

Finally he sighed.

"Okay," he said. "What do we do?"

CHAPTER

TWENTY-SIX

I led him back toward the Siren. As we drew closer, I gestured Venir toward us. The Christmas Elf hurried over, his fluffy white curls bouncing on his head. His large pointed ears quivered. In the dim lighting of the auditorium, he looked drawn and serious.

"You and KJ will instruction the reindeer to disrupt the link between the Siren and the sea beast," I whispered. "Send it to the South Pole."

Venir nodded and moved back toward the reindeer who still surrounded the trapped Siren.

KJ gave me a final questioning look. It was the most him he'd looked since I found him, the same skeptical, wry expression that lifted his left eye brow and curled one corner of his lips almost into a smile.

My brother was still in there, flaws and all. I gave him a nod.

Then it all fell apart, like a shattering Christmas bulb.

Snorts and stomps sounded behind KJ. The reindeer were getting agitated. Both Mallory and Venir were trying to calm them but they continued to get more and more upset. Then behind them, I noticed the water in the huge aquarium sloshing back and forth.

Damn the halls, we were too late! The sea beast was already coming.

Then a chorus of song burst forth.

The Siren had chewed through the scarf.

The slight smile on KJ's face vanished. He almost folded in on himself. Misery flashed across his face then disappeared beneath a mask of blankness.

Behind him, Venir and Mallory had frozen in position. The muscles on Venir's face twitched as he tried to fight but Mallory had been completely overpowered. He had a blank, dreamy look on his face. His hand hung loose at the sides of his body.

Even the reindeer stood frozen, entranced.

I hadn't secured the Siren well enough and it was going to be our doom.

Wait a minute.

Why was I still able to have a coherent thought? Why was I even still able to look at her and even move?

I angled around KJ, stepping around Mallory. From this

side, I would be able to come at her from behind. Maybe I could secure the scarf around her mouth again.

It still didn't answer how I was able to resist her. I'd felt it affect me before. Sort of.

Was I becoming more resistant with each exposure to her?

It still didn't answer the why question.

The Kringle line was supposed to only have one child. Yet here I was. Someone outside the rules. So maybe the rules didn't always work on me.

Just one more step.

Tentacles erupted from the aquarium, spraying water everywhere. I felt myself get drenched again. I swiped water from my eyes...

Multiple tentacles reached out. They grabbed several reindeer who didn't make a sound as they were yanked off their feet. One each slithered around Venir and Mallory. Another headed toward KJ.

Through the now soaring song of the Siren, I heard her laugh.

Triumphant.

All my plans, all my efforts, wasted and useless. Like I was.

Nothing I had ever done had come to anything.

Now I'd led my friends straight into disaster. Once they were dead there would be no one to stop Ligeia and the sea beast from taking the North Pole.

Nothing to stop them from breaking down the barrier that protected the Human Realm.

Nothing...

Except me.

Because her song didn't have sway over me any more.

Ligeia wasn't important. Her song was weak and fading. Already I could hear the harshness in the notes, the breaks in the melody. Too much breathiness. She'd never be able to hit the high notes.

I focused those thoughts on her and I could see her falter. Somehow she'd linked herself to me, forcing her thoughts into me but it hadn't occurred to her that I'd be able to send my own thoughts back.

And I knew just how to hit her. Pick on all the little flaws in her song and show her how they were expanding.

Her eyes narrowed with weariness. Uncertainty filled her song. With each hesitant chord, she stumbled further.

I turned my back on her. She wasn't even important enough to focus on any more. I had something else to contend with.

The sea beast.

More water sloshed from the top of the aquarium as another couple of tentacles flopped over the top edge. The suckers pressed onto the tile floor. The thick muscles of the tentacles bulged as they tightened.

In the dimness, I watched as a huge body began to rise up.

The sea beast had decided to fully reveal itself. No longer

just showing its many tentacles. A domed head rose up, streaming water off its grey, glistening surface. A single, huge eye blinked, iris dilating into a tiny point even in the dim light. It probably was used to light in the depths of whatever ocean it had been called forth from. Near the bottom of the body, close to the tentacles, was an opening that looked like a mouth. Rings of teeth glistened. The opening expanded and contracted, like it was anticipating tasting one of the items its tentacles had enveloped.

And one of those tentacles had almost reached KJ.

I darted forward. Water splashed up with each step. The fishy, sour stench filled my nostrils. I grabbed KJ's arm and jerked back.

The tentacle swiped inches from his face.

We staggered just out of reach. Shrieks filled the air. The sea beast howled in anger that I had denied it its prize.

Yet it had grabbed Venir, Mallory, Comet, and Dancer.

As the Siren's song faltered, the other reindeer scattered throughout the auditorium. Blitzen and Cupid took to the air, hovering near the ceiling. Rudolph and the others spread through the seating area, forming a ragged semi-circle, just out of reach of the tentacles.

Behind KJ and I.

Which meant we were still within reach.

KJ still slumped against me. He shook his head, coming out of his stupor.

Good thing as the sea beast was making another grab for us.

I tightened my grip on his arm, pinching his skin hard enough to make him wince. I had to get his attention, make sure he was hearing me.

"Go right," I yelled.

A tentacle slashed forward. I jumped left. Pushed KJ to the right.

He skidded, landed on his knees.

The tentacle lashed toward him.

He hunched, dropped his head.

The tentacle sailed above him.

Missed.

We couldn't keep dodging forever. We had to do something. But my idea to disrupt the link between Ligeia and the sea beast hadn't worked. It was too late to try to send it somewhere else.

I had to deal with it here and now.

Even as it tightened its grip on my friends.

I had to do something. But what?

I felt helpless as I watched the tentacles waving in the dimness above the aquarium, wrapped around Venir and Mallory and the two reindeer. As the Siren's song faltered, they had all woken. Mallory and Venir struggled, shouting for help. Comet and Dancer bleated in fear.

I couldn't watch but I had to. I'd failed. It was my fault.

No. Not yet. I couldn't give up. Not when my friends needed me. Not when KJ needed me.

But maybe it wasn't all up to me, or at least not just me.

KJ had already climbed to his feet although he still swayed a little. His hands were closed into fists.

"Get Rudolph," I said. "Distract it."

"What are you goin' do?" KJ said.

I glanced back at the sea beast's glittering eye. I couldn't tell if it understood us but I didn't want to take the chance.

"You'll see."

KJ nodded. He flicked a gesture at Rudolph. The reindeer leapt to his side. KJ climbed onto his back and they soared into the air, just as another tentacle reached for them.

I managed to stagger back as it swept the air before me. I felt the sucker brush my cheek as I jerked my head back.

Too close.

It was swinging back, closer now. The chairs were at my back. No way I could scramble over them in time.

An outraged bleat sounded. Hooves flashed in front of my face, kicking at the tentacle as it reached for me.

The tentacle reared back.

Blitzen landed on the tile floor before me. He swung his head, antlers slashing toward the tentacle.

I leapt onto his back.

Blitzen launched into the air.

The floor tilted. Gravity grabbed at me. I felt myself sliding. I lunged for Blitzen's neck, wrapped my arms around it as the reindeer spun to avoid a slashing tentacle.

The world spun around me. I caught sight of the sea beast, tentacles waving as it tried to grab at us. I glimpsed KJ and Rudolph darting just out of reach as well. Movement blurred as the remaining reindeer also leapt forward. Hooves and antlers slashed and punched at the waving tentacles.

It was definitely something, but I knew it wasn't enough.

We had to do more to bring this creature down.

And I had an idea of how to do it but it was going to take all of us. Together.

As Blitzen soared above another reaching tentacle, I waved across the room at KJ. He and Rudolph were on the other side of the creature. The glow of Rudolph's nose blazed form and I noticed how several tentacles waved in front of him, as if to ward the reindeer away.

Then I noticed the single eye blinking and water as the massive head tilted away.

Of course!

Being from the great depths, the sea beast would not be used to strong light or loud music, or anything that would assault the senses.

Sure the Siren's song sang to it, communicated with it, but I couldn't imagine that it would like some other kind of music.

Say, for instance, loud, boisterous Christmas carols.

KJ *did* like Jingle Bells.

KJ nodded to show he'd noticed my wave.

"Light 'em up," I shouted. "Rudolph, go for the eye."

Even from across the room I could see the smile blossom on KJ's face. He hunched over the reindeer's neck. As one, he and Rudolph darted around several waving tentacles and aimed for the single eye.

The yawning mouth gave a screeching roar. The head lifted and yanked forward faster than I thought possible. The mouth opened, sharp teeth flashing, reaching for KJ and Rudolph.

I closed my eyes and focused on my Christmas magic. With all the reindeer and a Christmas Elf nearby, I could feel it like a constant hum. As I focused, it seemed to leap up inside me.

I called every bit of Christmas to me that I could. I heard Christmas carols blaring in the air. Huge Christmas trees, sparkling with shimmering balls and shining tinsel. The sweet, delicious scent of Christmas cookies, candy canes, cinnamon, egg nog, and nut meg. Bells ringing. Choirs singing. Lights flashing, sparkling, shining.

And with it cold and snow. Big snowflakes drifting from the sky. Snow drifts piling on the sides of aquarium. Icicles hanging from the ceiling.

My head pounded. Pain laced through my temples and down my neck. My entire body shivered as it alternated between hot and cold. Christmas magic, always like a shimmering light in me, felt like a burning laser. I felt like I could barely control the force of it pouring through me.

I opened my eyes.

A row of Christmas trees penned in the sea beast. It slashed and hit at the trees but tinsel, lights and balls got caught up in the suckers, weighing them down, binding them. Comet had already managed to wiggle free and was now diving at the tentacle that held onto Mallory. As I watched, Comet speared the tentacle with his antlers then started thrashing his head back and forth. Brackish blood sprayed from the torn flesh.

The sea beast screeched. The tentacle spasmed and flopped open.

Mallory fell several feet to the floor.

He rolled, his trench coat flapping around him. He finally stopped, got unsteadily to his feet, and started to stagger toward the chairs.

Now I just had to free Dancer and Venir and make sure KJ and Rudolph hadn't been eaten.

I directed Blitzen to the left, skirting the wall as we angled toward the back of the sea beast. I caught a red flare off the right side wall.

Rudolph and KJ were fighting to free Dancer.

Then I spotted Venir, huddled against the head of the sea beast. Somehow he'd gotten out of the tentacle grip and run up the tentacle to the head.

"Let's get him, Blitzen," I said.

I felt the reindeer agree.

As one, we dove forward, dodging between the branches of two Christmas trees. I caught a strong whiff of fresh pine then a waving tentacle made us dart upward.

We wove back and forth, getting closer and closer to Venir. Closer and closer to the sea beast's head.

I stayed focused on Venir. I had to make it think that was our only objective.

At the same time, I kept an eye on the icicles jutting down from the ceiling. There was a particularly sharp one that I liked.

It reminded me of the pen KJ had used. The one I'd tried to use in the spell.

Even as I thought it, I could see the way the icicles shifted. How it looked less like an icicle and more like a pen.

The force of the magic pouring through me bucked as I tried to hold it back. It wanted to be let loose, wanted free reign. But letting it loose so wildly was just as bad as letting the boundary protecting the Human Realm down.

Wild magic had no place here, even if it was Christmas magic.

I was starting to see why it might be so dangerous to have more than one Kringle child in each generation.

Jingle Bells started ringing and the song began to play.

I focused on Venir. We dodged one more tentacle and came level with the spot where the Elf huddled against the sea beast's head.

I waved at him. Venir saw me. His eyes were wide with terror, his face pale and shaken.

He hesitated a moment then raced forward. He took two steps and leapt into the air. His arms flailed around him. His panicked yell filled my ears.

Then I felt him land on the reindeer's back behind me.

Before he started slipping off.

I reached back, grabbed his pant leg and jerked.

Hard.

I felt him slam against me. He wrapped his arms around me, squeezing my diaphragm.

Then a tentacle slammed against Blitzen's head.

We went spinning through the air.

I felt Blitzen's confusion and pain as the images swirled around us. Lights and sound were overpowering. I had a hard time drawing a breath as something squeezed tighter and tighter.

Had a tentacle grabbed us? Was it already hauling us toward the huge mouth?

I heard soft whimpering. Venir. It was his arms crushing me. I had to unpeel them from me so I could catch my breath.

Blitzen hovered above the sea beast's head, slightly to the back, where its one eye couldn't see him. As the reindeer shook his head, I saw blood on his muzzle.

I tugged him forward. He continued hovering in place, not wanting to move.

"Just a little more ahead, Blitzen," I coaxed.

He gave a snort, blowing droplets of blood into the air. Finally he drifted forward. Another two tentacles waved closer and I felt the reindeer stiffen, getting ready to dart away.

But I couldn't let him. Not when I was to close.

"Get him out of here," I said to Venir behind me.

Before the Elf could reply. I let go of Blitzen's neck and leaned over to the left.

Way over.

And found myself falling in the air, aiming right for the top of the sea beast's head.

TWENTY-SEVEN

The flesh was soft and spongey when I landed but still hard enough to knock my breath from me. I lay gasping, clinging to the top of the sea beast's head. Already I could feel my body start to slide.

I dug my fingers in, felt thin hairs tickling my palms. Wiggling, I managed to pull myself upright, enough that I could sit without sliding.

From my vantage point, I could watch as the sea beast battled against my friends. The various reindeer darting forward like sparks jumping from a Christmas fire. The huge trees had formed a protective barrier but already they were starting to look battered by the constant slashing from the waving tentacles. As I watched, one of the suckers latched onto the top of a tree on the left and yanked it, tearing off the top quarter.

KJ on Rudolph swept across from left to right, leading several reindeer in a buzz, aiming for the creature's eye. Five tentacles flicked up, scattering the attack.

Giving me my chance.

I hopped to my feet but stayed low, feet wide apart to stop from slipping. I'd grown up in snow and ice. I was well practiced at staying on my feet in slippery situations.

I shimmied closer to the back of the creature's head. Above me, in the twinkling, shimmering light I spotted several icicles, including the one I had focused on before. As I squatted on the sea beast's head, I reached out of it, drawing it toward me with Christmas magic.

Underneath me, the creature jerked.

I fell backward, landing on my rump. A swirling rage flashed through me, turning everything around me inky blue. I blinked and light flooded back.

The sea beast's magic. I'd felt it, just as it felt mine.

Now it knew I was up here.

Already several tentacles were reaching upward, converging on my location.

Now or never.

I reached out.

For the icicle. For KJ's pen. For the candy cane Mother would give us when we cleaned our rooms. For KJ's pen.

For the telescoping arm that let Dad put the star on the top of the Christmas tree that they decorated every year right outside the Elves' workshop. For the rugby-like ball thrower that KJ used to throw a ball for the reindeer when they played a type of soccer in the air. For KJ's pen.

For the cane that I had taken from a rouge faerie in my other life, that had bonded to me and saved my life.

The tentacles flailed around me, swatting away all the magical things I conjured. Just missing the one thing I'd called more than the other's.

KJ's pen.

It felt solid and real in my right hand. I clicked the top, felt the tip protrude. Ready to write.

Ready to finish this.

I bent forward and jammed the pen into the back of the sea beast's head.

And let KJ's words flow.

The creature shrieked, mirroring the Siren's answering scream. I felt the essence of KJ's message flow through the pen, the excitement, the caution, the anxiety, the concern, the hope, and finally the request for help. Its own song of a new relationship gone wrong, destroyed by something unspeakable.

Poured directly into the sea beast's brain.

The tentacles that had been reaching for me began to flail wildly, slashing back and forth. I ducked down, pressing my cheek against the creature's slimy head.

I looked around.

All the tentacles were flailing and shuddering. No longer in a coordinated attack, they were still just as dangerous in their frantic bucking motions.

KJ motioned the reindeer back, out of reach. They all hovered in a semi-circle, jerking back when a tentacle got too close.

To my right, I spotted Venir on Blitzen. They tried to dart closer but were forced back by two waving tentacles.

I held onto the pen. And felt the message flowing through it weaken.

Beneath me, the beast stirred again.

Regaining its coherence.

It hadn't been enough.

I tightened my grip on the pen and jammed it in further.

Maybe I had something to add to my brother's message.

I closed my eyes on focused.

On all my cases, all my reports. A charity fraud. A goblin. Stone bodies. A possessed troll. A rogue faerie, hunting Dad. The Yule Lads, distorted by a spell. Cursed ground. Falling into a void so deep it was enough to almost trap me.

And the feelings. The pain, the fear, the anguish, the horror, I poured it all out into the pen.

I felt the sea beast shake beneath me like an earth quake. The howling rose to a fever pitch, drowning out even the shrieking call of the Siren. Then I felt something slam into me, sweeping me off the top of the creature's head.

For a moment, I hung holding onto the pen like a climber's anchor. Then my fingers slipped. I lost my grip on the pen.

I felt myself falling. Falling.

Then there was only darkness.

MY CHEEK BRUSHED AGAINST SOMETHING SOFT AND COOL AS I turned my head. It didn't feel like the sea beast's head. I pressed my hands down on either side of my body, found I was lying on my stomach. The surface felt soft to my palm and smooth.

I pushed myself up and opened my eyes.

In the dimness it took a moment for my eyes to focus. The walls were way too close to be the auditorium. I saw a dresser against the wall. Curtains covering the window.

I sat up completely and felt the bed sheet puddle in my lap.

My bedroom at the North Pole.

My stomach tightened. What had happened? How had I gotten here? Had we beaten the Siren and the sea beast? Had I imagined it all?

Where was KJ?

The thought drove out any fuzziness left in my brain. I yanked the covers back and jumped out of bed. I grabbed whatever clothes were closest and was out the door within a minute.

From downstairs, I smelled pancakes and sausages.

My stomach growled and my mouth watered even as anxiety spiked inside me. What reality was downstairs waiting for me now? The last time I'd woken up disoriented, no one remembered my brother.

Would they remember me this time?

Would it even be my family?

Was there even a Toronto for me to return to?

Deep breath. Stop. I would only find out by going down there.

My bare feet sank into the carpet as I crossed the living room toward the kitchen. As I reached the door, I saw the kitchen table tucked in beside the window.

Someone sat with their back to me. Someone in a red flannel shirt.

All the saliva dried in my mouth.

Dad peered from around the figure and spotted me. He waved me forward.

"Look who's finally awake," he said.

The figure turned.

KJ.

He looked like he always did in his red flannel shirt, except I could see dark smudges under his eyes. The lines at the sides of his mouth were a little deeper. His expression was a little flatter, less inclined to smile or scowl.

At least the lack of a scowl at me was an improvement.

But I didn't like that flat expression.

"Hello?" I said.

"Closer to good afternoon, sleepy head." Mother crossed the kitchen from the stove. She held a plate of sausages in her hand. The aroma seized me and drew me forward. Sharp spices, sizzling meat. The sausages looked huge in front of me.

Mother shoved me back. Her voice sparkled with laughter.

"These are for everyone, not just you. Sit down."

She pointed with the spatula across the table at the seat under the window. I hurried to obey her. The sooner I did the sooner I'd get sausages.

As I sat, she rolled three sausages apiece onto my Dad's plate, my brother's plate, and mine.

Before she'd even managed to turn away, I'd chomped my way through one of mine.

Dad chuckled. "A little hungry, huh?"

KJ frowned, with a slight look of disgust.

That almost looked like one of his normal expressions toward me. But I could make him do better.

I reached toward one of his sausages.

"Hands off," he snapped. The scowl he gave me was every inch KJ.

That was better.

I let myself eat half of my second sausage, savouring the delicate spices and meaty texture. I licked the grease off my lips.

"So what happened?" I asked. "The sea beast, the Siren, are they gone? Is everything back to normal?"

Dad bowed his head toward his plate. Mother turned to me from the stove.

"We'll discuss everything after breakfast," she said.

I knew better than to push. More often than not, she had the final say of things in this house.

The food was piled high on the table. Pancakes with two types of syrup, more sausages, fruit, hash browns so crispy they crunched all the way through. I felt like I drank a gallon of coffee and ate three plates full of food before I couldn't stuff any more into my mouth. When the mounds of food turned into a stack of empty plates, Mother waved her hand, sending the plates streaming across the kitchen to stack themselves in the sink. She remained at the table, sipping her tea.

She exchanged a look with Dad. He chewed his last bit of pancake and then dabbed his mouth with a napkin. Then he cleared his throat.

"The Siren and the sea beast are gone from this Realm," he said. "The Council has taken charge of them. They are too dangerous even for the Underwell although what you did diminished them quite a bit."

I nodded. "What about this reality? Is it...the same?"

I glanced over at KJ. His expression was stony. All the delicious food seemed to curdle in my stomach. My chest felt tight. Did they remember him for real? Was I still stuck as the heir?

Did I still have my life?

Mother placed a hand on KJ's shoulder.

"We remember your brother again," she said. "And we remember not remembering him." Her grip tightened on his shoulder. "I'll never forgive the Council for hiding him from us."

"As far as we can tell, the world has returned to how it was," Dad said. "We remember both ways but it does not appear that the rest of the world remembers the same."

I let out the breath that I didn't realize I was holding. The world had returned to how it was, that meant I had a home and a private detective business to go back to. Friends that would remember me, whose lives would be back on track. Venir, Palle, Mallory, and Shirl.

I had my life again.

Cheering seemed like a bad idea though.

"It has been very difficult," Mother said. "It's going to take us all time to recover from this assault." She rubbed my brother's shoulder. He bowed his head and I caught a meaningful glance pass between him and Dad.

Dad cleared his throat and opened his mouth to speak but Mother held up her hand.

"Your brother has decided to step back," she said. "This ordeal has been a terrible strain and he needs to heal."

"He hasn't decided yet if it will be permanent," Dad said. "He's going to take some time to consider his options, but for now he's stepping down as heir to the Santa Claus title."

I pressed my palms to the table. They felt sweaty. My heart pounded in my chest. My stomach felt like it was filled with lead that might drag me crashing down through the floor into the centre of the earth. It took every effort to remain sitting upright and not sag down to the floor.

I cleared my throat. My mouth felt more parched than the dry winter snow.

"What does that mean?" I managed to squeak the words out.

Mother gave me a bright, cheery smile.

"You get to continue as heir," she chirped.

"I know it's been a challenge for you, Noel," Dad said. "But you're really getting the hang of it. In a couple hundred years it'll be old hat to you. By then KJ will have had a chance to make up his mind and if he decides not to come back, you'll be well positioned to take over."

"Not come back? Take over?" My voice felt faint even to my ears.

"Your father's been thinking of early retirement," Mother said. "This would be the perfect opportunity. We've always wanted to cruise the Mediterranean."

She reached across the table and took Dad's hand. He smiled and gave her a squeeze.

I had no moisture left in my body. No muscle tone either. I leaned against the back of my chair to stop from sliding off it.

"Retire," I said.

"*Early* retirement," Mother emphasized.

With slow, deliberate movements, KJ poured himself another cup of coffee. He added some cream and stirred it, then lifted the cup to his lips. He gazed at me with a bland expression, except...

Except for the malicious twinkle in his eye.

He swallowed a mouthful of coffee and then set the cup down on the table.

"I think we've scared the hell out of him enough," he said. His voice sounded strong, deep, with his normal touch of arrogance.

Wait a minute.

Mother and Dad burst out laughing.

KJ's lips curled into a grin.

Wait a minute!

"You were kidding?" I said.

"You think I'd let you take over?" KJ said. "You were a disaster. I barely took one step into the workshop before all the Elves descended on me, relieved I was back. I could slack off for the next thousand years and not do worse than you."

"Noel wasn't that bad," Dad said. "He might have gotten a better handle on it in a few hundred years."

"Maybe five or six," Mother said.

KJ snorted.

"Seven or eight?" Mother suggested.

"Hey, I was managing," I said.

KJ lifted his coffee cup. "You want to take over?" He cocked an eye brow at me.

"No," I said. "Not at all." I held up my hands. "It's all yours."

Mother dabbed her eyes. Dad nibbled on another sausage. Both of them looked lighter and younger than ever.

"But it is true that KJ is stepping back for a time," she said. "He does need a break."

"But I'm not going anywhere," Dad said.

"And it won't be permanent," KJ said.

"He just needs some rest." Mother rubbed his shoulder again. "So he's going to go to stay with you in Toronto for a while."

"Ah," I said.

"Unless you'd rather hang out here," KJ said.

"Nope," I said. "Toronto. Sure. I've got a spare room. You can stay as long as you like. As long as you come back here to take over for Dad."

KJ drained his coffee cup and set it down on the table. He slapped my back hard enough to almost send me spilling onto the floor. I managed to brace my legs against the chair legs to stop from falling.

"Great, I'm almost packed. We can leave after you brush your teeth."

He pushed back away from the table.

Mother gave me a beaming smile.

"I just know it'll be good for you both to spend some time together."

Good.

Time.

I gave her my best smile.

At least I was going home to Toronto, even if it was with my brother in tow.

Back to my life, back to being a private detective. Even with KJ there to sneer and grumble, I felt my spirits lifting. There was something to be said for finding your right place in the world and although I loved my family, it wasn't quite right here at the North Pole. Even with full access to my Christmas magic. Being back home in Toronto was the right place for me.

I picked up the pot of coffee to pour myself another cup.

I didn't feel the need to brush my teeth just yet.

My life would be waiting.

I could spend another few minutes here with Mother and Dad.

The coffee smelled rich and robust as I poured. Dad lifted his cup so I poured for him too. Mother took a sip of her tea.

And we relaxed in the bright sunshine of a North Pole day.

JOIN MY NEWSLETTER!

If you enjoyed this story, please consider taking a moment to review it or to recommend it to your friends. Reviews help other readers decide if a book is for them.

Sign up for my New Releases mailing list and get a free copy of the *Rebecca M. Senese Sampler*, featuring stories of science fiction, urban fantasy, mystery and horror. Enjoy them all!

Click here to get started: https://rebeccasenese.com/newsletter/

Santa's son is on the case!

Enjoy more Noel Kringle with The Noel Kringle Chronicles!

REBECCA M. SENESE
Santa Claus:
PRIVATE DETECTIVE
SANTA'S SON IS ON THE CASE.
THE NOEL KRINGLE CHRONICLES

REBECCA M. SENESE
SANTA MUST DIE!
THE NOEL KRINGLE CHRONICLES

REBECCA M. SENESE
THE CLAUS CONNECTION
THE NOEL KRINGLE CHRONICLES

REBECCA M. SENESE
THE TWELVE DEATHS OF CHRISTMAS
THE NOEL KRINGLE CHRONICLES

REBECCA M. SENESE
BABY, IT'S DEADLY OUTSIDE
THE NOEL KRINGLE CHRONICLES

REBECCA M. SENESE
DO YOU FEAR WHAT I FEAR
THE NOEL KRINGLE CHRONICLES

About the Author

Based in Toronto, Canada, I write horror, science fiction and mystery/crime, often all at once in the same story. I am the author of the contemporary fantasy series, the *Noel Kringle Chronicles* featuring the son of Santa Claus working as a private detective in Toronto. Garnering an Honorable Mention in *"The Year's Best Science Fiction"* and nominated for numerous Aurora Awards, my work has appeared in *Home for the Howlidays*, *Bitter Mountain Moonlight: A Cave Creek Anthology*, *Promise in the Gold: A Cave Creek Anthology*, *Unmasked: Tales of Risk and Revelation*, *Obsessions: An Anthology of Original Stories*, *Fiction River: Visions of the Apocalypse*, *Fiction River: Sparks*, *Fiction River: Recycled Pulp*, *Tesseracts 16: Parnassus Unbound*, *Ride the Moon*, *Tesseracts 15: A Case of Quite Curious Tales*, *TransVersions*, *Deadbolt Magazine*, *On Spec*, *The Vampire's Crypt*, *Storyteller*, *Reflection's Edge*, *Future Syndicate* and *Into the Darkness*, amongst others.

Find me online:
www.RebeccaSenese.com

www.NoelKringleChronicles.com
www.RebeccaSeneseBooks.com

facebook.com/Rebecca.M.Senese
bsky.app/profile/RebeccaSenese.com
x.com/RebeccaSenese
bookbub.com/authors/rebecca-m-senese
instagram.com/rebeccamsenese
goodreads.com/rebecca_senese
wandering.shop/@rebeccasenese